S0-BNH-340

JAWBREP

JAWBREAKER

CHRISTINA WYMAN

FARRAR STRAUS GIROUX

NEW YORK

Content warning: This book contains themes that might be sensitive
for some readers, such as parental alcohol use disorder and one scene in
which a parent slaps a child.

Farrar Straus Giroux Books for Young Readers
An imprint of Macmillan Publishing Group, LLC
120 Broadway, New York, NY 10271 • mackids.com

Our books may be purchased in bulk for promotional, educational, or
business use. Please contact your local bookseller or the Macmillan Corporate
and Premium Sales Department at (800) 221–7945 ext. 5442 or by email at
MacmillanSpecialMarkets@macmillan.com.

Library of Congress Cataloging-in-Publication Data is available.

First edition, 2023
Book design by Meg Sayre
Printed in the United States of America by Lakeside Book Company,
Harrisonburg, Virginia

ISBN 978-0-374-38969-7
1 3 5 7 9 10 8 6 4 2

For Jaime and Jenna.
I want nothing more in
this life than a better
world for you both, in
every conceivable way.
I love you forever.

Author's Note

The first time I had an inkling that something was "wrong" with my face was when a peer saw me whistling at school. I was a good whistler for a third grader—loud and mostly on pitch. I'd often whistle to the tune of my favorite video game (*Sonic the Hedgehog*, back then).

My classmate found my whistle funny. He said I looked like Bugs Bunny. What I hadn't realized until I went home that day and watched myself whistle in the mirror was how my front teeth hung over my bottom lip like pillars. I also didn't know until that moment that I didn't whistle like a person with a normal mouth, simply because my lips wouldn't close. My teeth made it impossible. After that day, I made sure I would never whistle publicly, with my severely buckteeth on full display for my classmates to weaponize.

The fact is, there was no concealing my teeth, whether or not I whistled. This "Bugs Bunny" experience snowballed into what would prove to be an emotionally debilitating time, particularly in late elementary and junior high school. Intense bullying (about my teeth, height, clothes, and hair) was a main feature of those years. Perhaps worst of all, there was almost no meaningful adult intervention, and a lot like Max Plink—the main character in this book—I was on my own trying to sort it out (or run from it). Also, like Max, I didn't often bother trying to get adults involved, as that usually made things worse. Too many times, I was personally blamed for the bullying I had endured.

I can't, however, pinpoint the exact moment when I started to figure out that my family was a little different from some of the other families I came across. My dad worked a hard physical job for the New York City transit system; my mom stayed home with my sister and me until we started school, and then she worked part-time for a doctor's office during our hours at school. When my sister and I became teenagers, Mom took the best position she'd ever been offered: a letter carrier for the United States Postal Service. Like my dad's work, her new job was very physically demanding and, at times, emotionally debilitating. She delivered mail in our neighborhood, to many of my classmates' home addresses. My peers' dads—many of them, anyway—were accountants and executives. Some were business owners. Many of my classmates' moms did not work outside the home. They often volunteered for the Parent Teacher Association, organizing and helping with all kinds of school events. This was something that stood out to me because my own mom wasn't available to volunteer at school—she had to work.

Financially speaking, Max's family is always in survival mode. I am intimately familiar with such difficulties and how scary it can be to watch them play out in parents' interactions with each other and, at times, their children.

My parents were teenagers when they had me, and not much older than that when my sister was born. We rented the home we lived in, and my mom and dad drove clunkers. Once, our car was stolen in the middle of the night (I was supposed to go on my first-ever early morning fishing trip with my dad that same morning). We lost another car in an accident. Our apartment building was broken into and our bikes—our primary source of summer entertainment—were stolen. My dad would often complain about "living paycheck to paycheck." My sister and I shared a bedroom and got on each other's nerves on a regular basis.

We lived for pizza Thursdays and the occasional family drive to New York's countryside, a region we referred to as "Upstate," where members of our extended family lived. At home, the four of us fought over the one bathroom that we all had to share. There was nowhere to go for privacy. My sister and I watched relationships with certain family members and friends come and go as toxicity and dysfunction took over.

I put my head down and did (mostly) well in school. I was helpless to do anything else. As a child, I couldn't fix what was going on around me.

In all of this, our parents did the best they could for my sister and me. They often did without, or racked up debt, putting their own lives and needs and goals on hold to make sure we had what we needed—including braces and school enrichment opportunities. And while it was clear to me that a lot of our peers lived very different lives, and I was insecure about this, my sister and I typically had what we needed. I would never—could never—say otherwise.

Back to those teeth and jaws: The statistics you'll encounter in this book are true. According to the American Association of Orthodontics, approximately four million Americans wear braces, and 80 percent of them are between 6 and 18 years old*, with similar numbers reflecting other countries (Germany**, for one example). Braces are normal. And for most people who wear them, I think, they're abundantly necessary. Putting vanity aside, orthodontic treatment can offset a lot of debilitating dental problems in adulthood—which is really the point of orthodontic treatment. (I would know—I've been in braces three separate times, topped off with double jaw surgery when I was thirty-three! My jaws were held shut with tight rubber bands for six to eight weeks. I'd never eaten so much ice cream—through a straw—in my life.)

But perhaps more sobering are the statistics on bullying. According to a 2019 report published by the National Center for Educational Statistics***, one out of every five students between the ages of 12 and 18 reported being bullied—including name-calling, insults, social exclusion, rumors, physical abuse, and other common forms. Recent data published by the Cyberbullying Research Center in partnership with the Cartoon Network**** reported that 49.8 percent of tweens (9 to 12 years old) said they experienced bullying at school and 14.5 percent of tweens shared they experienced bullying online.

Although I didn't come up in an age of social media, I know too well how it feels to be a part of such heartbreaking statistics. And as a teacher, I saw it happening with my students on a near-daily basis.

I wrote this book, in part, because I yearned to tell the kind of story that I wished I'd had access to as a child. The kind of book where parents and families don't behave well (as a rule, versus the exception); a book about the kind of bullying and heartache that children with craniofacial anomalies might experience. As Max says, "It's open season on kids with a mouth like mine." I wanted—perhaps needed—to write a book about what "open season" looked and felt like. But I also wanted to write a book about how hope, love, and friendship really do conquer all.

I also wrote this book because of my love for, and belief in, young people. If I can say one thing about my own experiences, it's that those tough times may have been hard, but they were also not forever and not insurmountable. Sometimes finding joy takes a lot of work. I hope you'll be inspired by Max's resilience and the support she receives from unexpected places.

Above all, I hope this story will encourage you to be what others may need in their toughest moments. We could all use a good friend or two. Thank you for reading Max's story.

With love,
Christina Wyman

* https://www3.aaoinfo.org/_/press-room/

** https://pubmed.ncbi.nlm.nih.gov/21486872/

*** https://nces.ed.gov/pubs2019/2019054.pdf

**** bullying/pdfs/CN_Stop_Bullying_Cyber_Bullying_Report_9.30.20.pdf

JAWBREAKER

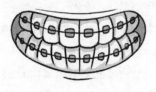

I

RUNAWAY TEETH

"I don't get why I have to go with you to Max's bucky beaver appointment."

My little sister sulks from the back seat of the car. I'm up front with Mom, who just picked us up from school because I have an orthodontist appointment. Alexis always whines when she has to come along, even though it means she gets out of school early.

"Why don't you shut up, carcass breath?" I bite back. Alexis is one year younger than me and she acts like a total baby when she doesn't get her way.

"What did I tell the both of you about name-calling?" Mom snaps. We're at a red light around the corner from the doctor's office. And it's exactly like Mom to ignore the fact that Alexis started the whole thing.

"You're right, Mommy," Alexis says, batting her eyes at Mom in the rearview mirror. "I'm sorry. I'll never do it again." Mom's face softens, and it reminds me of how Alexis always gets off the hook, no matter how badly she treats me.

It wasn't always this way with my sister. Not that long ago, we could be in the car together without fighting. We'd sing along to whatever song was on the radio and even make each other laugh. During longer rides we'd invent games to make the time go by and it was fun. We were never best friends, but we weren't enemies, either.

I stare out the window and clench my fists. It's bad enough that I have these appointments to begin with. About once a month I have to see Dr. Watson to get my braces tightened, which is about as much fun as it sounds. This means that my teeth and gums are gonna feel like they're on fire for almost one whole week. Then, just when the pain starts easing up, I'll have to go and do it all over again. And Mom usually makes Alexis come with us, which used to not be so bad. If the wait to see the doctor was long, we'd joke around or do our homework together while Mom looked at her phone. But lately, Alexis has been acting like coming to my doctor's appointments is the Worst Thing Ever.

I roll down the window just a bit, to get some air. It's the last day of January, and the icy wind seeps into the car as Alexis kicks the back of my seat.

"What's your *problem*?" I bark.

"Your train wreck of a face, that's what. It's *cold*. Shut the *window*."

"Enough!" Mom snaps again. "If I have to pull over, you'll both be sorry."

Even though a lot of kids at school wear braces, I still feel like a freak. I have something called a maxillofacial deformity. It sounds scarier than it is, and it looks scarier than it sounds. Basically, my parents call it a severe overbite, my orthodontist calls it an extreme overjet, and the kids at school call me Bucky Beaver (among other awesome and totally creative insults). My jaws fit together like mismatched puzzle pieces and my top teeth are spaced and overlap my bottom lip.

When I was eight or nine, my teeth pretty much started to do whatever they wanted, and now they look like they're running a race against my face. The doctor says that braces should Fix My Deformity, but I've been wearing them for a whole year and I still feel like my face is a hot mess.

Ever since the doctor glued these stupid brackets to my teeth I live on Advil and soft foods, and I can't do anything fun like bite into pizza (instead, I eat it with a fork—blah) or apples because it hurts too much and food gets stuck and I can do real damage to The Apparatus if I eat the wrong thing. I'm also not allowed to chew gum or eat hard candy, and I have to brush my teeth way more than normal to keep everything clean.

Oh, and thanks to the way my teeth jut out, my lips wouldn't close *before* I had braces. Now that there are chunks of metal glued to them, my mouth hangs open even *more* and I'm on constant drool patrol.

Whoever invented braces must have seriously hated kids. Sometimes I wonder if my orthodontist hates kids, too. She acts like plastering a bunch of metal to my teeth is No Big Deal.

"Ew, Mom, she's drooling again!" Alexis shouts from behind me. I glance in the side-view mirror—I didn't realize she'd been giving me the evil eye from the back seat. "You slobber like a Saint Bernard!" Her face twists with disgust.

I wipe the drool away with my sleeve and glare back at her.

"The two of you better knock it off if you don't want to spend this weekend in your bedroom," Mom warns.

This whole thing with Alexis being such a jerk really only just started when she joined me at junior high school last fall, which was right around the time that I got braces. Alexis is in the sixth grade, and I'm in the seventh. And my parents say that she'll need braces, too, in another year or two, so I really don't get why she makes fun of mine.

Again, Alexis kicks the back of my seat like a baby. "Ugly loser," she growls under her breath. I know Mom heard her because *I* heard her, but Mom doesn't do anything about it, and fifteen minutes later I'm sitting in the Chair of Doom.

2

THE CHAIR OF DOOM

I'm pretty sure Dr. Watson is the worst thing to ever happen to me.

Me and Mom walk into the doctor's office. I'm wearing my favorite T-shirt. It's white with black letters and says *There*, *Their*, and *They're* in large capital letters. Mom got it for me because she knows I get a kick out of grammar. Dr. Watson completely ignores it, which I expected, but I still find it annoying.

Most people comment on my T-shirts because of how out-there they are. I have a collection of sarcastic shirts that Mom is helping me build. If she sees one she knows I'll like, she picks it up for me if it's cheap enough—and only if it's school appropriate. My second-favorite T-shirt is a black one with white letters that say *Don't even*.

I set myself up in the patient's chair and Mom sits on the other side of the room just as Dr. Watson breezes in.

"Great to see you, Ms. Plink." Dr. Watson smiles at Mom. Her teeth are white and pearly against her brown skin, and her black curly hair is pulled back in a tight ponytail. "And you, Max. Any complications this time around? Unusual pain or discomfort?"

"No, but—"

"Open, please." Dr. Watson begins to poke around my mouth before I can get the words out. "Okay, close," she orders as she shoves the mirror up against the inside of my cheek. "I'm just looking at how your teeth and jaws are fitting together at this point. I think of them like puzzle pieces. There's a very specific way that your top teeth should sit over your bottom teeth."

She pauses and looks at Mom. "Today we'll start practicing with the headgear. We might need a maxillofacial surgeon down the road, to fully correct the malocclusion." Dr. Watson turns to me. "This is a surgery that would change the position of the maxilla, which is your upper jaw, and the mandible, which is your lower jaw. So, double jaw surgery in your case. But we'll have to wait and see. It might be a few years before we know exactly what needs to be done." Turning back to Mom, she says, "She has to be almost finished growing before we can make any final decisions."

My stomach churns and my mouth goes dry.

"You think I need *surgery*?" My eyes dart between Dr. Watson and Mom. This is the first time Dr. Watson has said anything to me about surgery. And I'm only twelve. Won't it be *years* before I stop growing? Like, don't people stop growing when they're twenty-five or thirty or something?

"Are my jaws *that* messed up?"

Dr. Watson throws Mom a curious glance, as if to say, *Have you all not had this conversation yet?*

She stands up from her rolling chair. "That's a good question, Max. A maxillofacial surgeon is a doctor who specializes in jaw restructuring. Um." She clears her throat. "Realignment. Remember, like a puzzle. Making sure your top and bottom jaws are even with each other, but also making sure that your top and bottom teeth align and fit together. This helps with chewing, swallowing, and sometimes even breathing. I know we've talked about this before."

Then she asks me to open and close my mouth a couple of times. "Some deformities correct without maxillofacial intervention, especially when you get in the game early enough," she says. I *hate* when she says deformities. Like, isn't there a better word? "That's why we're going to start using the headgear, like I mentioned the last time I saw you. We talked at length about that, remember?" Dr. Watson sounds a little irritated, like she doesn't want to be caught up in the drama of Mom not telling me things that she's supposed to tell me. I remembered that Dr. Watson said something about headgear about a month ago, and when I went home and googled it I was seriously hoping she'd forget. But this is the first time I'm hearing anything about surgery.

"This really sucks," I say under my breath, and before the words are even out of my mouth, I know I'm walking on thin ice.

"Max," Mom warns. "Watch your mouth." Her hands are clutched around her purse, like a gremlin or something is about to pop up from around a corner to steal it. She's young—the youngest mom of anyone in my whole grade, I bet—but her brown hair is graying, and her skin is super pale. When she's really tired, you can see some of the veins under the skin around her eyes.

The doctor sighs, like I'm the first kid ever to hate having braces. She bends forward, leaning over me. "Open, please."

I do as she says, and she pulls my lips back far away from my mouth. It doesn't hurt or anything. "Sometimes, Max, a person's lower jaw might overshoot their top jaw, and that's when this happens." Dr. Watson juts her bottom jaw out so that her bottom teeth overlap her top teeth. "In your case, your top jaw shoots way out over your bottom jaw."

I mean, I *knew* my mouth was messed up, but I didn't know it was, like, *surgery* bad. I squeeze my eyes shut because I can feel the tears and you're not supposed to cry in front of your enemies.

"So they basically have to smash up my face if things

don't get better? Sounds like a great solution." I open my eyes and see Mom glaring at me from her chair, in a *you just wait until we get in the car* kind of way. She always has a real problem with me asking questions, especially of Authority Figures, but this time, I don't hold back.

Dr. Watson shrugs. "Kids get orthognathic surgery all the time. You certainly wouldn't be the first. The surgeons reposition your jaws and wire them shut for a few weeks, so that everything can fuse in the correct place, much like broken bones. You can ask me whatever questions you might have. I'll make sure you get a pamphlet on the way out, if that'll help."

They reposition your jaws and wire them shut for a few weeks . . . like broken bones . . . the doctor's words knock around my head like Ping-Pong balls and I taste bile.

"What do you—" I squeak, but Mom interrupts me.

"Will it help my *wallet*?" Mom smirks like she's trying to be funny, but in a way I can tell isn't a joke.

Dr. Watson's eyes are nervous now, like she *really* doesn't want to be a part of family drama. I don't blame her. My family is nothing but drama, at least lately.

"Max, look here." She pulls her lower lip down and taps on her bottom teeth. Some of them are crowded together, like dominoes that started to fall over. "Sometimes, braces can't correct everything. See? This can still happen, many years after braces. As we get older, our teeth tend to do what they want to do, and we have to accept our imperfections. In your case, we'll just have to see how you do here. You're not finished growing, which makes things hard to predict. Bite down, please."

Dr. Watson examines one side of my mouth, and then the other. She looks at Mom. "As I've said from day one, Max is a complicated case. We'll just have to see how things develop. In the meantime"—she turns her attention to me—"we need to try the headgear we talked about last month."

I swallow hard. Having a skeletal deformity is a real blast.

"She mostly gets it from her father's side of the family," Mom says. "The women had horrible teeth. All of them."

I know that Mom wore braces, too. But I don't bring it up.

Dr. Watson glances at Mom and says, "Indeed, these things are often hereditary, for better or for worse. But we'll do everything we can to take care of Max, get this fixed, and avoid surgery." She opens a drawer and pulls out a contraption that looks a bit like a thin metal tube folded into the shape of a half-moon with two slim stems on each end. It has a strap running from side to side, like a slingshot.

Dr. Watson unhooks the strap. "This is the headgear, Max. Some of my patients call it a jawbreaker." She chuckles.

"Why?" I yelp.

Dr. Watson clears her throat. "It's not actually going

to break your jaw. You'll feel a little sore when you wear it because it's designed to gently reposition your top jaw. That's all that means. I used to have to wear one, when I was around your age."

She holds the headgear over my face. "For best possible results, you're going to have to keep this on for four to six hours during the day, and when you sleep. Open, please." I open my mouth and she somehow connects the brace to my back brackets. Then she secures the strap behind my head. It's a snug fit, and now I have more metal protruding from my face than I ever thought possible. I basically have a shiny metal orb around my head. You could probably stand me on the roof of your house to get a better Wi-Fi signal.

Dr. Watson holds a mirror to my face, and I wish she hadn't done that.

"I am *not* wearing this thing to *school*," I try to say, but my words come out all lisp-y and jumbled. It feels like the front of my face is being pulled through the back of my head.

"Everyone'll make fun of me," I try again, but it's hard to bring my lips together for certain words and I sound like I'm talking with my mouth full.

Dr. Watson shakes her head. "You don't have to wear it to school. You have to wear it *after* school, whenever you're home and not eating, and certainly when you sleep. This is our best chance at subverting the need for surgery down the line."

"It already feels like I got punched in the teeth," I grumble. It's like I have tiny little boxing champions in my mouth that are punching my teeth from the inside *and* the outside. But I can't block my face because the boxers are microscopic and invisible.

"Maximillia. Audrina. Plink. That's enough complaining." Mom's tone now has a real *one more time and you're finished* kind of feel to it, as if *she's* the one wearing weird metal bars around her head. She then turns to the doctor and asks, "How long will she need to do this?" like I'm not even here.

"Oh, I'd say about six months to a year. Maybe longer. It depends on how consistent she is." Dr. Watson looks at me. Her expression turns serious. "It also depends on how much she wants to avoid surgery and how soon she wants to get out of braces. If she wants to wear braces until she's thirty, then she'll slack off with the headgear." The doctor glances at the clock on the wall. I know what that glance means. She doesn't have any more time to deal with me.

"She'll be consistent," my mother says with a scowl. "I'm not paying for this if she's gonna slack off. We don't have the money for surgery."

The doctor makes me practice with the jawbreaker a couple of times, to make sure I know how to put it in and take it out. Turns out that there are these tiny tunnels attached to my back brackets that let the headgear's stems slide right into them. And not only did Dr. Watson give me the jaw-breaker, but at the very end of my appointment she tightened my braces, too, so now every part of my mouth is sore and will be throbbing by dinnertime.

Before we leave, Dr. Watson loads me up with dental wax. The kind you have to wear when your wires poke into the sides of your mouth and cause blisters. "Looking forward to seeing you in just a couple of weeks. It'll be a quick visit, to gauge your comfort with the headgear," she says, but by the time I turn around to say goodbye she disappeared down the hall.

Mom storms into the waiting room, which is full now with kids in braces and a bunch of tired-looking parents. Alexis is slouched in a chair. She scowls when she sees me, like the fact that I even exist is enough to annoy her.

"Let's go," Mom orders us. Fine with me. I can't wait to get out of there.

"But her face still looks the same." Alexis bats her eyes, all innocent-like. "Too bad."

3

SURGERY AND SECRETS

I'm in the back seat this time, because me and Alexis take turns. It's one of the few things we don't fight about because the rules are the rules: Whoever had the front seat in the last ride has to sit in the back for the next one.

When Alexis sits in the front she makes sure to push the seat all the way back so that I can't sit behind her. I mean, I could, but not without my knees banging up against the back seat. I'm tall for my age. The doctor says Off the Charts tall. I'm almost five feet eight and a whole head taller than a lot of the other kids in my grade. It just adds to the fun of having a deformed face.

Alexis starts cackling, but I don't really hear her. I'm staring at myself in the rearview mirror. The way my curly brown hair frizzes up like a cotton ball but I'm not allowed to wear gel or hairspray to smooth it down because my parents say I'm too young for hair products, like there's an actual law about it or something. My forehead shines when the light hits it and even from the back seat I can see my skin slick with oil. A new mountain of pimples cropped up on my cheek overnight, little red explosions over pasty white skin. Mom and Dad don't let me wear makeup, either, even though a bunch of other girls at school started wearing some. Even my best friend, Shrynn, started wearing a little bit of lip gloss, and her mom is super strict about these things.

I move down to my mouth. The way my top teeth jut out over my bottom like pillars. Once I start focusing on my mouth, all I can see is metal and teeth. It makes my stomach turn.

It's funny, in a not-funny way. I never had a clue that there was something wrong with my face until I started seeing Dr. Watson.

When I start to feel bad about my face—which is only about a million times a day—I play a little game with myself. I squeeze my eyes shut and make a wish:

Please, please, let me look like someone else when I open my eyes. Anyone else. I don't care who. Just not Max Plink.

"Max, are you listening to me?" Mom snaps.

"I, um—" I swallow. "Yeah." I didn't realize that she'd parked the car. We're home.

"As soon as we get inside, you are to put that brace on."

Alexis makes sure that I see the witchy expression she

makes before she gets out of the car and slams the door and skips off to the apartment building where we live.

And now I feel myself detach from my body. This happens sometimes, especially when I'm feeling angry and powerless. The way Mom orders me around. The way Alexis is super entertained every time I have to deal with something hard. The way Alexis and I don't even really look alike so she has no idea what I'm dealing with.

The way Mom doesn't even ask me how I'm feeling, and the way Dad will just pretend like everything's fine when it's the total opposite of fine.

⋛ ☆ ⋚

"WHY DIDN'T YOU TELL ME I MIGHT NEED SURGERY?" I yell at Mom as soon as we're inside. She has a scowl on her face, like *she's* the one who has to wear a jawbreaker. Like *she's* the one who might need to have her jaws ripped off.

I usually get in trouble for yelling at my parents, but I don't care this time. I see drops of spit fly out of my mouth, and I don't care about that either.

"We're having ravioli tonight." Mom takes off her coat and heads into the kitchen. She always makes a soft dinner on the same day as my orthodontist appointment, because she knows how much it hurts me to chew, and she knows how much I love ravioli. "We can talk about it after dinner. For now, I want you to think about your attitude. Not everyone has the opportunity to fix their teeth. Think about being more grateful. And you're on tomato duty." She turns away from me and calls out to my sister, "Alexis, you're on cucumber duty and I'll be checking your homework after dinner, so make sure it's finished."

"Whatever," Alexis mumbles before grabbing a couple of cucumbers, a plate, and a knife. "Gross," she says. "These are soft and practically rotten."

"There are kids who won't have dinner tonight," Mom growls. "Would you like to be one of them?"

"You're right, Mommy." Alexis bats her eyes. "I'm sorry." She rolls her eyes when Mom turns to hand me three large tomatoes.

Every night, Alexis and I are on some kind of dinner duty, usually something easy because Mom handles the bigger things. And this used to be okay, when we could stand next to each other and help Mom prepare food and maybe even talk about school and stuff without fighting.

A couple of years ago we talked about Alexis's art projects a lot while we helped with dinner. Mom would ask her questions and Alexis would show us something she was working on for school. When she had to make a portrait of one of her family members, she even chose *me*. I sat for almost an hour while she made a charcoal drawing, with cool little shadows around my eyelids, nose, and neck. It wasn't perfect, but it didn't need to be.

I remember how Dad had said, "Wow, Bug, that's a spitting image," which made Alexis smile so proudly.

Alexis got an A on her project, and when she brought it home at the end of the year, Mom framed it and hung it up on the kitchen wall, next to the table.

Now the drawing hangs there like a bad joke as Alexis angrily stabs the cucumbers and I rush through slicing the tomatoes just to get away from her.

"Alexis, get to your homework as soon as you're finished," Mom says. "Max, we can talk about your issues after dinner."

My issues. Because having a maxillofacial deformity is *My* Issue, and not being told that I might need surgery is *My* Issue.

"No, Mom," I say as Alexis dumps the sliced cucumbers into a bowl and storms off. I know exactly what's gonna happen. Mom'll get distracted with dinner and cleanup and checking Alexis's homework and saying goodbye to Dad before he heads out for his night shift. And then when I ask her about surgery, she'll say she's too tired to talk about it and that I should think about my *attitude* instead. And this exact thing will keep happening until she thinks I've forgotten about it.

But I'm not exactly about to forget that I might have to

get my jaws ripped off and bolted back on, like I'm some sort of plastic action-figure doll. "Why didn't you tell me?"

She opens the refrigerator. "I have to focus on dinner. Now put your headgear on and stop complaining."

"Mom, NO!" My cheeks are hot with anger and my voice is loud. Too loud.

"Don't you DARE scream at me," she hisses. "Your. Father. Is. Still. *Sleeping*."

Dad works nights for the city's transportation system and spends the days getting as much sleep as possible. We live at one end of Brooklyn—the end that connects to Coney Island beach, where you can see New Jersey across the bay. Dad said it takes two full hours for the train to get to its last stop in Queens, which is, like, completely on the other side of the city.

"THEN TELL ME THE TRUTH FOR ONCE! YOU NEVER TELL ME THE TRUTH."

Mom slams the refrigerator door shut and throws a head of lettuce on the counter. "This is the last time I'm gonna tell you to watch your tone and *lower your voice*." Mrs. Tone Police takes a deep breath. "But yes, fine, we didn't tell you about the surgery. There was no point in watching you get upset over something that might not happen anyway."

I can't believe what she's saying. "No point?""

"Maximillia," she says. Oh, have I mentioned how much I hate when she says my full name? I can't stand it. My name is so different from everyone else's in my family. Alexis gets to be Alexis, Mom gets to be Jackie, Dad gets to be Chris, and I get to be Maximillia because I was named after Dad's grandma, a woman I've never met. According to Dad, I also have her teeth. He'd always talked about how my great-grandma Millie had a wild set of chompers until her teeth fell out because she couldn't afford to take care of them. That was back in southern Italy, where she was from.

"And if you wanna blame someone," Mom says, "blame your father. It was his idea to not tell you."

"Oh, so now let's blame Dad." I slink against the wall. "How long have you guys known this might happen, anyway?"

The only sound in our small kitchen is the knife slicing through the lettuce and banging against the cutting board. "After your first round of X-rays," she says. "Just before Dr. Watson put your braces on. We talked after the appointment, when you were in the waiting room. And she wasn't sure, and she said you're a complicated case and that it will be a long time before we know anything."

So Mom and Dad have known for a year that I might need surgery, and they couldn't be bothered to tell me about it.

"What about Alexis?" I ask, but it's more like an interrogation. "She knows she's gonna have braces, right? Is she gonna need surgery, too? Or are you gonna wait until she's wearing a hospital gown to tell her?"

I can see Mom's jaw twitching. Her lips are in a flat line. "She knows she'll need braces, but she probably won't need surgery."

"Oh, well, goody for her," I say.

Mom puts on a pot of water for the ravioli. "It's really time for you to grow up, Max," she snaps.

"I'm not the only one," I mutter.

"That's it." Mom turns to me. "You wanna talk like that to *me*? You can forget about getting on the phone with Shrynn. You'll do your homework and you'll study, and don't even *think* about turning on the TV. Out of my kitchen. Now."

This is just like Mom, you know? I'm the one who might have to go through something big and scary and probably painful, but *she's* the one who gets to be upset.

And now I can't even tell my best friend what's going on until I see her in school tomorrow, because I'm grounded for having feelings. Whenever Mom's angry, she takes away everything I love the most. And the last time I tried to talk to Dad about it, he only said, *You need to listen to your mother*, like that's helpful. When's it her turn to listen to me?

There's so much I want to say back to her, and none of it's nice. I glance at my cell phone in the basket on the table. Its red light is blinking. I won't be able to check it until the morning, before Mom wakes up.

Alexis and I have our own flip phones, which is not at *all* embarrassing when everyone else has super fancy smart-phones. Our phone plans are prepaid, and we can't even take pictures or videos. We're also not allowed to bring them to school because Mom says there's no reason to have a phone with us when we're exactly where we're supposed to be and when the school won't let us use our phones during school hours anyway.

I storm out of the kitchen, through the living room, and into the bedroom I share with Alexis. I'm relieved to have the room to myself for once, because Alexis locked herself in the bathroom to talk on the house phone. The bathroom is off the kitchen, and I saw her sneak in.

I flop down on my bed and bury myself under my blanket. I wish for a different face, even though I know that those kinds of wishes never come true.

4
IT WASN'T ALWAYS LIKE THIS

My parents' bedroom is right next to mine, and I can hear their muffled conversation through the wall. Mom's voice is sharp and high pitched. Dad hasn't been awake for very long because his voice is groggy and he keeps saying, *Wait, what? What happened this time?*

I know they're about to start fighting because that's, like, their favorite hobby these days. But it wasn't always like this. Back a couple of years ago, when Dad wasn't working the overnight shift, he'd be home during normal hours, and sometimes we'd go for walks as a family and he and Mom would hold hands. If Mom was working a shift at the diner on a Saturday, Dad, Alexis, and I would walk there—just six city blocks—and sit in her section. Mom would laugh and squeeze his arm when he'd leave her a really big tip.

"I could run away with this," she'd joke.

"Only if you take me with you," Dad would respond.

But the walks and the random trips to the diner haven't happened since Dad started working nights. Now we don't see him nearly as much, and when we do, there's always Some Sort Of Issue.

I fling my backpack onto my bed. I have the bottom bunk and Alexis has the top. Our room is barely bigger than a closet and our bunk beds, dresser, and nightstand make it feel even smaller. Our shelves overflow with knickknacks, books, and dolls, and there are a bunch of posters on the wall of actors and singers and stuff.

Today's newspaper is folded up and sitting on my bunk, and that helps me feel a little better. Dad does that sometimes, especially if he knows there are a couple of stories I'll be interested in. He likes that I'm on the school newspaper. He says that I'm the writer in the family, which I guess is true.

If you do good in school, you girls'll have a much better life than me and your mother did, he always says. The way he says *mother* sounds like *muddah* and it's funny to me.

I pull my jawbreaker out of my backpack and stand in front of the full-length mirror that hangs on the back of our door. I examine my mouth and try to pull my top lip down over my teeth. Like, if I stretch it out enough it'll stay put, like Play-Doh. But when I let go, my lip goes right back to its original position.

But it's not all bad, I guess. When I force myself to focus

on the upper part of my face, I notice that I have high cheek-bones, a slender nose, and big blue eyes that stand out.

I step away from the mirror and pull down on the cuffs of my pants. It really sucks to be taller than almost all the other kids.

"This is why she acts like this." I can hear Mom's voice getting louder through the wall. "Because you let her get away with everything."

"Maybe she's right, Jackie." Dad's muffled voice comes through, clearer than before. "We probably should have told her. She's angry. And she's twelve. Kids get mad sometimes. The two of you used to get along. Why don't you try talking to her about it? Without yelling?"

My stomach churns.

"Well, Mr. Self-Righteous Child Psychologist, it was your idea not to tell her, was it not? And she has no right to talk to me that way, no matter the reason." Mom is seething now.

"Ohhh, you mean she snaps and argues and complains about everything for no apparent reason?" Dad's tone is tinged with the sort of fake surprise that sounds more like sarcasm than anything else. "I wonder where she gets it from!"

"Oh, so now it's my fault? Like everything else, right? Well, *you* can take her to her next appointment. Then maybe the doctor will at least know Max has a father who isn't *completely* useless." I hear their bedroom door slam. Mom stomps through the living room and into the kitchen. In the past, Dad would follow her. This time he doesn't.

Back when Dad first started the night shift, Mom would gently wake him up for work at around the time we got home from school. Sometimes, she'd make his favorite dinner—spiced pork chops and potatoes—because the smell would usually rouse him before his alarm. Before he'd leave for his shift, she'd tell him to be careful on the tracks and he'd tell her not to worry. He'd often come home with a bouquet of flowers that he got first thing in the morning on his way home as soon as the corner deli opened. Mom would set out snacks for him in case he woke up during the day and couldn't get back to sleep—something about his circadian rhythm being out of whack because Dad was up all night. If my parents crossed paths in the morning they'd kiss before Dad went to bed and Mom went to work.

None of these things seem to happen anymore. Instead of flowers, Dad comes home with a six-pack of beer, and instead of laying out snacks, Mom chain-smokes in the kitchen.

I lie on my bed and wrap my pillow around my head. When I was younger, my parents would argue only once in a while, but it was never loud and it wasn't scary and it didn't last for that long and it would always end with them laughing and hugging. Now they seem to argue every week. And it's the worst thing ever when I know they're arguing about me.

5
KEISHA TELLS MAX TO GROW A SPINE

Last night Dad left for work without eating dinner—but not before barging into my bedroom to tell me to Stop Giving Mom Lip. His pale skin was pink and worn-looking with windburn. It was super cold and windy this week, and he works mostly outside. So he looked angrier than normal.

Worst of all, he didn't ask for my side. He never asks for my side. What Mom says is pretty much the law. But he did give me a kiss on the cheek and say, *It's a lot quieter around here if you do what your mother says.*

Something about the way his breath smelled bugged me. It was sour and reminded me of beer.

After dinner, Alexis saw me wearing my jawbreaker for the first time. Her face got all twisty, like she'd seen a pile of rotting garbage, and when she called me antenna face, Mom came into our bedroom to tell her to clean up the kitchen, even though it was my turn. After Alexis stomped out of the room, it was just Mom and me. She handed me a soft package wrapped in tissue paper.

"I thought you might like this," she'd said. "I was saving it for Valentine's Day, but I thought you'd want it sooner. It's from me and your dad. We have something for your sister too, but she'll get hers in a few weeks. Don't tell her I gave it to you early."

I unwrapped the package. In it was a long-sleeved, light pink T-shirt with the words *To, Two,* and *Too* written on it in big black letters. I decided then and there that it's my new favorite shirt.

"And here's this, in case your headgear makes it hard to sleep." Mom had handed me a bath towel, and I knew that *hard to sleep* meant wet and drooly.

"Also some Tylenol or Advil, in case you need it during school tomorrow," Mom continued. She handed me a baggie with a tiny pill inside. There was also a folded-up letter. She cleared her throat. "And I wrote a letter for the nurse so that she knows you might have to take pain medicine, so make sure to keep it with you. There's also a note in there from Dr. Watson, just in case."

"Thank you," I'd whispered. We didn't hug or smile or do any of that warm and mushy stuff, like my best friend,

Shrynn, does with her mom. But I knew this was Mom's way of apologizing.

In this way, the night ended better than I thought it would.

⊰ ☆ ⊱

Now me and Alexis are on the bus on our way to school, which is one of my least-favorite places to be because I'm trapped like an animal in a cage.

"You have to see this thing that she has to wear in her mouth now!" I hear my sister cackling in the back row as the bus crawls down Kings Highway during rush-hour traffic. "She looks like a human antenna!"

The bus driver hits a pothole, and my insides bottom out and I taste English muffin–flavored bile. We only live five miles from school, but the bus takes about a half hour to get there because of all the traffic and stops.

My life in Brooklyn isn't like what you see in the movies about New York City. I mean, I guess maybe sometimes it is. There's lots of really good food and things to do and trains and buses everywhere. There's also lots of graffiti and concrete and noise and crime sometimes. But it's not like kids are allowed to do whatever they want whenever they want to. I've seen movies like that, where kids are always going on adventures around the city, and it's *totally* bogus—especially if you have strict parents like mine. Most middle school kids where I live take a regular yellow school bus to get to school. I'm not even allowed to take public transportation yet—at least not without one of my parents.

"You got a picture of it, right?" I hear another voice, this one a boy's. I'm pretty sure it's Vince Mazza. He's a major jerk. Last year, I had to cut a whole chunk of chewed-up gum from my hair after he smashed it into my head during lunch hour.

I squeeze my eyes shut and take deep breaths through my nose. I try to focus on my breathing to drown out what's going on at the back of the bus, like our yoga-obsessed gym teacher taught us to do when we're stressed. One, in . . . two, out . . . three, in . . . four, out . . .

It doesn't work. I pull out my pocket dictionary and flip to the *S* section. I'm a complete dork for vocabulary, and our English teacher taught us a word last week that really stuck with me.

Scourge. Noun. A person or thing that causes great trouble or suffering. For homework last week, Mr. Brace asked us to use it in a sentence. I wrote four.

(In no particular order.)

The school bus is a scourge.
My teeth are a scourge.
My sister is a scourge.
My life is a scourge.

These are interesting sentences, Mr. Brace wrote back. *Let me know if you'd like to talk*. After I read his note, I crumpled up my homework and threw it in the classroom garbage pail. Everyone knows that *interesting* is code for *alarming* or *concerning* or some word that could earn me a trip to the school counselor. And that's when I decided to never be honest in my homework again, because the last thing I need is for my teachers to call home to let Mom know that I'm being *interesting*.

"Bucky Beaver has teeth that should have their own zip code!" Carlay Prince's witchy voice floats from the back of the bus. She's best friends with Vince, and they're both in the seventh grade, like I am. "Come on, Lex, show us a picture of that thing!" she says, and I want to gag. No one calls my sister *Lex*.

"I, um . . . ," Alexis begins. "I'm getting a new cell that takes better pictures. Probably next week!" I snort. If she's getting a new phone next week, then I'm getting a Ferrari for my thirteenth birthday. But of course, Alexis can't admit she has a flip phone to the most popular girl in the seventh grade.

"Ugh!" Carlay groans. "I wanna see a pic of her new antenna! You *have* to text one to me! Imagine being so ugly that you need a doctor to rearrange your whole face!"

"I'll see what I can do," Alexis cackles.

"Maybe we can find a picture of a horse with braces," Vince says. "It's pretty much the same thing."

I hear more shuffling and laughter.

"Found one!" Vince shouts. "Look at all these horses!" He laughs. "There are, like, hundreds!"

"Her teeth should totally have their own social media account!" Alexis chimes in, a little louder now, like she wants me to hear her.

It's not supposed to be like this with sisters. Sisters are supposed to love each other to the moon and back, especially when things are bad. It's hard enough that I have other people making fun of me. To have my sister in on the joke is next-level humiliating.

"We should call it Max the Beaver!" Vince says.

"I like Bucky Beaver better," Alexis laughs.

"Lex, what if we just took a pic of you and used it to pretend that you're her?" Carlay asks. "You kind of look alike. We can make a pretend antenna out of tinfoil."

I hear Alexis make a gagging noise. "You want *me* to pretend I'm *her*? No way! And I *don't* look like her. You'd never even know we're sisters." The skin around my eyes and up my nose starts to sting but I don't want to sniff because I don't want anyone to know that I've started crying.

Alexis is right. We don't look that much alike. I mean, we have the same hair color and eye color and stuff, and she's pale like me and almost as tall as I am because she's only a year younger, but that's about where it all ends. Her hair doesn't look like someone glued a mop to her scalp, her pants don't fit her like she's constantly preparing for a flood, and she'll get braces eventually, but her teeth don't hang out of her mouth all crooked and weird.

She also has a lot more friends than I do, and a couple of months ago, as soon as she started junior high, she leeched onto Carlay and Vince like they all used to share a womb or something.

We take our final turn onto the avenue where school is. I'm relieved because soon I can race right into homeroom, and I don't have to see Carlay and Vince until later on in science class. It'll be about seven hours until we're on the bus again, but the afternoon bus is always noisier, and I can pretend that I don't hear them.

"Hey, Plink!"

I sniffle and wipe my eyes. Keisha Bell, our school newspaper's editor in chief, is the only person I know who calls me by my last name. I whip my head around.

"Back here!" she whispers. That's when I realize that she's sitting right behind me. She's peering at me through the space between the fake leather backrest and the window. Keisha's an eighth grader.

She shoves a bunch of tissues in between the space. I take them without looking at her.

"Why do you let them do this?" she asks softly. I don't answer her.

"I have a little sister," she continues. "This is not okay. Do you want me to say something?"

"NO," I say, a little too loudly. "No," I say again, softer. "It's not worth it. It's just how she is. It's how *they* are."

Keisha peers at me through the space. Her dark eyes match her brown skin and she's totally giving me her signature No Nonsense Look and I can tell she's not buying it. "They may be a bunch of troglodytes, but they're not allowed to use technology against another student. It's in the student handbook." I make a mental note to look up *troglodyte* as soon as I have the chance. "And bullying off school grounds is an actionable offense. Do your parents know about this?"

As editor in chief, it's just like Keisha to know the student handbook by heart. She's super smart and she's always writing some article or another about school rules and how they're either not fair or should be better or something. In the fall, Keisha wrote up a whole investigation called *The Rules for What Girls Wear Are Four Times as Long as the Rules for Boys: It's Time to Get Real About Sexism at Weiss Junior High*. It went viral on the school's social media account and got picked up by a major news channel. She even has her own social media channel that she calls K-Word, with a couple thousand followers. She's probably gonna be a famous writer someday.

"Just drop it, okay?" I sniffle. "There's no point."

"Well, you should write about it," she says matter-of-factly. "I'm telling you, people think twice about messing with you if they think you might write something about them. Besides, we need another op-ed soon. I can help, if you want."

"There's no way I'm writing about this," I scoff. I can only imagine what would happen if I wrote an entire story about *My Sister and Her Friends: The Scourges of Weiss Junior High.*

"If you don't wanna write about this, then don't," Keisha says. "But you'll have to grow a spine if you want to make it in journalism." She slinks back in her seat and puts a pair of heavy-looking headphones on before closing her eyes. I want to ask her who she thinks she is, but part of me knows she's right.

6
INTRODUCING MAX'S JAWBREAKER

The school rule is that we're supposed to go straight to homeroom from the bus. We're not even allowed to go to the bathroom without permission, even though there are ten minutes before homeroom starts. But I need to check my face because I know it looks like I've been crying.

There's a huge wall of scratched mirrors as soon as you walk into the girls' room. I want to ignore them, but I lose my willpower by the time I'm at the fifth and last mirror.

I study my reflection. The sight of my own face makes me nauseated. No wonder they make fun of me. With a face like mine, how could I expect them not to?

I'm still in the bathroom when the warning bell for first period rings.

⋟ ☆ ⋞

"Medusa's hair is like a sea of snakes. Simile or metaphor?" I'm fifteen minutes late when I burst into the classroom and Mr. Brace is pointing to the board, where he scribbled a few sentences.

"Simile," someone calls from the back of the room, before yawning.

"How do you know?"

"Because it says *like* or *as*," someone else groans.

I tiptoe over to my seat between DeShaun Stevens and Shrynn.

DeShaun cups his hands over his mouth. "Ooooooh," he says, like I'm in big trouble. But then he smiles and holds his bag of pretzels out to me under the table. We're not allowed to eat in class, but DeShaun somehow gets away with always eating in class, and he always secretly shares his snacks with us.

"Nice of you to join us, Max." Mr. Brace pauses at the board. He looks to be about my dad's age, and he has beads of sweat forming under his curly red hair. Mr. Brace gets really sweaty when he teaches, and his pale skin gets super flushed and splotchy, like he's just finished a workout.

"Sorry, Mr. Brace," I say as I rush to pull my books and notes out from my backpack. I'm even later than I would have been because I needed to stop at homeroom to let Mrs. Shipp know that I wasn't absent.

The last thing I needed was for the school to text Mom

telling her that I hadn't made it to homeroom. Mr. Brace stares at me like he wants an explanation.

"I . . . um." My face heats up as I try to figure out what to say. "Girl stuff." I mean, what was I supposed to say? That I spent the last half hour in the bathroom crying because my sister is telling everyone that I need to get my face rearranged?

Mr. Brace returns to the board. "TMI, Plink. But we're glad you're here."

⋛ ☆ ⋚

Instead of going straight to lunch, I convince Shrynn to come to the bathroom with me. Except, we don't go to the bathroom that's closest to the cafeteria. We go to the bathroom near the library, which is on the other side of the school. A lot of kids use the bathroom during lunch, and I need to avoid them.

"What gives, Maxi?" Shrynn rolls her eyes as I drag her by the arm down the hall. "I'm really hungry. And I told DeShaun we'd eat with him today. Keisha's joining us, too."

"They won't be mad if we're a little late," I grumble. The door is like a boulder and it takes my whole body to push it open. I peek under the stalls. The bathroom is empty and echoey. You can hear water dripping from the faucets and crashing into the sink.

My book bag has a deep inner pocket that I use when I need to make sure I don't lose things, like lunch money or painkillers for my mouth. But today, I brought my headgear with me to show Shrynn.

Her dark brown eyes widen as I pull the hunk of metal from my bag. Shrynn wears braces, too, but she doesn't look like she has something wrong with her face. She's way shorter than me—six inches or so—and has a super pretty smile. Shrynn doesn't have to think about constantly being on drool patrol, and the other kids don't bully her about *her* braces.

She pushes her long black hair out of her face and ties it into a low ponytail. I glance toward the bathroom door and notice a wooden stopper up against the wall.

"Just a sec," I say. I leap over to the stopper and stick it under the door, just to be extra sure no one comes in.

I strap the metal to my head. Shrynn winces, and now I can't look at her.

I don't know exactly what I was expecting Shrynn to do, but I guess I wasn't expecting her to recoil in horror at the sight of me.

"Maxi," she says softly. "That really sucks. Are you supposed to wear it in school?"

"No, I don't have to do that," I say. I try to speak through the metal but haven't gotten used to it yet, so I'm still speaking with a lisp. "I just wanted to show it to you. Because words can't really describe . . ."

"Well, if you don't have to wear it at school, don't worry—"

The bathroom door, the same door that took my entire body to open, flings open so hard and so fast that it bangs against the wall. Carlay Prince, Queen of the Seventh Grade, waltzes in with Alexis so close behind that she's practically in Carlay's back pocket. It's also Alexis's lunch hour but it never occurred to me that they'd show up at a bathroom clear on the other side of the school.

"No one ever uses this bathroom," Carlay says, but then stops short when she sees me and my metal in all its glory. Alexis bangs right into the back of her but Carlay doesn't seem to notice. Carlay brings her hands to her mouth like she stepped into raw sewage.

"EWWWWWW!" she shrieks. "LOOK AT YOUR TRAIN-WRECK FACE!" She whips out her phone and starts fiddling with it and now I have exactly three seconds to stop myself from becoming the star of her million and one social media channels.

Quickly, I yank on the jawbreaker, but I forget that it's still strapped to the back of my head and I yowl in pain. Alexis smirks but doesn't say anything.

Look at your train-wreck face.

Those were Alexis's exact words in the car the other day and now they're bouncing off the bathroom tiles, except they're coming out of Carlay's mouth.

"Come on, Maxi," Shrynn says softly. She helps me unfasten my jawbreaker's strap right as Carlay positions her phone at me. I yank the metal from my face and shove it into my book bag, remembering Mom's warnings that if I break it or lose it, I'll be in the kind of trouble I've never even heard of.

"Yeah, come *on*, Maxi-Pad," Carlay snarls.

Alexis peers over her shoulder. "Did you get a picture?" she whispers, and in this moment I feel such a burning hatred for my sister that I can barely breathe.

7

NO ROOM FOR ANYTHING EXTRA

It's the next morning and Alexis is scarfing down toast in the kitchen and waving a crumpled piece of paper. "Ma, I forgot to give you this," she says.

I'm a few feet away in the bathroom gripping a brush and trying to batten down my hair, but I'm only making it worse because it poofs out more and more with each stroke.

I'm also starving. Last night was my second full night with the jawbreaker and now I know how it got its name. I could barely crunch into my cereal this morning, so I had to have applesauce and soft cheese instead of cornflakes.

I never told Mom about what happened at school yesterday. I wanted to forget about it, and besides, I didn't think there was a point. Mom and Dad don't do anything when Alexis acts up right in front of them, so why would this be any different?

"What is it?" Mom asks. I hear her washing breakfast dishes. She leaves for work at the diner at around the same time we leave for school.

"The permission slip for the sixth-grade trip. We're going to the Museum of Modern Art. It costs fifty dollars for the bus and the ticket and lunch and stuff. It's due next week."

I know what's coming. Alexis takes art seriously. She has an easel propped up against the corner wall in our bedroom, with a bunch of paints and brushes that she keeps in a pencil box on the floor underneath it.

"I told you both at the beginning of the year that we don't have extra money," Mom growls. I hear dishes clinking in the sink. "We're still trying to catch up from a couple of years ago."

What happened a couple of years ago, when I was in the fifth grade, is that Mom lost her job at the pediatrician's office where she worked answering the phones and filing papers and stuff, because the doctor decided to retire and move away. This was also around the time when our elementary school started putting pressure on everyone to have their own computer at home, because of Junior High School Expectations. Mom and Dad didn't want us to fall behind, so they spent money they didn't have on a new computer, which also meant that we had to get internet, because that's how our teachers wanted us to submit some of our assignments. Even though my parents got the cheapest kind of computer, they still complained about the extra bill, and they never let us use it for anything but school.

Mom eventually found her job at the diner, but then Dad's car broke down and then our landlord told them that he was raising the rent, so they had to deal with that, too. This was also when I started seeing Dr. Watson, and the words *severe malocclusion* and *skeletal deformity* were suddenly a daily topic of conversation.

Also around this time, Mom started chain-smoking again after she'd already quit for a year, and she and Dad started fighting about everything.

"But Mom, if I go to the museum I can write a paper about it for extra credit and then bring my grade up in English! And besides, MoMA has a bunch of new exhibits and I really wanna see 'em! You *know* that this is important!"

"What's important?" Dad just got home from a night at work and now I hear him in the living room with his heavy work boots.

Mom ignores him. "Ask your teacher if there's another way to get your grade up. And maybe you should have thought about this before you started slacking off."

"I *don't* slack off," Alexis huffs. "I just can't stand the books she makes us read. They're not even interesting, and they're all about stupid stuff, so I fall asleep, and then we get a pop quiz. I don't know why she keeps making us read books about things that don't even happen here. And all the characters are dumb rich kids with dumb rich parents who live in big houses," she says, then takes an annoyed breath. "They have dumb conversations about their stupid idiot lives. So yeah, totally real-life stuff that I'm supposed to want to read about."

"Alexis Jane, you fall asleep in *class*?"

Uh-oh. Mom's voice rises about nine octaves, and I know it's time for me to get my butt to school.

"What's this about falling asleep in school?" Dad calls out from the living room. He's taking off his boots and they make a loud thud as they drop to the floor, like bricks.

Softly, I open the bathroom door and slink back to my bedroom to get my backpack. "Hi, Dad," I whisper as I creep past. He has deep lines around his eyes and he looks tired.

"Sorry, Alexis. You've seen the extras board," says Mom. "There's no room for anything extra this month."

The extras board is this white board that hangs up inside our front hallway, right opposite the door to our apartment. It's the first thing you see when you walk in and the first thing you see when you leave, unless you shield your eyes. The board has the word EXTRAS on top, in big blue capital letters. Sometimes, there's a number under it. The number represents the exact amount we have available to spend on extra things that month, like a new pair of sneakers or something. And with each extra thing we get, Mom writes it on the board and updates the number. She always tells us to check the board first before we ask for extras. Once we're at zero, we have to wait for the next month.

In a good month, if Dad works a lot of overtime or if they pay off a bill, there might be a hundred bucks to spend on extra things. But lately, the board has nothing but a big red zero on it.

When our friends came over it was really embarrassing, because a lot of times they'd ask what it means. When Shrynn asked, I told her that I didn't know, but that it probably had something to do with Dad's work.

I don't really have friends over that much anymore, anyway.

Mom's voice cuts through my thoughts. "We have too many bills this year as it is, and a payment for your sister's braces is due next week. If you're getting bad grades in English, it sounds like you shouldn't be going on a trip anyway. Get your grades up and *then* we'll talk," she says.

"Hey, Bean," Dad says to me. He sighs as he tugs on the low ponytail that I decided on for my hairdo. I smell that sour smell again and my gut twitches.

Mom rushes into the living room. "If you wanted to go on an expensive school trip, you should have saved your birthday money like we told you to," she calls out behind her. She looks at Dad. "Tell her, please."

"But I used it for other things that you told me to use it for!" Alexis's voice is high pitched and she sounds like she might cry. In a way, I feel bad for her because it's just like Mom to send us mixed messages like this. Sometimes she'll get mad at one of us for doing exactly what she told us to do.

"I don't have time for this." Mom snatches her coat and apron from the hall closet before lighting up a cigarette.

Alexis storms into the living room and glares at me, and I know what she's thinking. She can't go on *her* trip because of *my* braces.

"Why don't we talk about it later?" Dad says to Mom. Alexis looks at him hopefully.

"If you wanna argue with her, go right ahead."

"I have some overtime coming up; maybe we can work something out," Dad says.

"If you have overtime, we have bills to pay." Mom grabs her purse and slings the strap over her shoulder. "There's breakfast on the counter." She slams the door on the way out and the walls vibrate.

8

MAX HOARDS LUNCH MONEY

"There're other ways to get money. I think the school has funds," I say to Alexis on our way to the bus stop. It's an unusually warm winter day. I even want to take off my coat, but I know Alexis would tell Mom if I did. "Scholarships and stuff. In case someone needs money. You just have to ask your homeroom teacher for an application, and then she gives it to the principal. But I also have—"

"That's not for class trips," Alexis says as she glares at me. "It's for poor kids who need food and clothes and school supplies and stuff, and *we're* not poor. And besides, if you wanna ask the school for money, go ahead and embarrass yourself. I'm not about to ask the principal for a handout."

Alexis is wrong about the school money. The fund is for things that the principal calls needs-based.

But I had a feeling Alexis would respond that way, and I had a plan B. I feel the outline of my secret stash in my jeans pocket—leftover money that I keep hidden in my sock drawer. I brought it with me to school today in case Alexis wanted it for her trip. I thought that maybe if I helped her, she'd be nicer to me.

I take a breath. "I have leftover—"

"Just shut up about it!" she snaps. I wince. If my eyes were closed, I could swear it was my mother walking next to me and not my sister. The way their voices take on that razor sharpness, the way their words could cut glass. The way they're both angry for so much of the time.

"I hate you!" Alexis is shrieking now. We're close enough to the bus stop for the other kids to hear her. I see Carlay turn around from where she's standing on the corner with Vince. "Just don't talk to me! Go away!"

There's a deli right at our bus stop. I duck inside, trying to avoid my reflection.

I hide behind shelves piled high with bags of chips and stacks of newspapers. I study the newspaper covers. The headlines are nothing but crime and politics. Boring. But I pick up the *New York Daily News* because that's the one Dad reads and I think it would make him proud if he saw that I bought my own newspaper, even though I could use a computer to read the news for free if I really wanted to.

I hear the bus roar from down the street. I run my fingers over my jeans pocket and feel my small wad of cash and coins folded into a single sock like a wallet. I've been saving most of my lunch money for a few weeks. When I know Mom's not paying attention, I make my own lunch at home. If my parents knew I made my own lunch most of the time, they wouldn't give me money for it.

Lunch at school is three dollars, if you don't get any dessert. I have almost five dollars in my sock and another twenty-five hidden in my drawer at home. I feel like I need to save as much as I can, in case there's a school trip or something else that I want. I don't like to ask my parents for extra money, especially when the extras board says zero.

I pull out one dollar and two quarters and quickly place the newspaper on the counter. Maybe if I can read it on the bus I'll be distracted enough to not notice when Alexis and her friends start in on me.

9
SHRYNN'S PERFECT LIFE

"So you have to wear it for, like, sixteen hours a day?" Shrynn's lying on her bed on her stomach, with her feet kicking back and forth behind her. I'm sitting next to her as she runs her tongue over the brackets on her top teeth, like she's trying to imagine what it must be like to have your jaws reconfigured by an obnoxious metal rod.

Shrynn shoves some popcorn in her mouth, even though she's not supposed to because of her own braces. Popcorn is her favorite thing ever—especially the caramel-coated kind—and she hides bags under her bed because her mom would not be happy if she knew that Shrynn wasn't taking the Rules About Braces seriously. "And what does it feel like, exactly?"

It's Friday, thank goodness, and school ended about an hour ago. I usually go to her house on Fridays, unless I have an orthodontist's appointment. Going to Shrynn's house is one of my favorite things in the world because she's one of my favorite people, and the Li/Cheung family is really nice to me. But I also love going to Shrynn's because then I don't have to take the bus home after school. Andra—that's Shrynn's mom—picks us up. Andra's last name is Li, while Shrynn and her sister use their dad's last name, Cheung.

As soon as we shut the door to her bedroom, I pull the jawbreaker out of my backpack and strap it to my mouth for another fun game of show-and-tell.

"You'll wear it at Shrynn's," Mom said this morning, after I protested this New Rule. "Or you'll stay home. And *don't* lose it at school. I'll be calling Shrynn's mother to make sure you wear it, and at your next appointment, I'll be asking Dr. Watson about whether she can tell if you've been slacking."

I bit my tongue during Mom's lecture.

Then I think she felt bad about being so strict, because she said, "Look, I know it ain't fun. And you don't have to wear it in public. But if you want to go to your friends' houses after school, this is what you have to do."

At least she tried to soften the blow. She doesn't always.

"It basically feels like the front of my face is being pulled through the back of my head," I say to Shrynn. It's still kind of hard to talk through all the metal, but I'm getting used to it.

"That really stinks," Shrynn says quietly. "I guess that's why my mom was on the phone with your mom yesterday?"

I don't say anything. It's hard to talk about what my family can be like, even to Shrynn. And already my jaw is starting to throb.

"Well, hopefully you won't need surgery. My mom said your mouth would have to be wired shut if you do. Not a bad thing for the rest of us." Shrynn throws a pillow at me, and we both start laughing.

"By the way, Mom gave Amy and me permission to have a few people over next Friday. Like you, DeShaun, and maybe some people from newspaper club. She said she'd make cupcakes and order pizza." Amy is Shrynn's younger sister.

"So what do you think?" Shrynn says. Her birthday is months away, so I'm confused about why she'd be throwing a party. "What for?" I ask.

She shrugs. "Why not? Mom thinks Amy and I could use a winter distraction." Shrynn rolls her eyes. "Corny, but so what? We get a party out of it."

Having a little party at Shrynn's house sounds like the best thing in the fricking world, and it's all I can do to not do a cartwheel in the middle of her room.

"Amy might have some of her friends, too. That okay?"

"Of course it's okay," I say. "I love Amy. You know that." Amy is Alexis's age but she's nothing like Alexis. She's funny and silly and she and Shrynn really adore each other.

"Does your mom know what Alexis has been acting

like?" Shrynn asks. I know she's thinking about what she witnessed in the bathroom at school this week.

"Not really," I say. "I mean, she sees some things, but . . ."

"Alexis seems to be hanging around with Carlay and Vince a lot," Shrynn says slowly, quietly, like she's being careful about choosing her words. "Do you think your parents should know?"

Shrynn's known Carlay and Vince for as long as I have, so she knows how mean they are. *Everyone* knows how mean they are.

"It seems more like she's a tagalong," I snort. It's true. From what I've seen, it's more like Carlay and Vince put up with Alexis jumping at their heels like a puppy. And they only seem to really be into her when she's bullying me.

"I don't get it," Shrynn says. "I'm not saying that I'm perfect, or that Amy is perfect, but, like, I can't imagine my sister acting like that. And my parents would totally go nuclear if they knew that Amy was making fun of me and trying to get other kids in on it." She starts braiding her long black ponytail.

Amy and Alexis aren't friends, and it's not hard to figure out why. To Alexis, Amy is probably too nice, if there's even such a thing. To Amy, Alexis is probably too much of a goblin.

I slide down onto the floor, and Shrynn climbs down from her bed to sit cross-legged across from me. I think about how to respond, because I really don't know how to say that my parents are too busy or preoccupied or whatever to get Alexis to back off. Or how, if one of us does something Mom doesn't like, we both get in trouble for it.

On Shrynn's nightstand, I see a small silver frame that I hadn't noticed before. It's a picture of the Li/Cheung family, and it looks somewhat recent. The girls are standing in front of their parents, and they're all smiling, happy to be together. Well, Shrynn and her mom and dad are smiling. Amy is sticking her tongue out and trying to touch the tip of her nose, a total Amy move. And Shrynn has her arm around Amy's shoulder.

To be honest, I'm a little jealous of Shrynn. She just seems so happy all the time. Even her bedroom seems happy. She doesn't have to share it with her sister, and it's big and the walls are a bright yellow and she has her own artwork hanging up all over, mostly still life sketches of fruit and vegetables. Her bedroom sort of feels like a museum. One of Shrynn's sketches even hangs up in the dining room—it's of Amy biting into an apple. Alexis would love Shrynn's art, I think, but I've never told her about it. Alexis hasn't ever been nice to the people I consider my friends.

Just then, Amy comes barging into the room. "Mom made cookies!" she cries. "Chocolate chip! Mom almost *never* makes chocolate chip cookies unless you're coming over, Max. And we also have leftover pineapple buns!"

Shrynn's mom is standing behind Amy holding a plate

of cookies in one hand, and in the other, a plate with a few buns that look like bumpy bread rolls, except they're sweet and buttery—I know because I've tasted them before.

Shrynn, Amy, and Andra all have the same light tan skin, freckled noses, dark eyes, and thick black hair, except Amy's hair is wavier and cut shorter than Shrynn's.

"You remember these, right, Max?" Shrynn's mom says. "They're called bolo bao. One of our favorite desserts. The girls' grandmothers know how to make them from scratch, but not me. Thankfully we have that great Chinese bakery right near where their dad works." She places the cookies and buns on the floor, in front of Shrynn and me.

"They're called pineapple buns because of the way the crust comes out," Amy says, snatching one from the plate. She holds it out to me. "See? It's hard and bumpy. Like a pineapple."

I smile. "I remember," I say, forgetting for a second that I'm wearing my jawbreaker. And Amy must have been too excited about the cookies and buns to notice that I have this hunk of metal wrapped around my face, until now.

"Whoa!" she says. "Where can I get one of those?"

"Amy," Shrynn warns, "be kind. And by the way, please knock next time. You don't like when I go barging into your room, right?"

"But I *am* being kind. I want one! I want to look like Saturn! That's my favorite planet!"

I burst out laughing. Science is Amy's favorite subject, and it's just like her to have a favorite planet.

"Um, don't you think *Earth* should be your favorite planet, you loony tune?" Shrynn teases.

"Maybe you'll have one next year, when you have braces," Andra says. She sits down on the floor to join us. Amy plops down between her mom and Shrynn and grabs a cookie now that she's done eating her pineapple bun.

Shrynn's mom takes a bite of a cookie and looks at me. She smiles, but her eyes are laced with concern. Andra is way older than my mom. Something like ten years older. But she has a lot less gray hair than my mom. And she's dressed really nicely, in black slacks and a white blouse with ruffles in the front. She's wearing pink fuzzy slippers now, but when she picked us up from school, she was wearing heels. Andra is an accountant and Shrynn's dad is a pharmacist, so they have to dress all fancy-like for work. From what Shrynn has told me, her mom gets off work before we get out of school, but she also goes in super early.

"How does your mouth feel today, Max?" she asks.

I unhooked the jawbreaker so that I could eat a pineapple bun. "It's okay, I guess. No big deal." I don't want to complain to Andra after she went through the trouble to give us dessert.

"Can I see it?" Amy holds out her hand for my jawbreaker. I lift it from where it sits in my lap and examine it.

"There's not really anything to see," I say. "It's just a stupid metal bar that connects to my braces."

"Amy, these things are not toys, and I'm sure Max wouldn't want you touching something that has to go back in her mouth." Andra's voice is stern but kind. In fact, I've never heard her yell at Shrynn or her sister and I've known them for, like, a hundred years.

"Bummer," Amy responds. "Well, can you make sure I get one when I have to have braces?" She wraps her arm around her mom's, and I laugh again.

"We'll see what the orthodontist says," Andra replies. She winks at Amy and then turns her attention back to me. "It's really normal, Max, to go through something like this. It's also really normal to be frustrated with it. It's hard work that your orthodontist is doing, to make sure that you don't have problems later on in life." She strokes Amy's hair. "Everyone has a bone or two to fix at some point. Your bones just happen to be in your mouth."

"You should tell her about your crown, Mom!" Amy says. She's on her third cookie now.

"Your crown?" I ask.

"Oh, yes, a silly tooth in the back of my mouth. It was weak and it needed a crown." Andra opens her mouth wide and points to a back molar.

"She also has a couple of fake teeth," Shrynn says, smiling. "Like, two totally fake chompers right at the front."

"Really?" I gape. Andra smiles. All her teeth looked real to me.

She points to her bottom teeth. "Bicycle accident, when I was a teenager living in Hoboken, New Jersey. It was stupid, really. I had a lollipop in my mouth. And back then, it took them weeks to make new teeth! I walked around like a jack-o'-lantern—at school, out shopping, everywhere!" The four of us laugh.

"Which is totally why we're not allowed to be on our bikes or Rollerblades with candy in our mouths," Amy comments, rolling her eyes.

"I got very lucky," Andra says.

"It probably could have been much worse," Shrynn says wisely.

In this moment, I feel like I belong. Even better, I feel like everything's going to be okay. And like maybe the jawbreaker will do its job and I won't have to have surgery.

For the first time since I got my headgear, I actually don't mind talking about my teeth.

"Mom, can we take a picture?" Amy digs into her pants pocket for her cell phone. She pulls out a pink case with yellow daisies on it.

"Only if it's okay with Max."

"Can you wear your Saturn ring?" Amy nods at my headgear. "What's it called, anyway?"

My stomach drops. Amy wants me to wear my jawbreaker in a picture. That's like . . . evidence. Documentation. Proof.

"It's—I call it a jawbreaker, but—"

"COOL!"

"I don't think Max wants to wear it in a picture," Andra says softly. "And that's okay."

"It's *very* okay," says Shrynn. "Amy, don't be a pest."

"But it's so cool!" Amy is practically screeching. "How could you *not*? Every science nerd I know would be so jealous!"

I look down at my headgear. I guess I don't need to make such a big deal about it. And Amy is such a good kid—I figure that I could at least give her this one thing.

"On one condition," I say.

"*Any*thing," she says with a grin.

"You can't share it with anyone or let anyone see it. Only us."

"Deal. As long as we also get your T-shirt in it."

I look down. I forgot that I'm wearing a white T-shirt that says *YOU'RE HILARIOUS* in black block letters, with a yellow, grim-looking emoji underneath.

Amy holds out her hand. I shake it wildly and we both giggle. I can trust Amy like a sister. I mean, like the sort of sister I wish I had.

I strap my jawbreaker to my mouth and Shrynn and Amy stand on either side of me, wrapping their arms around my waist. Andra takes Amy's camera and holds it out in front of us.

"Say cheese!" she says.

"No, say Saturn!" Amy protests.

"We can't smile and say Saturn at the same time." Shrynn rolls her eyes.

"Challenge accepted!" Amy takes a deep breath.

"SATURN!" we all screech. It turns out, you can absolutely say *Saturn* and smile at the same time.

10

A FAMILY ON FIRE

Friday night is pizza night at our house, and it's also the one night a week that we get to eat dinner with Dad without him having to leave for work because his schedule is a little different on Fridays. He works straight through a Thursday night shift into the day shift on Friday, and by the time he gets home he's exhausted but in for the night.

Between hanging out with Shrynn and going home to a pizza dinner, Friday is probably my favorite day of the week and today feels especially good.

But I know something's wrong as soon as I get home. I can see it in Mom's eyes.

First of all, there's no pizza. Mom made grilled cheese, which is more like a backup dinner. She's also glaring at Dad, but he's acting like he doesn't notice. Alexis is sitting on the couch playing with Mom's phone, which is how I *really* know something's going on. Mom never lets us just play with her phone unless she really wants us to be distracted.

"What's going on?" I ask.

"Why don't you girls go to your room for a few minutes?" Dad says. "And shut the door behind you."

Without arguing, me and Alexis head to our room. Something in Dad's voice means business.

Alexis sprawls out on her bunk bed with a bottle of nail polish, and I camp out on my bunk with the newspaper that Dad left for me until I remember that I forgot to do something.

I get up and rummage through my book bag to find my jawbreaker. I fasten it to my braces, and for the first time, Alexis doesn't say anything about it. Maybe it's boring to her now, which is fine with me. Alexis bores easily.

"Because Friday night is *family* night, not your friends' night." I hear Mom's muffled voice through the wall and my stomach churns.

"Sometimes I need time to myself, Jackie. You know, like the kind of time you get on your days off when the girls are at school. Just some time away. Is that so bad?"

"If you need time away so bad, maybe you'd like to have it permanently. You're a *husband* and a *father*, Chris. Or did you forget that fact?" There's a pause. "How could you be so selfish?"

I hear Alexis sigh from the top bunk, but we don't say

anything to each other. It's weird to have a sibling who knows exactly what you're going through, but who you can't talk to about it. Who you can't talk to about *anything*.

"You know, it would be a lot easier on me if you were home more," Mom continues. "And your breath smells like alcohol. How *dare* you come home smelling like that? I'm tired of covering for you. *Tired* of it!"

"Jackie, calm down. Do we need the neighborhood knowing our business?"

Mom starts yelling like the house is on fire. "You don't get to tell me to calm down when you smell like a six-pack." There's a pause. "I want you gone," she seethes. "You hear me? *Gone*." My gut's in knots and I hear her flick her cigarette lighter, even from a room away. Pretty soon, the house will smell like cigarette smoke. Dad *hates* when the house smells like cigarette smoke.

"You know we can't afford for me to live anywhere but here," Dad says. "We already talked about that."

Wait, what? Mom and Dad have talked about splitting up? That's news to me.

"Then you'll be on the couch," she barks. "And we'll save, and we'll cut more, because I can't live like this. I *won't* live like this."

"What will we cut, exactly?" Dad's voice booms through the walls. "Every penny is spoken for. You know we can cut your chain-smoking habit, right? That'll free up about a hundred bucks a week right there."

I feel Alexis shift her body on the bunk above me. She's probably facing the wall and covering her head with a pillow. That's what she usually does when Mom and Dad fight. I wish I could also put something over my head, but a blanket or pillow would just pull on my jawbreaker and make my face ache.

I hear Mom storm into the living room. My fluttery happiness from the afternoon is gone and now I want to be anywhere else but home.

"Max, Alexis, in the living room, now," Mom orders. The smell of cigarette smoke creeps under our bedroom door.

I sit up from my bunk. Alexis hops down from hers. I open our bedroom door first. The living room is right on the other side. I can feel Alexis on my heels. When the house is on fire, you don't ask questions. You do what you're told.

When I open the door, Dad's sitting on the couch. Mom's apron is in her hands and her jacket's on, like she's leaving for work. Mom never works on Fridays. Like Mom says, Friday nights are family nights. Even if Dad's in bed early, at least we're all home together.

"I'm working on Friday nights from now on," Mom says. "We need the extra money. When I get home, I expect dinner to be eaten and the dishes to be cleaned and put away. Max, you wash, Alexis, you dry."

"But—" Alexis protests.

"Jackie, stop," Dad says. He sounds defeated.

"You're on dinner duty tonight," she snaps at him. "Make sure Max wears her headgear to bed and check with Alexis about what homework she has to do this weekend. You can help her plan so that she gets everything done on time." Now she's talking like we're not even in the room.

"But you're not even on the schedule," Dad says, sharper this time.

"I am now," Mom bites back. "I'm picking up an overnight shift at the diner. We're short-staffed and they always need someone on Fridays. I'll be home in the morning."

"But *why*?" Dad says. "There's no need for this. And I don't want you walking home at that hour."

"You stopped caring about what I need a long time ago." Mom turns on her heel. The door slams and the walls rattle, and I hear Alexis sniffling as she turns back to our bedroom, slamming the door behind her.

It's not just our house that's on fire. Our family is, too.

⋛ ☆ ⋚

"Why didn't you call me Saturday?" Shrynn asks. "I called you Saturday afternoon *and* Sunday. And why weren't you at lunch?" It's Monday, the Monday after Mom stormed out, and we're sitting in newspaper club. Our paper is totally online, and the room has laptops at each seat. It's the last class of the day and there are only about ten of us and it's my favorite.

Because it's the first full week of the new month, we spend a lot of time figuring out what our stories should be. And then, because we produce two newspapers every month, we divide our stories across the issues and leave room for anything that might crop up in between. Dr. Dodge, our newspaper club adviser, calls them editorial meetings. Keisha takes notes on the whiteboard and they stay up there all month long.

But today I'm distracted and I just want to be by myself. The thing is, I know Shrynn called me this weekend, but I told Mom that I didn't want to talk to anyone. We had a test today in science class, and then I skipped lunch. To be honest, I've been avoiding her.

I don't know how to tell Shrynn what happened last Friday.

I want to forget about my braces and my jawbreaker and my parents' money problems and the constant fighting and the fact that Mom worked her first overnight shift ever and Dad spent the night in his room with dinner getting cold in the kitchen. I want to forget about how another beer can appeared in the recycling bin every time I went into the kitchen for something. I want to forget about how Alexis did all her homework without being told and about how I did the dishes without being reminded and how Alexis dried them with a flimsy dish towel, silent as she stood next to me, one of the few times in recent memory that we've worked together without griping and bickering.

For practically the whole weekend no one said a word to one another.

I especially wanted to forget that Mom said Dad smelled like alcohol. I'd hoped I'd been imagining that sour stench.

We learned about alcoholism in school when my science teacher showed the class before-and-after pictures of someone's liver after they'd been an alcoholic for a bunch of years or something. The alcoholic liver was a different color and a different shape from the healthy liver and looked, well . . . sick. My teacher did the same thing with a pair of lungs. He showed us a picture of healthy lungs, and then he showed us a smoker's lungs. The smoker's lungs were the color of charcoal and all crinkly looking, and I figured that's what Mom's lungs must look like because she smokes a lot—especially when she's annoyed. And people who have sick livers and messed-up lungs could get *really* sick and maybe even die.

But there's one thing that I can't stop thinking about, no matter how hard I try.

"This is all. Your. *Fault*," Alexis said through clenched teeth on Friday night. She stood in the middle of our bedroom in her pajamas. Her hair was wild and her face was red and puffy. "They don't even want to stay *married* because of you," she said as she choked back a sob and threw herself facedown onto her bunk bed.

That night, that terrible, no-good, awful Friday night, I fell asleep thinking about the Li/Cheung family. About how Amy's face lights up with happiness and the way Shrynn puts her arm around her sister when they're standing together at the refrigerator looking for a snack. I thought about Andra's soft voice and gentle face. I don't see Shrynn's dad, Daniel, as much. He's tall with lighter skin than Andra and thick black hair. When I do see him, though, he always seems happy to be home with his family. He'll walk through the door after work and give Shrynn and Amy a hug while their mom stands in the background smiling.

I don't know how to tell my best friend, my friend with the most perfect family in the world, that my own family is falling apart.

11

THE JOURNALISM COMPETITION OF A LIFETIME

Thankfully, I don't have to. Not yet, anyway. As soon as the bell rings, Dr. Dodge gets things going so we have to stop talking.

"Good afternoon, esteemed staff reporters!" he calls out. He stands up from behind his desk. Dr. Dodge is tall and thin and probably the snazziest dresser I've ever seen. He always wears a suit to school, topped off with a silver watch that practically glows against his brown skin. Today he's wearing a light gray pin-striped suit and shiny black leather shoes.

I can't help but notice his teeth, because I notice everyone's teeth. His are pearly and perfect and for the thousandth time I'm wondering if he's ever had braces, but I'm too shy to ask. Dr. Dodge looks like the kind of guy who might have been on his way to model for a magazine and then took a wrong turn and wound up advising the newspaper club at Weiss Junior High School instead. He also teaches seventh-grade life science, but I don't have him for science because I have Mrs. Neast.

The class quiets down. "We have a couple of announcements. K-Word, why don't you get us started?"

Keisha stands up and smiles. She's very professional looking, in a black blazer and turtleneck and red suede flats that look like ballet slippers. "Thanks, Dodge." He lets the newspaper club members call him Dodge. "First, let's not forget that it's time for New York's Rising Star journalist competition." She checks her phone, which is where she keeps her meeting notes. "The deadline's in eight weeks."

"I'd like to jump in to say a bit more about this," Dr. Dodge says, standing from where he was sitting at an empty student pod. "For anyone who thinks they might want to get involved with journalism someday, this is the competition for you. The winners get chosen by Jordan Slade personally. If you win, you'll get to shadow Jordan for a day this summer at Brooklyn's very own Channel 5 News. She announces the finalists and winner on the air sometime in late spring."

My heart leaps. Jordan Slade is a super well-known journalist and I love her story. She's always talking about how her parents were poor but pushed her to do well in school and how she climbed through the ranks in journalism. By the time she'd finished high school she had two internships under her belt and Channel 5 loved her so much that they paid for her to go to college, which was something she wouldn't have been able to do without the studio's help.

Mom knows how much I liked watching Jordan on TV in the mornings before school, so she even read her memoir and shared the most important parts with me. According to Mom, Jordan wrote a lot about how she had to work harder than other people—the kind of people who start out with money and connections and don't have to fight as hard for the things they have.

"That could be you," Mom said, back when she used to say nice things to me. "You could be the next Jordan."

"It's a serious opportunity," Dr. Dodge continues. "For the first time in the competition's history, they're requiring video essays instead of written ones, whereas it used to be the applicant's choice. And remember, it's open to students across the city, so there'll be a *lot* of applications. The winning video gets posted to the news website and winners get a five-hundred-dollar prize to spend however they want."

Shrynn and I share a glance. I bet she's interested in applying. I mean, most of the kids who are on the newspaper would probably want to do something like this.

Normally this kind of competition is something I'd really

want to do, but there's no way I'm submitting a video essay. No way in the *world*. The last thing I need is for my face to be on TV or the internet. Mom and Dad have always warned us about that kind of thing—what goes on the internet today stays on the internet forever. The thought of my face, my mouth, my teeth living online until the end of time makes me want to cry. Especially because I *know* it would wind up in the wrong hands.

Besides, it would be too weird to compete against my best friend for something so important. And even though the scholarship money would be nice, Shrynn can have it for all I care.

"This used to be a competition without a prize," Dr. Dodge continues, "but Jordan worked really hard to make sure to change that part so that all kinds of kids from all different backgrounds were recognized for their hard work." I stare at my fingers because I know exactly what Dr. Dodge is getting at. "And you all won't have to worry about competing against Keisha, being as she won last year and previous winners are not allowed to compete again." Dr. Dodge laughs like he told the funniest joke ever, but none of us laugh with him.

Keisha shrugs. "It's true, but I wasn't gonna say it." And then we all laugh because Keisha made it funny.

"Any questions?" Dr. Dodge asks. A sixth-grade reporter half raises her hand.

"What if we don't have great video equipment?" she asks, when what she *should* ask is, *What if we don't have the right equipment for this competition? And how is it fair to compete against kids who do?*

"I'm sure we can work it out with the AV club," Dr. Dodge says. "Students borrow equipment for their projects all the time, as long as it's school related." The AV club is for the kids who like video production. The newspaper club works closely with them (we call them the AVCs) when we have a project that's heavy on the audiovisual stuff. Carlay and Vince are AVCs, but I've never had to deal with them, thank goodness.

"Any other questions?"

I zone out while other kids ask stuff like how many people can be in their videos and how long they have to be. Part of me wishes that I could just write the danged thing, because then applying would be a no-brainer. I'm good at writing and I don't need any special equipment to do it. And if I won, I wouldn't have to worry about my face being on the internet for the world to see.

"I'll help you with yours if you help me with mine," Shrynn whispers.

"I'm not gonna do it," I whisper back.

Shrynn's eyes bug out. "What? *Why?* This is totally your thing."

"I know, it's just . . ." How do you tell your best friend

that you're too embarrassed about how you look to record a video?

"Let me know if you'd like to kick around ideas for your applications," Dr. Dodge says. "I'll hand out the forms when announcements are over. Read the instructions carefully—they'll probably answer all of your questions. Keisha, what's next on the agenda?"

"First, any ideas for stories for the next issue, or future issues? I have some, too, so let's get a list going." She makes her way around the pods to the whiteboard and uncaps a marker.

Shrynn raises her hand, and I see her cheeks flush. She can be shy in class sometimes.

"I . . . I think I'd like to do something on divorce," she says quietly. "Kids whose families are going through a divorce. For a future edition." Dr. Dodge nods slowly as Keisha positions her marker to the board. I look at Shrynn but she doesn't bring her eyes to meet mine.

"An essay or a reported feature?" Keisha asks.

"Oh, um," Shrynn stammers. "Reported. Just reported. Thanks."

"This sounds like a strong project," Dr. Dodge says kindly. "Let's talk about which issue it should be in, okay?"

Shrynn nods. "Thank you," she says softly.

Does Shrynn somehow know what's going on with me at home? Does she have some kind of best-friend ESP? I mean, it's not like I'm wearing a tattoo across my forehead that says, *Hi! My parents hate each other and have talked about splitting up but can't afford to do it. What's going on in your life?*

Mom's words to Dad swim across my brain. *I want you gone.*

"We also need another opinion piece." Keisha writes *Op-Ed* on the board. "Max, you're great at this. Want to take this one? It can be whatever you want. We'll need it by the middle of next week."

I hide a smile. "Sounds good," I say. I write *Op-Ed* in my planner.

Keisha makes a list of more stories and their assigned staff writers. Theft in the locker room. The new school rule about fining ten dollars to students who use their cell phones in class without permission. Cutting our lunch hour short by fifteen minutes so that we can add class time onto major subjects. And a few other things that I had no idea were happening. Shrynn takes on the story about theft in the locker room. And most of the staff writers are handling at least two stories each. I feel weird about only having the op-ed to work on, but my internet connection at home really stinks. And besides, I get no privacy because Mom makes us use the computer in the living room ever since Alexis was caught on social media, which we're totally not allowed to have.

"Oh, one more thing," Dr. Dodge says. "I agreed to help Mrs. Neast with something. The sixth-grade science teachers are having their showcase in about six weeks and she'd like to run a montage on loop, with pictures of all the science-y things that we do around school. The AV club agreed to lead the project, but it couldn't hurt to have a few more hands on deck. You'd just have to help gather some images with your phone. Mrs. Neast said that the science teachers would be happy to consider your efforts for extra credit, which sounds like an easy way to get some bonus points. Any takers?"

Shrynn and a couple of other kids raise their hands. I'd like to contribute because I wouldn't mind extra credit for science, but I don't have the right kind of phone. Keisha writes their names on the whiteboard under the words *Science Montage*.

When she's finished, Dr. Dodge stands back and admires the board. "And this, folks, is why we're an award-winning online newspaper. The hardest-working biweekly in the whole city." A few of us clap, and Dodge bows because he's goofy like that. "Thank you all for your good thinking with our next couple of issues."

"Don't forget to take a picture of it, in case someone accidentally erases it," Keisha says. Everyone, even Dr. Dodge, takes out their phone and snaps a picture while I doodle in the margins of my spiral notebook.

"Okay, all, here are the Channel 5 competition applications. They're also available online, but I wanted to print them out so that they stay on your radar." Dr. Dodge passes out the forms.

Shrynn gives my sleeve a quick tug. "Well, you might not want to do it, but I think we should apply together," she says.

"I'll think about it," I say, even though I won't. My mind's made up.

12

FRIDAY NIGHTS AT SHRYNN'S HOUSE ARE NO MORE

It's Friday morning and five whole days since Dodge introduced the journalism contest, which means it's five whole days closer to the deadline.

But who cares? I'm not applying anyway so it doesn't matter. But every time I tell myself that it doesn't matter and that I don't care, a twinge in my gut tells me that it does, and I do.

As I pack my book bag, I hear Mom moving around in the kitchen. I think she's annoyed about something because she's smoked three cigarettes since she woke up.

I haven't told Mom about Shrynn's party because I go there every Friday anyway. And because Friday night is pizza night at our house, I figured she wouldn't mind if I had pizza at Shrynn's instead. Mom's fiddling around with her purse when I approach.

"Mom, can I—" I begin. She looks up at me.

As soon as I start to speak, Dad comes barging through the door from his night shift, which was pretty good timing because then I can tell the both of them at the same time.

"Before you go to sleep," Mom says to Dad, "don't forget that you're on dinner duty after school today."

"Hello to you, too," he grumbles as he shakes off his work boots. They hit the floor with a thud.

"Shrynn's having some friends from the newspaper club over. I'm supposed to go to her house after school. Like I do every Friday? I was going to ask you if I could eat dinner over there, too. Pizza."

They both look at me like I'm speaking a foreign language.

"I don't think it's a good idea," Mom says. "Your father is working a lot of overtime in the next few weeks. Fridays and Sundays will be the only time he gets to see much of you and your sister."

"But I don't get it," I say. "I see Shrynn almost every Friday. You know that."

"And your friends are more important than your dear old dad?" Dad says as he tugs on my ponytail. I'm not sure but I think I smell a whiff of beer.

"It's not that she's more important, but the whole newspaper's getting together at her house today." If this is some sort of New Rule, this rule where now I'm not allowed to have a life on Fridays, why haven't they said anything?

"You'll have to choose another day," Mom says. "Fridays and Sundays belong to your father now. It's the new arrangement under the circumstances."

"*What* circumstances?"

"That's none of your business," Mom snaps. "Now stop asking questions and let Shrynn know that you'll have to see her on a different day."

"And you can tell me all about the newspaper over pizza dinner tonight," Dad yawns as he makes his way over to the bedroom to change out of his work clothes.

Tears spring to my eyes even though what I really want to do is scream. Lately I feel like a bottle of soda that someone shook really hard and the cap is about to explode right off the top.

"And here's your lunch," Mom says. She hands me a paper bag.

"What do you mean? You know I eat the school's lunch."

"You have to start bringing your own lunch to school," Mom says. I hear Alexis lock herself in the bathroom. "Alexis, too. I bought a bunch of cold cuts and made you a turkey-and-cheese sandwich with a small salad. I put honey mustard on it," she says lightly. "You can probably dip your sandwich in the dressing, too! My customers at the diner order it that way all the time; I bet you'll like it."

I glance at the extras board. It still has a big fat red zero in the middle of it. But that doesn't matter as much when I get to save my lunch money. It's my secret stash. It makes me feel secure. How am I supposed to save if I'm taking lunch to school now?

"But why?" I swallow hard. "Can I get the money from Dad instead?"

"Do *not* ask your father for extra money. Every dime we make has to go toward expenses. And we spoke with a financial adviser," she says with a shrug, like I know what a financial adviser is. "We're taking a look at the bills in the house. It's cheaper to make lunch at home instead of buying it every day, so that's what we'll do. And besides, it's healthier." She opens the bag to show me what's inside. "There're grapes and goldfish crackers, too."

"Oh, goody!" I say. "How lucky am I?"

"Excuse me?" Her head snaps up. "Watch it, little girl," she says. "You *are* lucky. Do you know how many kids don't even get lunch, let alone the hot breakfast you just ate? Me and your father work our butts off to keep food in your stomach." She fidgets with her cigarette lighter, positions a cancer stick between her lips and inhales deeply. "*We* do without so that *you* can have what *you* need."

Someone should tell Mom that that's called Choosing to Have Kids, I say to myself. But I don't dare say it out loud.

"And are you gonna stop buying cigarettes? Is Dad gonna stop buying beer?"

And before I can duck, before I can shield my face or even turn my body or step backward, the back of Mom's hand lashes against my right cheek. My flesh stings, and I don't move, I *can't* move, so I just stand there, staring at the floor. I don't look at her. I *can't* look at her. My veins pulse with betrayal. And possibly hatred. And a deep, aching sadness.

This isn't the first time Mom's hit me, but it's been a while. At least a year, I think. She used to hit us more, especially when we were younger. Usually at home, if we weren't listening. Sometimes she'd yank us by our hair and drag us to our bedroom if she was really mad, or she'd pinch our skin or grab us by the arm real tight.

"Take *that* with you to school," Mom hisses. "Now put your lunch in your book bag and get out of my face."

Alexis emerges from the bathroom just then, her wavy hair in perfect little tendrils held back by a thick headband. It reminds me of Carlay. Carlay is the queen of headbands. I've never seen Alexis wear one before.

She pauses and stares at us. My cheek still stings.

"What's going on?" she asks. Her voice is small, like she's afraid to ask.

Mom thrusts a brown bag of lunch at Alexis. "Take your lunch and get to school."

Alexis snatches the lunch from Mom's hand and glares at me. I'm in trouble, so Mom takes it out on Alexis, too. That's the way it works in our house.

I leave for school, my plans for my perfect Friday forgotten with a single slap.

13

MOM'S SECRET

It's the following Monday afternoon and now we're seeing Dr. Watson for the first time since I got my jawbreaker. Alexis is home with Dad so it's just Mom and me.

I'm super tired today because I had a nightmare last night. Another one. In most of them my teeth fall out of my head and then grow into the size of buildings and then chase me down the street and I wake up in a sweat with my jawbreaker flung across the room. I think my nightmares picked up ever since I had to start wearing this extra chunk of metal.

But I don't tell Mom any of this because we haven't spoken much since the other day. Since the smack. It's fine. I mean, is it even necessary to talk to our parents? Just because we live together? Maybe we just won't talk to each other until I move out when I'm an adult.

And anyway, if I did tell her, she'd probably say she has

bigger fish to fry. She and Dad have been yelling at each other so much lately, especially since Dad's been out on the couch. Even though he and Mom are basically on opposite sleeping schedules, she still wants him to sleep in the living room.

I saw a news story where psychologists and other Important People say that parents are not supposed to fight in front of their kids because it's damaging to our mental health. One lady who wore a white lab coat even said that it could be damaging to a kid's brain to be exposed to screaming and yelling all the time. She said it sets off our fight-or-flight reflex, or something like that.

Well, the Important People would probably tell my parents to cut it out. All they do is fight these days, and it's like they don't even care who's watching or how it makes me or Alexis feel. Sometimes it feels like the walls are shaking when their arguments get really bad.

Last night was no exception. It was Dad's night off and he came home late with a six-pack *and* smelling like beer.

"How dare you? How *dare* you?" Alexis and I had been in bed for a couple of hours by then and Mom didn't even *try* to keep her voice down.

"I don't know what you're talking about," Dad had said. "It's not like I drove home. What's the problem?"

"What's the *problem*?" Mom's voice was even louder and more like a shriek. "This is the third day in a row that you

"So I guess . . . ten to twelve hours including when I sleep?"

Dr. Watson scrunches her eyebrows. "And yet, it seems like it still hurts. Hmm." She pauses. "It's been over a month since we last saw each other, right?" She checks her folder. "You should be acclimated to the headgear by now. The idea is, once you're used to it, we can make minor adjustments along the way until you're exactly where you need to be."

"Max has been complaining that it still hurts," Mom says from the other side of the room, in a tone like it's my fault.

"Close, please." I do what the orthodontist says. She examines my mouth with her mirrors. It aches a bit when she pokes around.

"There is one of two things going on here," Dr. Watson finally says. "Either your jaw is not taking to the treatment, or you're not wearing it as much as you say you are. Either scenario doesn't bode well for avoiding surgery."

Ugh. *Busted*. I pull my hood over my face and stare at my hands.

"Maximillia Audrina Plink," Mom growls from her seat. "The truth."

I swallow hard. Dr. Watson looks at me. "I think I've been taking it off in the middle of the night."

"What do you mean, you *think*?" Mom barks.

"Let's explore this before we jump to conclusions," Dr.

Watson says quickly. For the first time since I met her, she feels more like a friend than an enemy. "Tell me more about what's going on."

I take a deep breath and describe how I've been having nightmares pretty much since I got the jawbreaker, and when I wake up, the danged thing is across the room.

"Or maybe you're not wearing it during the day?" Mom snaps. "When I'm at work and can't monitor?"

"I do, *too*." I'm trying not to cry now. "Put up a camera if you want to."

"Then why didn't you tell me this was happening?"

"Maybe because Max felt like she might be in trouble for something that's partially out of her control," Dr. Watson says gently but firmly. Mom glares but doesn't say anything more. It feels nice to have another adult stand up for me. "There's an easy solution to the nighttime problem, Max," she says. "I see it all the time."

"Is that true?" Mom asks. Her tone is a little softer but not by much.

"It's called unconscious removal," Dr. Watson says. "When a device is especially uncomfortable, we might remove it in our sleep without realizing it." She turns to me. "You say you put it in right before bed?"

"Yeah," I say. "Usually. After I brush my teeth."

"That actually might be the problem." Dr. Watson smiles at me. "The headgear will always feel a bit sore when you first put it in, but the soreness should go away once you're used to it. The trick is to not go to sleep when it's still feeling sore. That's when we run into trouble. Our unconscious minds want to relieve the pain, and we wind up taking off the appliance in the middle of the night without realizing it. You might take a little Tylenol before bed, just as a crutch, until we really nail this down."

I like how Dr. Watson says *we*. Like we're in this together, and it's not just me against my teeth and jaws.

"Now," she continues in a fake stern voice, "I can't say why your headgear is winding up clear across the room. Most of my patients wake up on top of it, or with it next to them. You must be playing baseball or soccer with yours."

I smile. Mom rolls her eyes, but I think I see relief flash across her face.

"So let's agree to start over." Dr. Watson pats my shoulder. "Wear it a couple of hours before bedtime, say, put it on right after dinner. Give the soreness time to settle." She turns to Mom. "If there are any problems in between now and our next visit, don't hesitate to call or make an earlier appointment. We'll troubleshoot together. Let's be sure to arrange another visit for a couple of weeks from now, to check your progress with keeping the headgear in place overnight."

My heart feels lighter, but Mom's quiet as we leave the office.

"I'm sorry, Max," she says as we climb into the car. I'm about to keel over because Mom's not exactly one to apologize.

"What for?" I ask softly.

Mom doesn't say anything at first. "For a lot of things." She doesn't mention the smack specifically, but I wonder if she's thinking about it. "For everything. For the fact that you even have to go through this to begin with."

Mom's never been this honest with me before. Or this . . . what's the word? Humble, I think. She sounds humble.

In a way, it's nice to have Mom all to myself.

"I just really want this headgear thing to work for you, the way it worked for me growing up. I really don't want you to have to go through surgery and eating through a straw for a month."

"Wait a minute," I say. "You had a *jaw*breaker?" I knew that Mom had to have braces when she was a kid, but she's always blamed Dad's side of the family for my bigger dental problems.

Mom nods. "Braces and headgear." She starts the car and then lights a cigarette. I roll down the front windows. "It was a lot different back then, though. Everything was a lot bulkier. A lot more noticeable and barbaric than it is now. I was also the only one in the family who needed them, and your aunts and uncles thought it was hilarious."

Mom doesn't talk much about her brothers and sisters, or their kids (my cousins), and we never see them.

It's always been a little confusing to me, when my friends talk about their big families and how everyone gets together all the time. Shrynn's family is *huge* and she has something like twenty cousins.

"Why didn't you tell me about that part?" I ask.

Mom's quiet for a long minute. "I figured things were so different now that it wouldn't really matter. But it doesn't seem that different at all." She puffs on her cigarette. "I remember wearing it for a year or so. I even had to wear it to school. I got in a lot of trouble for taking it off when I wasn't supposed to. My mother used to wait outside for me after school some days to make sure I was wearing it."

"But if you knew she'd be there, why didn't you just put it on before school got out?"

"I never knew exactly when she'd be there, and sometimes I took my chances," Mom laughs. "I usually walked home from school. And this one time she was waiting and I had no idea."

"So what happened?" I ask.

"She kicked my little butt. And when my father got home from work, he kicked it all over again. They were mad that I was wasting their money."

I'm sad for Mom. It must have been really hard to wear

a jawbreaker to school, and then to have her own parents punish her for not doing it right. "I can't believe you never told me," I say.

"They're painful memories, Max," Mom says. "The kids were cruel. They got away with a lot more than kids do these days. Now there are even *laws* about bullying. There was no such thing when I was growing up. And I never wanted to tell you about any of that because I didn't want you to assume you'd go through the same thing I did."

Mom and Dad have always talked about how little their families had. Dad even told stories about how his mom—my grandma—went without eating sometimes, just to make sure that he and his siblings had food. Mom told similar stories, especially when she thought me and Alexis were being ungrateful.

"How did you and Dad have braces?" I ask carefully. "I mean, how did your parents afford them?"

Mom shrugs. "It was just something we needed. And when your kids need something, you do what you need to do to make it happen. Your grandparents scrubbed toilets and did odd jobs. They took out credit cards and borrowed money from friends. They sold things when the bills were due. We ate peanut butter sandwiches for weeks on end. Whatever it took."

I mull that over. The last few weeks are starting to make

some sense, when I think about what it was like for my mom in her own family, growing up.

"Mom," I say. My heart thuds against my T-shirt, but if I don't take this opportunity to say what needs to be said, I might lose it. "Please don't smack me anymore." The words barely squeak through. "I mean, I know your parents did, but please—"

We've just turned onto our street. I watch Mom out of the corner of my eye. She reaches for her cigarette box and doesn't say anything. But the way her eyes glisten tells me that she's listening.

14

THE BEST PART OF DOUBLE JAW SURGERY

It's Thursday afternoon, a few days after my visit with Dr. Watson and my talk with Mom.

The house is quiet when I get home because Dad's asleep and Alexis had permission to go straight to her friend Kristy's house from school.

With the freedom to use the computer without Alexis breathing down my neck, I know I should churn out an op-ed or two for newspaper club, especially because I never turned in the one I said I would at the start of the month. But I have other things on my mind, and my club responsibilities will have to wait.

I make a mental note to work on it tomorrow during lunch and ask Mom if I can jump on the computer to look up the jaw surgery that I might have to get.

"Why don't you wait until you know you need it?" She looks up from her cigarette and bills.

"Because I want to be prepared," I say. "Just in case."

"If you want to torture yourself, go right ahead," Mom says. She's been a little softer with me since our talk the other day and I race out of the kitchen and into the living room before she changes her mind.

Dad doesn't have to be up for his night shift for another hour, which is right about when Alexis should be home for dinner. So the way I figure it, I have a solid hour of privacy to search about Double Jaw Surgery on the internet.

Within a few minutes, I'm starting to wonder if Mom was right. There are about a million websites that talk about the different kinds of surgeries orthodontic patients might need. I click on one that has a cartoon skeleton dance across the page.

So you need double jaw surgery, the site says. *Talk to your doctor about your options.*

The screen morphs into an animation of a skull sliced in two, with its upper and lower jaws being fitted together, and you can see screws placed all throughout its gums.

Dr. Watson never said anything about screws.

I click on images because I want to see if there are actual pictures of actual people who got the procedure, and not a bunch of animated dancing skeletons.

I'm greeted with hundreds of before-and-after pictures,

which are pretty cool. You can see how the surgery really changed the shape of their jaws, and their teeth look like shiny perfect pearls.

But as I scroll down, I see pictures of people who are right out of surgery. Their faces are swollen to the size of basketballs, and they have dark, ugly bruises under their eyes. Their jaws are held tightly together with rubber bands connected to their top and bottom brackets and the patients look like they're clenching their teeth. One girl even has dried-up blood caked in the corners of her lips, and it makes me want to puke. The pictures make it look like the people are in pain and helpless.

I soon regret even doing this.

I hate when Mom's right.

I click out of the pictures and go back to the websites.

I scroll all the way down, but all the websites look exactly the same, like orthodontists all pay the same person to handle their online presence or something. But then I see the link to a weird-looking web address at the bottom of the page.

Igotdoublejawsurgery.com

I click.

Hi, I'm Dean, the website reads. *I got double jaw surgery to fix my crazy jaws. Welcome to my blog.* There's a picture of a young guy—a teenager, smiling, with a girl around his age standing next to him. She has her arm around him and she's smiling, too. They're both wearing hiking clothes and sturdy-looking boots, as if they expect to be walking over sharp rocks and heavy brush. They have a dog with them—a yellow Lab, I think—and they're standing in the woods somewhere. The caption under the picture says, *Me, my friend Ashley, and my doggo, Cooper. Banff, Canada.*

And of course I notice that Dean's teeth are perfect. They're more than perfect. Like he belongs in a toothpaste commercial.

I look at the clock. Fifteen more minutes before I lose my privacy. Dad's been shifting on the couch, which I know means that he's starting to wake up. The tone in Mom's voice sounds like she's about to hang up the phone. And I know I'm going to hear my sister thunder up the stairs to our apartment any minute now.

I read quickly through the tabs on Dean's website. *Start here*, the first one says.

I click on it. The new page leads me to what seems like a million links.

The day I found out I needed double jaw surgery
Preparing for double jaw surgery
The best part of double jaw surgery (I snort at that one, and Dad shifts on the couch again.)
My double jaw surgery is tomorrow and I'm totally freaking out
The first days after double jaw surgery

Two weeks after double jaw surgery

I skip down to the last link. It says, *Two years after double jaw surgery*. It's the last update and seems to be the end of his blog. I do some quick math. I think Dean might be close to twenty years old.

"Wow," I whisper to myself. He must not be thinking about his teeth anymore if he's not updating. I can't imagine a world where I'm not thinking about my teeth. I click on the link that says, *The best part of double jaw surgery*, and begin reading.

OK, hear me out, gang. Do you want to know what the best part of double jaw surgery is? I'll give you one guess. No, it's not the results. Great results are a given. Your doctor wouldn't make you go through this process if your teeth and jaws weren't going to look and feel awesome in the end.

Nope, the best part of getting double jaw surgery is . . . (drumroll, please) . . . all of the ice cream you get to eat for months on end! I can't begin to tell you how many chocolate chip cookie dough ice cream shakes I had across those first eight weeks. Keeping your calories up is really hard to do with your jaws wired shut, and my parents were totally on the ball with the ice cream. I actually got sick of ice cream toward the end, if you could believe it.

I softly laugh out loud. I couldn't imagine being sick of ice cream.

"Hi, Maxi-Pie," Dad mumbles. I jump out of my seat. I didn't realize he was awake. He sits up and rubs his eyes. "Wuddya doin'?"

I hear Mom hang up the phone and Alexis charge through the door. The smell of macaroni and cheese wafts into the living room.

Dang it. No more privacy tonight.

"Hey, Dad," I say, glancing at the website again. I need to remember the exact address so that I can find it in school tomorrow. I've already decided that I'm going to spend lunch in the media lab to read more about Dean's story. "Nothing much. Just looking up things for school."

But I'm not sure he hears me. He gets up to use the bathroom and passes Mom on his way. They don't say anything to each other.

The news story said not to fight in front of your kids. But they never said a thing about pretending your spouse doesn't exist in front of your kids. If fighting affects kids' brains, I wonder how much damage happens when parents ignore each other.

15
IT'S OPEN SEASON IN SCIENCE CLASS

It's Friday and I haven't had a chance to talk to Shrynn all week because she hasn't been in school. She's barely responded to my texts with anything other than, *Sorry, haven't been feeling great, talk to you later*. And she never responded when I texted her saying that I couldn't come to her newspaper party last week.

I didn't want to keep bugging her so I waited for her to text me, but she hasn't and I'm starting to get worried.

Missing school is totally not like Shrynn. And I never got the chance to ask her about how her party went. It must have been pretty low-key because the kids in newspaper club haven't said a word about it, and neither has DeShaun, who usually has something to say about everything.

I still haven't had the chance to tell Shrynn that we have

to find a new day to get together after school now that Fridays at her house are permanently off-limits because of Mom and Dad's Creative New Arrangement.

But Shrynn also didn't show up to English last period, and now I'm on my way to science trying to decide if I should ask Mom to help me figure out what's going on. But when I arrive, Shrynn's sitting in her usual spot, looking sad and exhausted.

I'm on my way to talk to her when DeShaun holds out his hand for a high five.

"Heyyy, Plink-Meister!" he says. "Want a pretzel?"

"No thanks, De," I say, smacking my hand against his, even though I just saw him last period. That's the thing about DeShaun. He'll high-five you all day long if you let him.

DeShaun is thin with dark skin, and he wears round glasses (when he's not wearing contacts), slacks, a sports jacket, and leather shoes to school, almost every day. He's totally cool and has a ton of friends.

"What about a cheese doodle?" he asks. He gestures to the assortment of snacks that is splayed out all over his desk, and I laugh.

"Maybe at lunch," I say. I finally rush past DeShaun and over to my assigned pod—a group of four desks I sit at with Shrynn and two other girls.

"Shrynn!" I call as I fling my book bag onto my seat. "What the heck—"

But Mrs. Neast decides to start class before the bell even

rings, and now I can't talk to Shrynn like I want to. Like *I need* to.

"Good morning, budding scientists! It's time to get started!" Mrs. Neast screeches.

I see Carlay roll her eyes from a pod across the room while Vince claps his hands and stomps his feet and shouts, "YAY!" Carlay shrieks with laughter, and half the kids haven't even stopped talking to one another. Shrynn rubs her temples and looks like she wants to fall asleep.

Mrs. Neast is pale and frazzled looking, even more so than usual. Her gray hair is sticking out in a million different directions. She's wearing a thick, scratchy-looking gray sweater, purple corduroys that end above her ankles, blue nylon socks, and sneakers that don't match. The sneakers don't even *almost* resemble each other. One is a pink low-top Nike with black shoelaces, and the other one is a white high-top Sketcher with orange shoelaces.

Mrs. Neast may seem super kooky and not very organized but there's one rule that she's a stickler for: *no passing notes during class*. She doesn't really notice when we try to whisper to each other, or if we're doodling in our books or something. Sometimes I feel like you could strip naked and streak across the room and she probably wouldn't notice, especially if she's teaching something about science that she's *really* into. But if you pass a note and she catches you, you're in for it.

Still, I take my chances and rip off a corner of my loose-leaf paper. I write, *Where were you all week? Are you okay? How was the party?* and pass it to Shrynn.

Shrynn's wearing her glasses, which she almost never does because she has contacts. She takes my note and writes something down before passing it back to me.

I'm okay. Just not feeling great. I decided not to have the party. Anyway, what animal do you think Neast will make us worship today?

I laugh. Fridays in science are Ecosystem Day, where we learn about the biomes and habitats of different wild animals. I look up at Shrynn but she's doodling in the margins of her notebook. I can't help but think she's avoiding me. But at least now I know why no one seemed to talk about the party this week.

I write back, *Maybe we'll learn about Zealous Zebras? I have the notes from English if you want them. Oh, and next week's vocabulary.* The word *zealous* is on our new vocabulary list and I thought my note was pretty clever. I push it over to her and she gives me a half smile, like it hurt to even do *that* much.

Mrs. Neast approaches our table. "Time for some new seating assignments!" she barks, clapping her hands.

"Dandrielle," Mrs. Neast says to one of the girls in our pod. "Can you please change seats with Carlay? I'm trying out a new floor plan today." She wriggles her eyebrows. "I like to shake things up a bit."

Dandrielle shrugs, grabs her backpack, and moves to Carlay's old chair on the other side of the classroom. Carlay plops herself down in the seat next to me with a thump and rolls her eyes. Then she inches her chair as far as possible away from me, like she's afraid of catching something.

Carlay is wearing jeans, black leather boots, and a deep purple long-sleeved shirt that flows out at the bottom. The color somehow makes her black hair look even darker. She looks like she's dressed for a dance party and not science class. Her dark eyes almost match her hair, and her skin is like cream. Carlay is part Italian, like me—but there's no similarity on Earth that would result in us being friends.

Vince throws his pen at Carlay as soon as the teacher turns her back. He bleached his hair white again and in a few weeks he'll have dark brown roots and white tips that he thinks Looks Really Cool, when it really just makes him look like a skunk.

"Once again, budding scientists!" Again Mrs. Neast claps sharply. I rub my own hands, imagining that hers must be stinging by now. "Time to get down to business. Your mid-year grades have been submitted and some of you could afford a little extra credit." She looks meaningfully at Vince and he scowls at her. I stifle a snort.

Carlay leans over in her seat so that she's inches from me. "You should do a science project about your really awesome teeth and hair." She smirks as she curls a lock of her own hair around her fingers. "Also, where'dja get that T-shirt? The donation bin outside the grocery store?"

I look down. I'm wearing a T-shirt that Mom gave me last fall. It says *DON'T*.

I feel my cheeks burn.

And for once in my life, I think of the perfect comeback.

"Oh yeah?" I whisper. And just as I'm about to really zing her, I feel a thick trail of drool escape from my lower lip and run down my chin and for the love of everything I can't believe this is fricking happening.

I wipe it away with my sleeve, lightning fast, but it's too late. Of course it's too late. Carlay does her witchy shrieky laughing thing, and Vince whips his head around, his eyes demanding to know what he missed.

"EW!" Carlay calls out. "Max just drooled all over herself! She's worse than a dog!" And now everyone's eyes are on me and whatever it was that I wanted to say to put Carlay in her place vanishes somewhere deep in my stomach. Shrynn casts me a sympathetic look from across the table.

"Okay, everyone, that's *quite* enough!" Mrs. Neast claps her hands again. "It's time to get on with things." Everyone *else* heard what Carlay said, and Mrs. Neast is gonna act like she didn't hear a thing?

"It's Friday—who can tell me what that means?" Uh-oh. Mrs. Neast gets that starry, far-away look in her eyes.

"Tomorrow's Saturday," Vince groans.

"Thank you, Vince. What else?" Mrs. Neast says, exasperated.

"It's Wild Animal Day," someone else says from across the room, sounding bored and almost like they're in pain.

"Indeed, I think you mean that Friday in my class is Ecosystem Day, my favorite part of the seventh-grade curriculum!" Mrs. Neast grabs a stack of papers from her desk. "Today, life-scientists-in-training, you will become acquainted with . . . drumroll, please," she says, nodding at Dandrielle, who Mrs. Neast knows is a drummer for the school band. Dandrielle rolls her eyes and starts drumming on her desk with her pointer fingers.

Mrs. Neast inhales sharply. She's way too excited about wild animals. "The industrious . . . *dunh dunh dunh* . . . *beaver*!" She hands out a packet to each student, and the only thing I want in the entire world, right this very second, is for the floor to open up and swallow me whole.

Vince shakes with laughter. "You get to sit in a bucky beaver lodge!" he calls out to Carlay. He positions his two front teeth over his bottom lip like a beaver.

Carlay shrieks and buries her head in her arms, which are stretched out on her desk. Her shoulders heave. I can't tell whether Mrs. Neast is ignoring them or if she doesn't notice their behavior at all.

"Beavers, dear ones!" she continues. "Today's lesson is in honor of my cat, which, as you know, is a tabby named Beaver." She smiles, all proud like. "Did you know that beavers have really big teeth? Yes, *indeed*. And because their teeth keep growing, the blessed beaver must stop to file them down once in a while." Mrs. Neast clasps her hands together like beavers are the coolest invention in the fricking world. "And most importantly, most fascinatingly, they increase biodiversity by building dams and lodges that attract other animals, insects, fish, and wildlife! Today we're going to learn all about it."

Blessed. Fricking. Beavers. That's one way to describe them. Mrs. Neast bends over to scratch her shin, which is exposed because her pants are so short. I notice that she has long black hairs shooting out of her legs, like a furry spider. But I bet Mrs. Neast wouldn't even *think* to have a Furry Spider Ecosystem Day.

She straightens and continues lecturing. "They actually have to chew on tree trunks and branches to keep their teeth from getting too—what on earth is so funny?" Mrs. Neast's eyes are wide as she stares at Carlay. "Carlay, this is not what I had in mind for this seat change."

And this is how I discover that Mrs. Neast is basically clueless. Any teacher should know what Carlay and Vince are laughing at, especially if I'm one of their students and they're teaching about stupid beavers. You don't go teaching a lesson about beavers when you have a student that the school's biggest bullies call Bucky Beaver on the regular. A lesson on beavers is like open season on kids with a mouth like mine.

A couple of kids look at me. I feel Shrynn nudge my foot under the table, her way of reminding me that she's there, but a lot of good that does.

Carlay lifts up her head. She has tears streaming down her face from the kind of laugh that eventually has to come out of your eyeballs because there's just too much of it. "Noth—nothing, Mrs. Neast," she says, trying to catch her breath. She wipes her eyes. "Sorry."

Mrs. Neast nods, still clueless. "Please turn to page one. I'd like a reader to introduce us to the magnificent life of the industrious beaver."

Vince raises his hand, practically jumping out of his seat.

Mrs. Neast nods at him. "Thank you for volunteering, Vince. Please begin."

Vince clears his throat dramatically, like he's about to give a presidential speech. "The wondrous beaver is famous for its large buckteeth." He clears his throat again. "The mystical beaver's awe-inspiring teeth are no match for tree ba— tree *bar*— *Tree. BARK.*" He barely finishes the sentence because he glances at Carlay, who has practically fallen out of her chair, and now he's falling out of *his* chair. "Beaver teeth are up to an inch long," he continues reading. "And beavers even look like some humans."

I freeze. That last sentence isn't a part of the reading. I hear someone across the room laugh, and then another. It's only a couple, but it sounds like an entire chorus.

"What on earth has gotten into you all today?" Mrs. Neast barks. "If you don't stop this nonsense right now you will all have an extra essay to write for homework!"

Carlay starts doodling in her notebook. She scribbles something, rips off a piece of light pink designer paper rimmed with some kind of weird gold thread (because of course Carlay only takes notes on pretty paper), and flings it at me. I unfold it, even though I know I should just throw it in the garbage because if Mrs. Neast catches me with a note, I'm toast. In large, looping handwriting, it reads,

1. Did your mom procreyate with a beever?
2. You should get a DNA test to see if your part beever.
3. Is you're mom a beever, to?

Shrynn grabs the note from me and reads it. Her eyes grow wide and her lips form a thin line, like they do when she's really upset. She turns the note over and scribbles a response with her purple pen, positioning the paper so that I can see it better. I read what she's writing:

1. procreate (misspelling)
2. beaver (misspelling)
3. you're (contraction)
4. beaver (again x2)
5. your (possessive)
6. too (homophone)

0/6 Do over. And if you're going to insult my best friend, the least you could do is learn how to spell. Your grammar needs work, too.

As Mrs. Neast fights for the class's attention, Shrynn folds the note into a neat square and slowly pushes it across the desk to Carlay.

A fatal error. She wasn't fast enough. My heart seizes as I see Mrs. Neast catch Shrynn breaking the cardinal rule.

"Shrynn Cheung, are you passing notes in my classroom?" Mrs. Neast moves quickly to stand behind Shrynn, practically right on top of her, and Shrynn's hand is still touching the note, so she's caught totally red-handed. Mrs. Neast snatches it out from Shrynn's fingers. "It's always something with this group. Everyone, complete your packet in silence. Shrynn, please see me in the hall."

16
SHRYNN GETS INTO TROUBLE

I don't remember the last time I felt so sick. Shrynn never gets in trouble at school. I mean, *literally* never. And when she gets up to follow Mrs. Neast into the hall, her cheeks are pink and her head is down. Shrynn's in trouble for sticking up for *me*, and all because I don't know how to stick up for *myself*.

I raise my hand, but Mrs. Neast's back is to me, and she and Shrynn are almost at the door. So I call out. "But Mrs. Neast, it's not—"

She whips around. "Would you like detention, too?" she snaps. Carlay smirks behind her hand as Mrs. Neast and Shrynn leave the room.

Detention. Shrynn's getting detention and it's all my fault.

Once Mrs. Neast shuts the door behind her, Vince stands up from his seat and positions his front teeth over his bottom lip. "Hi, everyone, my name is Max Stinks and

I'm part beaver." He speaks like his teeth are glued to his bottom lip. "Someone help me find a tree. My teeth take up my entire face, and I need to trim them down!" The kids at his table howl because Vince is a real riot.

"I have a pencil!" Carlay shrieks. She digs around in her book bag, finds a pencil, and whips it at me.

I want to think of a clever comeback that will shut them up for good. Something that'll make them leave me alone and stay away from my sister. But I got nothing. So instead, my face heats up and my armpits feel all sweaty and I stare at my hands and suddenly I hate the T-shirt that Mom got for me and I want to take it off and throw it in the garbage, but then I'll probably just get arrested for public nudity or something, which is exactly what I need.

I glance around the room. It seems like everyone is laughing, but that's not true. Not everyone. Some of the kids aren't even paying attention to Vince, and DeShaun is giving him the evil eye.

Last year, right as I'd just started the sixth grade, Mom had the news on while she was making dinner and there was a segment about kids and bullying. There was this lady wearing a lab coat who came on to talk about how you need to act like you totally don't care what your bullies are saying, because if you don't care, they'll just get bored with you and leave you alone and find someone else to bother. That you can always say something like, you're entitled to how you feel but that doesn't mean that your words will have the power to affect me. I remember how she nodded like she knew exactly what she was talking about and like we'd be total idiots not to take her word for it. She called it Taking Back Your Power.

By then, Vince and Carlay had already started in with me, especially on the bus, saying stuff like, *Hey, Maxi-Pad! It looks like your teeth won a race against your face!*

After I saw that news story, I thought really hard about a comeback for when they cornered me again, so that they would know that I totally didn't care about what they thought of me. I didn't have to wait long.

"Hey, Horseface!" Vince had said after Dad dropped me off at the bus stop one morning. It was really embarrassing because his car is a puke-y green color and practically the size of a yacht and the muffler is so loud you can hear us coming from a mile away. "Nice car! Did your dad have to get something that big so that it could fit your teeth?"

"I'm sorry you don't like my face," I had said back to him. "But I like it just fine, thank you very much." I'd followed the news program's advice *perfectly* and held my breath, waiting for some sign that my new nemeses were going to find something else to do now that I'd taken back my own power. I promised myself that I'd tell Mom and Dad all about it, because they were always telling me to stick up for myself and this time I'd finally done it.

Vince's face scrunched up something ugly before he fell to his knees and howled with laughter. Carlay was also doubled over, with tears rolling down her cheeks. And then a couple of other kids started laughing. It wasn't supposed to go this way. The news story said so. The nodding, finger-pointing, lab-coat-wearing lady said so. You were supposed to be able to come up with something clever to say that was literally bully proof. But apparently the news people and nodding-lab-coat-lady never met Vince and Carlay.

Vince had jutted his top teeth over his bottom lip and shouted my words back at me. "I'm sorry you don't like my face, I'm sorry you don't like my face," he chanted on the bus the entire way to school and continued when I saw him in the halls and in class, with Carlay egging him on. I think maybe he stopped about a month later, when he got bored with it and discovered an insult that was more fun, like calling me Horseface Max from Beaver Town or something.

I never trusted the news again after that. At least not the stories that pretend to know stuff about kids.

Mrs. Neast and Shrynn come back into the classroom just as the bell rings, and Carlay and Vince bolt, their backpacks bouncing as they dash for the door. Shrynn's face is splotchy, like she'd been crying.

"Hey," I whisper when she makes her way back to our table. "I'm so sorry."

"It's not your fault," she sniffles.

"Shrynn-Meister, that was totally bogus," DeShaun says from behind me. "I *know* that it wasn't your fault."

"Mrs. Neast wouldn't listen," Shrynn says.

"Not cool," DeShaun says. "I'll walk you to your next class and"—he lowers his voice—"you can tell me all about Planet Neast."

Shrynn smiles all shy-like at him. "Sure. Thanks."

"Do you have detention?" I ask.

"No. But I have to write an essay."

"About *what*?"

She shrugs. "I don't know yet. I get to choose. But it has to be about science. And it's due Monday. I'm going to start it over lunch. I'll be in the media lab, so I won't be able to hang out today, okay? I'll see you later, though." Shrynn smiles at me, and her eyes are sad and swollen as she shoves her books into her bag and races out of class with DeShaun.

For the second time since science started, I feel like Shrynn's avoiding me. And because she won't pick up her phone, I haven't had one single chance to tell her that Friday afternoons can't happen anymore.

I take my time gathering my things. I'm waiting for the last few kids to leave. I have to do something to make this better. To make things right for Shrynn.

Now it's just me and Mrs. Neast in the classroom. She's erasing the whiteboard and I approach her from behind.

"Mrs. Neast?" I say softly.

She gasps and chucks the eraser at the floor. "I didn't realize there was still someone here. You scared me half to death!" She wipes her hands against her pants and looks at me. "You're going to be late to your next class if you don't hurry."

"I'm sorry, I, it," I stammer, then take a breath. "It wasn't Shrynn's fault," I say. "She was sticking up for me."

For a few seconds, Mrs. Neast closes her eyes, like she's frustrated. When she opens them, she says, "Thank you for your concern, Max. I understand that you and Shrynn are friends, but I'm not at liberty to discuss student affairs with other students. I've been teaching for thirty years. If I've earned anything, it's the right to trust my own instincts, don't you think?"

I was really hoping Mrs. Neast would ask me what I meant when I said that Shrynn was sticking up for me. But of course she didn't.

Before I can say anything else, she's already turned her back to me and started writing something on the board for her next class.

As I turn to leave the room, I take the crumpled-up ball of light pink paper out of the wastebasket that sits next to Mrs. Neast's desk. She might not care about who started the whole thing, but I do.

17

DAD JUST DOESN'T GET IT

"I'm gonna have the worst science project ever," Alexis starts whining as soon as we get to the pizzeria. She just found out about the sixth-grade science fair at school today, and I have the feeling it's the only thing we're going to be talking about over dinner. "And the whole school is gonna know it," she says. She looks at Dad. "There's gonna be, like, an assembly. Everyone will be there, families, too. My teacher's calling it the inaugural science showcase, whatever the heck that means." She takes an angry bite of pizza.

"I think inaugural means the first of something," Dad says, hiding a smile. "By the way, are we invited?"

It's Custody Fridays With Dad (which is my private nickname for what is now my least-favorite day of the week) and I'm still thinking about what happened with Shrynn in science class today, and I've been dying to call her but I can't because we left with Dad almost as soon as I got home. But I *have* to talk to her to make sure we're okay.

"My project is gonna be terrible and the whole world is gonna see it!" Alexis buries her head in her hands.

"Why do you say that, Bug?" Bug is Dad's nickname for Alexis.

"You have to *hear* what the other kids are talking about doing," Alexis says. "They're talking about using their computers and phones and stuff. One kid is talking about making an app that does your homework for you. Another kid is talking about inventing another social media website."

"Yeah, because we definitely need more of *those*," Dad teases.

"Well, they'll probably get good grades and extra credit and stuff because at least they can use those things," Alexis says hotly. "I'll probably have to use cotton balls and Popsicle sticks and an empty egg carton for my project, like a first grader, because our internet connection is the literal worst and Mom says I can't bring our laptop to school because it's the only one we have and we can't afford a new one if it breaks." She takes another angry bite. "I'll never get a prize if I can't do what the other kids are doing."

"Our connection works just fine," Dad says, rolling his eyes. "Can't you save your project at home and show it on a school computer? Besides, doesn't the school give everyone access to a laptop?"

"Dad, using the school computer is *embarrassing*," Alexis says. "No one takes home a school computer if they don't have to."

"And they're pretty terrible," I chime in, my mouth full. "They're old, even when they're *new*."

"And slow as *molasses*," Alexis grumbles.

"But you *do* have access if you need one," Dad says.

"You're missing the point, Dad," Alexis says. "The other kids have their own computers. And even if I *did* take home a school computer—"

"Our internet connection is terrible," I chime in again. For once, me and Alexis agree on something.

"Our internet connection barely works for anything other than email," she says. "How do you not know this?"

"And forget about having more than one program running at the same time," I say. "I can't have our school newspaper site open at the same time that I need to do research. It's impossible."

"And if we *both* have projects at the same *time* we have to take *turns*." Alexis folds her arms over her chest. "It's so *dumb*."

"If it's so *embarrassing*," Dad says, using air quotations, "can't you do your project *at* school and use the school's connection?"

"Dad! No!" Alexis's face is red and she has tears in her eyes. "You just don't get how unfair it is. No one else has to do it that way. Why should I have to do my work over lunch when everyone else gets to do it at home?"

"I'm sorry, Bug. I don't know what to tell you. We can't afford upgraded technology or bigger utility bills right now." Dad takes a bite of his pizza. "You'll have to do your best with what you have. We all do. There will always be people who have more than we do." He pauses to put more red pepper on his slice. "And there are also a lot of people out there with a whole lot less than we have. We should feel very fortunate, because we *are* very fortunate." Alexis rolls her eyes again, like she can't speak without her eyes rolling at the same time. But she gets away with it because she gets away with *everything*.

"Maybe you should come up with a topic first," he says, "and then we can figure out how to make it happen. What does it have to be on?"

"*Anything* about science or technology. There aren't any *rules*," Alexis huffs. "And it only has to be an *idea* that either helps you understand something better or solves a *problem* or something for the scientific *community*. It doesn't even have to be, like, *finished* or anything. It just needs to be an *idea*."

"Well, that makes things easier," Dad says. He and Alexis start brainstorming possible topics, and I zone out and finish my pizza. All of Alexis's talk about the science fair reminds me of the journalism competition and Jordan Slade. But

Alexis is required to participate in the fair. Thank goodness the journalism competition is optional for me.

"Dad?" I ask. Alexis is still going on about project ideas. Now she's talking about a girl whose father is a chemical engineer, and the girl wants to work with her dad on inventing a chemical that makes dog poop dissolve so that you don't have to pick it up and put it in a plastic bag. Something about how plastic is destroying the environment.

"*I* was talking to Dad," Alexis snarls.

"What is it, Maxi-Pie?" Dad says. I like when he calls me by my nickname.

"Why aren't you and Mom getting along anymore?"

"I need to talk about my *science* project," Alexis barks.

"We can talk about both, Alexis." Dad's tone is stern, but also soft. He pauses for a long minute. "Me and your mom were really young when we got together, Maxi. We were kids. You remember me telling you about that, right?"

"Yeah," I mumble. It's true. They were teenagers, and still in high school when they first met.

"And we probably did a few things that a lot of people don't do until they're adults. Like get married, move out . . ." His voice trails off.

"Okay?" I just want him to get to the point. I already know all of this stuff.

"And we didn't have a lot of support. And we made a lot

of mistakes. That's why I'm always telling you girls to get your education first."

"This is boring," Alexis says.

"Alexis, you're being rude," Dad says. "Don't say stuff like that to me, it ain't nice." I'm surprised that Dad even said anything to her. She usually gets away with being a total ghoul.

"You're right, Daddy." She bats her eyes at him and he laughs. When Dad looks away, she sticks her tongue out at me like a baby. "By the way, *ain't isn't* a word."

"You're right, Bug."

If Alexis can make my parents laugh first, she gets away with being a jerk most of the time. It's a talent I don't have.

"So things are hard right now," Dad continues. "It happens all the time. I'm sure you have a lot of friends who have parents who hit rough spots."

Shrynn is really the only close friend that I have, and her parents are perfect.

"Two of my friends have parents who aren't together anymore," Alexis says through a mouthful of pizza. "Angel and Kristy. Kristy's mom even has a *boyfriend* who *lives* with them now, which is totally weird."

The idea of Mom suddenly getting a boyfriend make me wants to puke up my pizza.

"It's time to go home," Dad says, gathering up his trash.

And I can't tell for sure, but I might have smelled beer on his breath the entire time we were at the pizzeria, especially in the beginning, before he masked it with dough, sauce, cheese, and pepperoni.

It isn't until much later that I realize that Dad didn't answer my question. Not really.

☆

Back at our apartment, Dad gets comfortable on the couch and he's snoring within a half hour. I'm careful not to make noise and even tiptoe past him when I have to use the bathroom.

Alexis goes to bed before I do. And as I climb into the lower bunk, with my jawbreaker strapped to my mouth, I know Alexis is awake because I can hear the faint sound of pencils scratching against paper. She's sketching. When Alexis can't fall asleep, she pulls out her sketchbook, hides under the covers, and makes art.

"You don't need fancy things for the science fair, you know," I say. I hear the scratching pause. "You can draw something. Maybe something about the brain, because the brain is science, and how art and the brain and science work together or something. And then you can use a computer to make an interactive 3D model." To be honest, I have no idea what I'm talking about.

After a few seconds, the scratching picks up again. And I'm not sure, but I thought I heard her mumble *thanks*.

18

MAX CHANGES HER MIND

It's Sunday, and Alexis is in our bedroom with her paints and easel and Mom's in the kitchen tidying up before she leaves for work. I'm wearing my jawbreaker and a T-shirt that says *Lucky Me* and I'm tiptoeing around Dad, who's stirring on the couch. My mouth aches, but if I don't want my parents on top of me about it, and if I don't want surgery, I have to work harder at wearing it more. Basic facts.

I scoot past Dad and step into the kitchen. "Can I text Shrynn?" I ask Mom as I reach for my phone in the basket. "I have to ask her something." I hadn't told Mom about what happened at school with Shrynn, and I want to check on her. I also want to talk about the newspaper.

To be honest, I've been really slacking off lately. Between everything going on at home, my jaws feeling like they're on fire, and then Shrynn getting into trouble at school because of me, I just haven't had the headspace to get much done.

"One second," Mom says. "I want to talk to you about something before I leave."

Mom pulls a piece of paper from the pile that she keeps on the table. It's yellow and crumpled and I recognize it instantly. The guidelines for the Channel 5 journalism competition.

"I was changing out the bag in the trash can and I found this at the top," she says, handing it to me. "Are you going to apply?"

I shake my head. "No," I say. "I don't think so."

Mom closes her eyes for a few seconds. That's her Frustrated Look. "Max, why not? This is right up your alley."

"Because I don't want to be on video," I whisper. "I can just do print."

"Wait a minute," Mom says. "You want to work in news someday, but you don't want to *ever* be on video? Do you think you won't ever be asked to do videos, or be in pictures, even if you're a print journalist? And what if you wind up at a major station? How's that supposed to work?"

I hear Dad let out a loud yawn in the living room. "Come on," Mom says, taking me by the arm. "We're talking about this with your dad, *right* now."

Mom can be super confusing sometimes. When she's mad, we know to stay out of her way. But when she's focused on something, especially if it involves me or Alexis, she harps on the issue—especially if it's something school related.

And if she's bothering to talk to Dad about it, that means she's serious.

"You're awake," Mom says to Dad as we move into the living room. "Maybe you can help me explain something to Max." Mom shoves the piece of paper at him. I stare at my fingers. I feel like I'm in trouble even though I haven't done anything wrong.

"A journalism competition," Dad says, yawning again. He looks up at Mom. "So what's the story?"

"The story," Mom says, "is that Max won't apply because it requires a video to enter. And she doesn't want to be on camera."

Dad reads the guidelines. "That's a silly reason not to shoot for a dream," he says. "Isn't this what you want? To work in journalism?"

"And if she won, she'd get to meet Jordan Slade, the lady who's on TV every night," Mom says.

"How am I supposed to put my face out there, like it is?" I say. "If I won, everyone in Brooklyn would see my video on the news. I'll be Bucky Beaver forever." I flop down on the couch across from them. "I'm too *scared.*"

"Maxi-Pie, this is your *life* you're talking about," Dad says. He sounds incredulous, like he can't believe what he's hearing.

"Your *future*," Mom chimes in. "Do you have any idea how good something like this looks on a college application, especially for kids like you? I've read articles about that, you know. You really want to stand out so you can get as many scholarships as you can. Besides, Max," she says as she sits on the couch next to Dad, "this is your *dream*."

I'm reminded of all the times Mom and Dad would talk to Alexis and me about our goals. We'd sit together in the living room, Mom and Dad next to each other, and Alexis and I would talk with them about what we wanted to be when we grew up. Alexis has always wanted to be a famous artist, and I've always wanted to be a writer. Mom and Dad would talk about the importance of going to college. Sometimes we'd talk about this stuff over ice cream, or during a walk on a nice day. It all feels like a lifetime ago, but seeing Mom and Dad next to each other on the couch reminds me of the way things used to be.

"Max," Mom says, her hands on her knees. She leans forward. "There's nothing wrong with your face. At all. Do you understand me?"

"Yeah, what's that business about, anyway?" Dad says. "You look like every other kid your age. You're *all* a bunch of weirdos and most of you have braces and all of you grow out of clothes after a week. I can barely tell you apart sometimes." He smiles and Mom's smiling, too.

"Chris, that's not true," Mom says. "They're just kids. Kids go through stages."

"Yeah, weirdo stages," Dad says.

"And you went through one, too," Mom says. "Or did you forget when you had all those pimples?"

"I just don't want people to make fun of me," I whisper.

"Max." Dad turns to me. "People are always gonna make fun of you," he says. "That's what people do to each other. They just did it to me the other day, on the job. Some guy I work with made fun of the size of my head." Mom brings her hand to her mouth and laughs.

"Really?" I squeak. "What did you say *back*?"

"I told him that he should see the size of my foot up his butt."

"*Chris*," Mom says. She swats at his arm but she's laughing the kind of laugh that grows and grows until it comes out of your eyes, and it feels exactly like it used to, when all of us were happier and she and Dad got along.

I'm cracking up, too, as I picture Dad with the guys he works with on the train tracks, all of them in their big heavy work boots and white T-shirts, their nails and skin caked with grease. I can feel drool trickling out of the side of my mouth and I don't even care about wiping it away.

"That's nothing," Dad says. "And *then* I told him—"

"Max, what we're trying to say is that you should think about applying for this opportunity," Mom says.

"Yeah, kiddo," Dad says. "This is your chance to do the things we never got to do."

"Well, there's another thing," I say carefully. "I don't

exactly have the best equipment. My phone can't take video, remember?"

"So what are you getting at?" Mom says. Her tone is stern now.

"Just that I'll need a phone or something to actually *do* the project." I feel like I know what's coming.

"Don't they have equipment at school?" Dad says.

I shrug. "I mean, I know the AV club has equipment, but it's bulky and old and used mostly for in-school stuff, and because it's super outdated most kids use their cell phones anyway."

"Max, you know we can't afford to get you a new phone," Mom says.

"I'm not asking for a new phone," I say. "But it would be a lot easier if I could borrow yours."

Dad rubs his hands over his eyes and looks at Mom. "I can't take the risk. If you break my phone, or you lose it, it'll be months before I can buy a new one."

I look at Mom pleadingly. I mean, *they're* the ones who want me to do this. Shouldn't they find a way to make it easier?

"With your father working nights, I agree. We can't take risks with his phone," she says. I was just beginning to think that maybe I *do* want to enter the journalism competition.

"When's the application due?" Mom asks.

"Six weeks or so," I say.

"You can use my phone at home," she says, "but outside,

you'll have to borrow someone else's phone. Or . . ." She stands up. "Use the school equipment. It might not be perfect, but it's available. Both you and Alexis need to figure out how to be comfortable using the resources available to you, even if it's not the latest and greatest thing.

"By the way." Mom pauses. "I feel like I haven't read one of your op-eds in a while. Have you stopped writing?"

I can't tell my parents that writing for the newspaper has taken a back burner to everything else—including worrying about *them*. They'd be livid if they knew I was obsessing over Adult Issues like their fighting and money problems. I should have predicted that they'd notice that I haven't churned out an op-ed lately, especially Mom. She's always really liked my essays, ever since I started writing for the paper in the sixth grade.

"I've just been busy with schoolwork and stuff," I say. Mom eyes me, like she's trying to decide whether she believes me.

"We all have to find the time to do the things we love," Dad says with another yawn.

Mom grabs her coat and purse from the hallway closet. "It's time for me to go. Max," she says, and looks over her shoulder at me. "I hope you'll think about this. The competition, your articles, all of it. There's no excuse to not take these opportunities." She glances at Dad before shutting the door behind her. "I'll be back at the usual time."

I've gotten so used to Mom and Dad arguing that I can't help but notice the absence of friction in the air. It feels good. I grab my phone from the basket on the kitchen table to text Shrynn about the competition.

I'm gonna do it, I type out, my heart lighter.

⋛ ☆ ⋚

I can smell the paint fumes seeping out from under my bedroom door. With Alexis working on her art and Dad watching TV, I ask if I can use the computer.

"But I thought it was too old and dumb and slow?" he says. But then he tugs on my ponytail. "Go ahead."

I pull up igotdoublejawsurgery.com, the blog by the guy who had the same procedure that I might have to get. Before now, I hadn't had much of an opportunity to really dig into it. I click on his very first entry.

I found out a week ago that I'd need surgery, which was my entire reason for creating this blog. (So hello from Canada and thanks for stopping by, whoever you are!) When the doctor said, "Dean, now that your bones are finished growing, I can officially say that you're a candidate for double jaw surgery. We've been suspecting this for some time," it was like I'd suddenly been cast in a real-life horror movie, starring me against my mouth and only one of us comes out alive in the end. According to the doctor, there was no other way forward. That surgery was the only way to fix my alien jaws. (TBH, they didn't say alien jaws. Those are my words, and the words of some of the not-so-nice kids at school.) No one really knows this, but after my mom brought me home, I laid down in my bed and cried. I was super scared and angry. Almost two years into treatment and I need surgery anyway? What a crock. A sick joke, you know?

I was angry at my parents for never telling me that this would be a strong possibility. I was angry at my doctor for acting like surgery is no big deal. (Um, hello? How is getting your face sawed in half not a big deal?) Most of all, I was angry at myself. Why couldn't I just be born with a normal mouth? Like, lots of kids have braces but I was the only one of my friends who needed actual surgery to complete the job.

I didn't realize I'd been drooling. I wipe it away with my sleeve and keep going. It's almost like I'm reading about my future self.

Mom made my favorite dinner that night—spaghetti and meatballs, extra parm and soft Italian bread!—and after I had a good cry I felt a little better. My parents reminded me that we had talked about the possibility of jaw surgery in the very beginning, but I must have forgotten. I was really busy with school and hockey back then, so maybe I wasn't really listening. I mean, I'm still super busy now with hockey and grades, but I've always sort of had a bad memory.

Or maybe I blocked it out entirely, which is what my therapist says people do sometimes when they're scared.

The way I deal with worrying is to overload myself with information (that's what my mom says, anyway). And I really wanted to start this blog because I couldn't find anyone else (other than doctors) who were talking about their jaw surgeries and what their actual experiences were. I was tired of the videos of animated skeletons that they probably use in dental schools. I wanted stories about real-life experiences, and I couldn't find any. No good ones, anyway. Nothing that walked you through the whole entire process. So hopefully my blog is unique. If it's not, let me know in the comments and I'll figure out how to make it better. Just don't ask me for blood and guts and gore. Because that's gross.

So, without further ado, my name is Dean H (I promised my parents that I wouldn't use my full name, and I should probably listen to them because they're the ones paying to host this site— Hi, Mom! Hi, Dad!). I'll be getting jaw surgery within the year, and I might be in braces for another year after that. Which makes a total of four years in treatment. Thanks for coming along for the ride!

I hear Alexis stirring on the other side of our bedroom door. She might want to hop on the computer soon, and because I've been on for a while Dad will probably make me get off to give Alexis a turn.

I scroll quickly through the comments under Dean's entry. There are a ton of people thanking Dean for his blog and talking about how worried they are for their own surgery and how much he's helped them be less afraid. It's like a whole community of people with the same mouth issues I have. People who totally get it. Dean also responded to most of the comments, and he seems super kind and encouraging, like a wise older brother or friend.

It's honestly not that bad, he says under a question about pain. *I was expecting it to be way worse. Check out my post-surgery posts if you haven't already. I talk all about it there.*

"I want you guys to see it." My bedroom door is open, and Alexis is standing in the doorway. I close down the computer.

"See what?" Dad yawns.

"The start of my science project." Alexis's voice is small, almost shy-like. She's staring at her hands.

Me and Dad go into the bedroom. Alexis's new art is propped up on the easel in the corner. Open jars of paint are strewn on newspapers that cover the floor. The smell of paint and chemicals and fresh art fills the air. It's almost the end of February and the windows are closed and have plastic covering over them because it's chilly out and the heat is on. Dad gets grumpy if we leave windows open when the heat's running, which is why he covers them in plastic at the start of the winter. Something about heating the neighborhood and wasting his hard-earned money.

Alexis stands at her easel. She has her science book propped open and she's painted a huge black outline of a brain, and different parts are colored in with different paint colors. It's pretty cool looking, to be honest. Alexis is really good with color and shadows and stuff, and the painting looks like a real live brain, with all the folds and ridges and things. The words *This Is Your Brain on Art* are painted at the top of the page in black block letters, and tiny explanations about the different brain parts are written in script along the margin of the page.

I know she'd never admit that I had anything to do with it, but I'm really happy that she went with my idea.

"It looks like a really good start, Bug," Dad says. "When's it due?"

"In about four weeks," Alexis said. "And it's just a draft for now. I'll start working on the final product soon and I'm also gonna figure out how to make a 3D version, where the different parts of the brain light up on the computer screen. My friend Kristy says she has a computer program that I can use at her house." Alexis looks at me. "Do you know if Weiss has touch screens?"

"I'm not sure," I say, hiding a smile. "But I can text Keisha and ask."

"Well, ya did good," Dad says. "Make sure you show your mother."

Alexis pushes her painting back against the wall, and me and Dad head back into the living room and past the extras board.

Dad shudders. "I hate that thing," he says. He lifts my chin with his finger and now we're looking at each other eye to eye. "Your mom left food in the fridge for us to heat up," he says. "How about you put together dinner for you and your sister?"

"But what about you?" I ask. Mom never said anything about me putting dinner together before she left.

"I'm gonna head out for a bit," he says. "And catch a breather." He pulls out his wallet and digs around until he finds a ten-dollar bill. He puts it in my palm. "Just don't tell your mother. Got it? When you see her tomorrow, you tell her that I made the best leftover macaroni ever. Add this to your stash."

Yikes. Dad knows about the money I keep in my sock drawer? "But how did you—"

"You really need to stop worrying about finances, Maxi. That's our job, not yours. And you should listen to your mom more. She wants to help you. To be involved in your life, you know? Her own mother wasn't very involved. She wants something different with you girls. Something better."

It feels good to hear him saying nice stuff about Mom.

"I've decided that I'm going to enter the journalism competition. I'll tell Mom tomorrow, when I see her," I say. "And I'll get started on some newspaper club work and I'll show her that, too."

"Good girl." He pauses. "I'm gonna run down to the deli. I'll be back in an hour or so. And Max?" Dad looks at me but doesn't say anything.

"Yeah?"

"You don't need to tell your mother that I went out, okay?"

"Right," I say. "Got it."

But when I try to write a new op-ed for newspaper club, I can't, because I'm wondering where Dad really is. I've never been in a position to have to help keep his secrets from Mom.

19

SOMETHING'S UP WITH KEISHA

"So you changed your mind about the journalism competition!" Shrynn says through a mouthful of turkey-and-cheese sandwich. It's the last full week of February and the day after my talk with Mom and Dad about the competition. Shrynn and I are sitting in our usual corner of the cafeteria, in between the exit and a table of sixth graders. Some of the sixth, seventh, and eighth graders have the same lunch hour, which means Alexis and I eat lunch at the same time this year, but she's at a table across the room.

I know I should be in the media lab right now catching up on newspaper club work, but I really want to talk to my best friend. *Maybe this afternoon or tomorrow*, I tell myself.

DeShaun's sitting next to Shrynn, peeling a grapefruit. Sometimes he sits with us, and sometimes he sits a few tables away with a different group of kids. I'm glad he's sitting with us today because my teeth hurt and I know he'll take my mind off it.

"All right, Plink-Meister!" he says in between chugging his chocolate milk and reaching for a high five. DeShaun's lunches are so predictable. I've never seen him without chocolate milk, a peanut-butter-and-jelly sandwich, and a monster-size grapefruit. "Shrynn told me all about it. Is one of you gonna be the next Jordan Slade?" He wiggles his eyebrows at me. "Cool shirt, by the way."

I look down to remind myself of which T-shirt I chose today. This one is red with the words, *Oh, just great*, in large white letters.

"Thanks," I mumble. I examine the lunch that Mom made me. It's a plain cheese sandwich, pretzels, and milk in a jug, but the milk is always warm by lunchtime and it's gross. I skip over the sandwich and milk and go straight for the little baggie of pretzels.

"What do you think your topic will be?" Shrynn asks.

"I'm not really sure," I say. Deciding to enter was hard enough.

DeShaun raises an eyebrow, picks up his grapefruit, and pulls his arm back like he's about to throw it at me. "Don't *make* me make my grapefruit orbisculate on you, Plink!"

"Huh?" I say.

"What does *that* mean?" Shrynn asks.

"I've been waiting for an excuse to use *orbisculate*. I saw it on a news show the other night. You guys are journalists, right? Don't you watch the fricking *news*?"

"But what does it *mean*," I say.

"How do you nerds not know what *orbisculate* means?" DeShaun pulls off a slice of the fruit and squeezes it. The juice squirts across the table and some of it lands on my sandwich.

"Hey!" I yelp. But Shrynn's giggling.

"See? My fruit just orbisculated your sandwich!" He bangs his fist on the table and howls with laughter. Me and Shrynn look at each other. She shrugs. I offer DeShaun a weak smile.

"Geez," DeShaun says, rolling his eyes. "I guess we're not in the mood to learn about the best word ever."

"Sorry, De," I say. I totally don't have an appetite, but I pick up the sandwich.

And then I hear a shriek from a few tables away and look over. I notice Carlay standing against the wall, buried in her cell phone, right next to a sign that says NO CELL PHONES with a big red X through it. She has one purple suede boot propped up on a bench while my sister stares at her from a nearby table, like a puppy begging for attention.

"Hey, Bucky Beaver!" I hadn't noticed that Vince walked by to dump his tray into the trash. He looks at me and shoves his top teeth over his bottom lip and makes a chomping motion. "I saw a picture of a train wreck this morning. It reminded me of your *face*."

I can feel my cheeks heat up. The sixth graders sitting at the end of our table snicker and glance at me.

"Clever, skunk-boy!" DeShaun jumps to my defense. "You come up with that all by yourself?"

But Vince is too far away to hear him. And when he gets back to their table, Carlay high-fives him. Not wanting to be left out, Alexis also holds up her hand and Vince gives it a quick smack.

Drool trickles down my chin and I wipe it away, lightning quick. I whip out my pocket mirror to make sure I got it all.

"You want me to get my grapefruit to orbisculate on him, Plink-Meister?" DeShaun's eyes are kind.

"That's okay," I grumble. "He's not worth it. But thanks."

"Ignore him," Shrynn whispers, and touches my hand. "Vince doesn't have braces. He's in no place to judge."

I know she's right. Braces are normal. We're in middle school.

But even though Shrynn's my best friend and pretty much my favorite person in the whole world, I can't bring myself to look at her. So I look past her instead, and that's when I notice that Alexis, Carlay, and Vince have somehow gotten hold of a bunch of tinfoil, probably from someone's lunch. They formed the foil into half-moon–shaped orbs, exactly the way my jawbreaker is shaped, and now it's jutting out of their mouths and they're doubled over with laughter.

I gather my tray. "Guys, I'm gonna go. I have to finish my

math homework," I lie. My homework is finished, but I need to leave the cafeteria before I choke the bully out of my sister.

"But I wanted to tell you about my—"

I turn to leave before Shrynn can finish. I pass Keisha on the way out. She's sitting by herself with a book at a table near the exit, which is super unlike her. She doesn't come to the cafeteria that often, but when she does, she's usually surrounded by eighth graders.

"Hey, Keish," I say. She looks at me and nods.

"What's wrong?" I ask.

"Do I look like something's wrong?"

"Jeez," I say under my breath. "Sorry I asked."

Keisha takes a deep breath. "Sorry," she says. "I didn't mean to be rude."

"It's okay," I say, turning to the exit. "You don't have to talk about it. I was just going to the media lab, anyway, to do some—"

"In a way, there's not much to talk about," she says. "But tell me this—if the school were having a seventh-grade dance, would your mom let you go?"

"A seventh-grade dance?" I say. "Do we even have those?"

"No, we don't, only eighth-grade dances, like the one happening in three weeks. But it's a hypothetical. If there was a seventh-grade dance, would your mom let you go?" she asks again.

I shrug. "I guess so. If I really wanted to. And as long as I had a way to get there and back. And if it was free." And if she knew that adults would be there to chaperone, but I don't say that part because I don't want to sound like a dork.

"So . . . she *trusts* you, then," Keisha says.

"I mean, yeah, I guess so." Mom and I don't always get along, but I think she trusts me. I've never really given her reason not to.

I look at Keisha. She's staring into space.

"Is everything okay?" I ask.

"Just forget I said anything," she says, turning back to her book.

I shrug and check the time. There are twenty more minutes left of lunch. What I really need to do is get started on some newspaper assignments, but I head to the media lab to read more of Dean's blog instead. Knowing that other people deal with the same things I do doesn't fix everything, but it definitely makes me feel better.

I click on a tab titled *Shocking Things About Maxillofacial Surgery* and read Dean's entry:

So, I knew that getting braces was common. Almost all of my friends have them. But I had no idea how common orthognathic surgery actually was (that's a fancy way of saying jaw surgery—and the "g" is silent, by the way). As soon as I found out that I needed to have this procedure, I started looking up statistics, hoping it would help me feel better. And it did, a little bit. Did you know that 15 percent of orthodontic patients have the sort of abnormal bone structure that braces can't correct by themselves? Lucky us, right? That's according to a famous hospital in the U.S. called Johns Hopkins.

At first, 15 percent didn't sound like a lot, but then my dad said that if he had a 15 percent chance of winning the lottery, he'd play it every single week. That made me laugh. But it also made me think. A lot of us are walking around out there, staring down the possibility of jaw surgery. It's nice not feeling so alone.

Dean listed other statistics, like the chances of complications happening after surgery (up to 40 percent)—especially if you don't follow the doctor's orders. But he also talked about how 92 percent of patients are happy with their surgery after more than six months have passed. He writes,

I like those odds. Especially if getting surgery means that my jaw won't cause me problems in the future.

≥ ☆ ≤

I was so focused on Dean's blog posts that I didn't realize there was another tab called *Q & A with Dean.*

I've been getting a lot of questions since I started
this thing, so I wanted to create a separate page
to address some of them here. I can't believe how
many of you actually read my thoughts! Thanks for
being here.

I skim the questions and answers that Dean posted. It's sort
of like reading an interview. Most of the questions are about
pain and recovery. Dean says that his mouth honestly didn't
hurt that much after the surgery, but recovery was slow and
annoying because he had to sleep sitting up for a couple of
weeks to control the swelling. He also had to eat all of his
meals blended, through a straw, even chicken, which seems
gross. (How do you even *eat* chicken through a straw?) But he
also talks more about all of the ice cream shakes he had after
his surgery, which sounds like a *huge* perk.

I glance at the clock. I have three more minutes of reading before the bell rings. I'm about to close out of the blog
when the last question catches my eye.

Dear Dean,
    Hi from California! I'm in middle school and I
don't know yet, but I might need to get this surgery.
But I wear braces right now and I'm also wearing
headgear. My question might sound like a weird
one, but how did you deal with bullies while you

were in braces? Ever since I got mine, they haven't left me alone. Do they ever stop?

Thanks, M.

Did I write to Dean in my sleep or something? The only difference between me and the writer is that I'm not from California.

Thanks for your comment, M. I'm super sorry that people aren't being very nice to you. I know exactly how that feels. The kids at school were . . . well, my parents read this blog so I'm not gonna use the words I want to use. Let's just say that they could have been nicer. Much nicer. It was pretty tough for a while, but my parents helped me through it. I have the best family in the world. The only thing I can really say is to be bigger than the bullies. You never really know what's going on in someone else's world, right? If it gets really bad you might have to tell someone like a school counselor or something. Find someone you can trust. It's been a while since I've been in middle school, but I can say that it blows over eventually. Lean on your friends and just do the best you can. Braces are temporary and super common, but unfortunately, so is bullying.

Something clicks in my brain. I know exactly what I want my application to be about and it's all thanks to some guy in Canada who I've never met.

"I hope that's research for new op-ed ideas. We have deadlines on the horizon and I need you to start pulling your weight, Plink."

I yelp. I had no idea Keisha had been standing over me. "What's that?" She nods at the screen. I close down the page. I don't want to talk to Keisha about it.

"Keisha, not cool," I whisper-bark. The media lab teacher is watching us from her desk, and I don't want to get kicked out for talking too loud.

"What's not cool is you blowing off deadlines," she says.

"I . . . I can't really think of anything."

Keisha stares me down. I look away.

"Do you think Jordan Slade would accept that as an excuse?" she says. I know Keisha's right.

"Keish, I—"

"We haven't had an article from you in weeks. It's *my* newspaper this year, Plink. Next year, it'll be someone else's. You can mess around then. But you're not about to make me look bad. Not with everyone watching."

"But who's—"

But before I can ask Keisha who she thought was watching, she turns on her heel and storms out of the lab, her purple book bag bouncing angrily behind her.

20

MAX GETS A SECOND CHANCE

For the first time ever, newspaper club is the last place I want to be. It's only been a couple of hours since I ran into Keisha in the media lab, and I don't want her to have another opportunity to tear into me.

And when I arrive, I'm in such a bad mood I don't even want to see Shrynn.

"What's wrong?" she asks as soon I plop down next to her. I really don't want to bother her with my problems because I know that something's been wrong in her world, too. Last week, when our English teacher told us what was going to be on the next test, Shrynn didn't even take notes. She doodled little flowers in the margins of her notebook paper instead. Then she called me later that day to ask me about what was going to be on the test.

Calling me to get the work after she'd already been in

class is *totally* not a Shrynn move. If anything, I'm the one to call her.

"Nothing," I say, shrugging. I force a smile. "Hey, maybe we'll get together this weekend and work on our—"

"Max, let's have a little chat, you and me, out in the hall, okay?" Dr. Dodge comes up from behind me. His tone is kind but serious.

There's a small desk with two chairs in the hall outside the club's classroom. Dr. Dodge gestures to one as he takes the other.

"I think we've known each other for a good long while, Max," he says. He's kind and gentle, but that's Dr. Dodge's way. He doesn't have to raise his voice for you to know that he's about to lay down the law.

"Why don't you tell me what's going on? I've noticed that you're taking on less and less. A lot less than the other staff reporters, even. We all have to pull together, you know."

"I know, Dodge, it's just—"

"Just what?"

"I have a lot of things going on right now, and it's been kind of hard to concentrate."

"I see." Dr. Dodge taps his fingers on the table. He pauses for a long minute. "Max, if you need to—"

Just then, the big double doors that lead into our wing open with a bang. Carlay and Vince charge through them.

"Hmm," Dr. Dodge finally says to them. "You appear to be lost. If my memory's correct, the AV club meets during this time, but they're two wings down." I hide a smile. Dr. Dodge doesn't play around. "Do you need my help finding it? Or should I call your teacher to let her know you're here?"

"No—no, Dr. Dodge," Vince says. He looks like he's trying not to laugh. Carlay nibbles on her thumbnail, but I can still see her witchy smile.

"Be on your way, then."

Dr. Dodge waits until they turn around and disappear through the double doors again before turning back to me.

"If you need to pull back from the paper for a little while, don't be afraid to say so," he says.

"Wait, what?" I squeak. "What do you mean, pull back? I love the paper. I don't want to leave it."

"Hold on, Max," he says. "There's no harm in taking care of other things that might need more of your attention right now. The paper will always be here."

"But Dodge," I say, "I really want to be a part of it. It's just been a little hard lately, but I'll do better." I look him in the eye. "I promise."

"It's entirely up to you, Max," Dr. Dodge says. "You're always welcome in the club. We all need to hold each other accountable for the things that need to get done."

Just like Dr. Watson, Dr. Dodge uses the word *we* even

though I know he means *me*. It makes me feel better about the whole thing, like he's got my back.

"And I want you to think really carefully about the assignments you take on. Just be honest with yourself. If you can only do an op-ed here and there, that's perfectly okay. Just tell us so. Or tell me privately, if you prefer. But try not to pull a disappearing act with your work, okay?"

"Okay," I whisper.

"So, about that Channel 5 journalism competition. Have you started your application yet?"

"No." I swallow. "I wasn't sure I was going to until recently."

"That's a pretty big project you're procrastinating on."

"I know. It's just—I couldn't really figure out what to write about until . . . well, until just now."

"Want to run your topic by me?" He smiles.

"Keisha was sort of a help with it." I figure if Dr. Dodge can go back and tell Keisha that I said she'd helped me with something, maybe I'll be in good with her again. "I think I'm going to do it on bullying. And braces. And how the two sort of go together."

"Ah, I see." Dodge smiles. "I remember those days. Too well."

"You had braces?" I say. I don't know why I'm so surprised. Dr. Dodge's teeth are totally perfect, and most people aren't born with perfect teeth. At least that's what Dr. Watson told me.

"I had the works. I had to wear this little rake-shaped thing on the roof of my mouth, too, to train my tongue to move correctly when I spoke. The kids all called me metal-mouth, train-track face, you name it. Now my son needs the same thing."

"So, you think it's a good topic?" I ask.

"Better than good. One of the better ones I've heard. You should really get started thinking about what you might want to say about it. And . . ." He pauses. "You might think about talking to Keisha. Get some pointers. After all, she was last year's Rising Star. She knows what it takes."

"But there's one problem," I say. I don't like to talk about these things with most people. It's embarrassing. "My phone can't take videos. I might have to use my mom's, but I'll also probably have to use the school's equipment, and . . . what if that means my submission won't look as good as other people's?"

"Max, students borrow the school's equipment all the time, for all sorts of reasons. In fact, I used one of the computers just the other day for a teacher project I'm doing for the principal. Just focus on doing the best project you can, okay? Jordan Slade won't know what hit her." Dr. Dodge stands up. "Now let's get back to work. We still have thirty minutes."

But I have one more thing I need to ask. "Dodge?" I say. "It's probably too late, but would it be okay if I submitted an op-ed first thing tomorrow morning? I can write it tonight. I promise." It's true. Dad will be asleep when I get home and Mom will be at the diner until right around the time Dad wakes up. I'm pretty sure I overhead Alexis ask Mom if she could go to her friend's house.

A whole afternoon with privacy is exactly what I need to bang out an op-ed, and I know exactly what I want to write about.

Dodge smiles. "It wouldn't be an award-winning paper without Plink's ink." He pauses. "I just thought of that myself. You like it?"

I giggle. "Yeah, it's pretty cool."

"All of the articles are scheduled to post online at seven tonight. So if you can email it to me no later than six, I'll make sure to include it. As long as this is the only time we're working on something so last minute, I'm okay with it."

"I can do it," I say.

21

SOMETHING TO THINK ABOUT

I submitted my op-ed last night, just a couple of hours after my talk with Dodge, and I. Can't. Stop. Smiling.

I smiled walking with Alexis to the bus stop even though she pretty much ignored me the whole time; I smiled when Keisha ran up to me and wrapped me in a big bear hug and apologized for being so intense; I smiled as I climbed onto the bus, even as Vince tripped me and called me Bucky Beaver and Carlay laughed like a screech owl.

I usually do pretty good with my schoolwork, but I don't always *feel* good about my schoolwork, if that makes sense. I mean, most of the time schoolwork just feels like a bunch of assignments that don't matter much, like identifying adverbs or knowing how to do algebra or memorizing the timeline of some war that happened a zillion years before I was born.

Maybe school is just this thing we have to get through

before the important stuff happens? I don't know. What I do know is that writing for the newspaper feels different, especially when I know I've written something good.

Dad's words echo in my brain, and now I think I understand what he means. *We all have to find the time to do the things we love.*

I smiled my way through the whole morning and straight through English, even as Mr. Brace piled on a whole bunch of work.

"Your journal responses are due next Monday," Mr. Brace says a few minutes before the bell.

I pull out my planner and write the words BRACE/ JOURNAL under next Monday's date, and then I write MEDIA LAB because I'm going to have to make it a point to print the assignment before class, because that's how Mr. Brace makes us hand in most of our work.

Every few weeks or so, Mr. Brace makes us write a journal entry after we knock out a couple of chapters of whatever book we're reading. Right now, we're reading S.E. Hinton's *The Outsiders*. It's this popular book by a super famous author who wrote it when she was a teenager or something. They even made a movie about it, which Mr. Brace is going to show us when we finish reading. It's a really good story, about a bunch of brothers who are supposedly from the wrong side of the tracks. People call them Greasers, because they don't have a lot of money and their hair is all slick and greasy-looking and stuff, at least from what it says in the book. And they're kind of wild and they get into a lot of trouble with this other group called the Socs, who are basically a bunch of well-to-do kids who live in big houses on the better side of town and wear nice clothes and stuff. I relate a lot to the main character, this kid called Ponyboy, because of the way he feels responsible for everything. He feels totally responsible for protecting his brothers from conflict with other people—especially the other gang in their town—and deals with constant stress in his life.

I think that's what makes a good book. When you can actually feel what the characters are feeling, even though they're not real.

Mr. Brace likes when we get really personal in our journals, and for this next journal entry he wants us to write about whether people can be redeemable. As in, is there such a thing as a totally good or completely bad person, and can people change? Should people be given second or third or even fourth chances? It makes me think of Alexis, and Mom and Dad, and even myself. I mean, I hope that people can change. It would be really weird if who you are at eleven or twelve is the same person you are when you're fifty or something.

"And typing it up is optional," Mr. Brace calls out as the bell rings.

He's never said that before.

"Yes!" DeShaun pumps his fist in the air. He turns to Shrynn and me. "My printer broke last week," he says. "Now I don't have to rush around to type up this stupid journal."

"There's no such thing as stupid journals," Mr. Brace calls from his desk as the class packs up. "Only stupid comments." But then he winks at DeShaun, so I know he's not mad.

"See you both at lunch later?" DeShaun asks.

Shrynn looks at me. I nod.

"I guess," I say, thinking of Carlay and Vince. I was in a good enough mood to ignore them this morning. But I don't know if that will last through the day. "I mean, I kind of like going to the media lab better."

Shrynn and DeShaun share a look, which makes me think they've been talking about me.

"Mm-hmm," DeShaun says. "So you have to give up your lunch because of those idiots?"

"How'd you know?"

"It's pretty obvious, Plink," DeShaun says. He pauses. "They're not as cool as they think they are, you know. But you running away in fear definitely gives them what they want."

"I don't run in *fear*," I sputter, but DeShaun had already turned to leave.

"I'll be in the cafeteria at lunch," Shrynn says, tugging on my sleeve. "Hope to see you."

"We'll see," I say. "We still have, like, fifty other classes before lunch anyway, so maybe we don't have to harp on it right now?" I shove my books into my backpack and make a mental note to cross out MEDIA LAB on my calendar.

"You're right," Shrynn says. "Let's forget it for now."

We walk by Mr. Brace's desk on our way out. He smiles wide and calls out, "My Language Arts comrades!" Shrynn and I look at each other and giggle. Mr. Brace can be totally weird. "Max, can I have a second?"

"Um, yeah, sure," I say. "I'm not in trouble, am I?"

Mr. Brace smiles. His plaid sleeves are rolled up to his elbows and he has a pencil tucked behind his ear. "Not that I know of!"

Shrynn heads toward the door but I grab her arm. "Don't go!" I hiss.

Mr. Brace smiles at Shrynn. "You can stay, if you'd like." He picks up a sheet of paper. It's a printout of my op-ed with handwritten notes along the margins. *Certain School Policies Are Harder for Some Students Than for Others, by Max Plink.*

"Thanks for writing this," Mr. Brace says. "It came out online in time for the seventh-grade teacher meeting this morning, and we made sure to give it a read." He pauses. "Talking about it actually took up a lot of the meeting. We're really grateful for your perspective. It helped us look at things a little differently, and we're going to rethink some of our requirements."

Shrynn squeezes my arm and lets out a little squeal. "Tha—thanks, Mr. Brace," I say. I wasn't sure that any teachers actually read our articles.

"We hope to hear more from you," Mr. Brace says. He hands me his printout of my article. "I thought you'd like to look at my notes. Keep up the good work."

Certain School Policies Are Harder for Some Students Than for Others
by Max Plink

Last week, all five of my teachers required us to either print or submit our work online. And that's okay, because of high school expectations, right? Our teachers talk a lot about preparing us for "The Real World." Except, for some students, these policies are an undue burden. Not every kid in school has a working computer, and not every piece of equipment that the school offers is updated with the latest software and working 100 percent of the time. According to Mr. Adam Freitz, Weiss Junior High School's technology teacher, we have enough computers for approximately 75 percent of students. "It's an issue we're working on," he said in a school newsletter published earlier this year.

Hadn't considered that. Thanks for this.

That's cool—but what about the other 25 percent? How many kids without the right technology are left in the lurch, and what are they supposed to do while the school works on this issue?

A lot of food for thought here, Max.

It doesn't stop there. Even those of us who don't rely on school computers might not have a great internet connection at home. Some of us might not have a connection at all, and others might not have printers. Those of us with broken computers or bad connections at home are left scrambling to meet our teachers' requirements, all in the name of high school expectations and beyond. Some teachers mark us down if we don't hand in printed assignments.

The funny, not-so-funny part is that the issue of having access to the stuff we need won't magically go away just because we're in high school. The problems might still be there. Then what? At that point, how much burden might be put on students in the name of college expectations, and how can schools and teachers make things more equitable while making sure we're all prepared for these expectations?

Great question.

But it's not just about computers and useless Wi-Fi. There are other school policies that seem to favor some students over others, like honor roll being tied to mostly perfect attendance, and cutting down our lunch hour where a lot of kids catch up on the assignments that they couldn't do at home. Some teachers who mean well ask us to use our phones during certain lessons, to make things fun, but that only works if you have a smartphone and the right plan. Not all of us have what we need to participate fully.

Yikes. This really is a big problem. I admit we haven't been thinking much about this. Thanks for shedding light on it.

Even small things like extracurriculars after school are hard for some students because they have to take the school bus home. Not everyone's parents are able to pick them up from school after activities that run late. This leaves out a whole bunch of kids who might want certain opportunities but can't have them.

How much are the teachers and administration

at Weiss Junior High School thinking about these issues? And how many students are being left behind in the name of school policies and high school expectations?

Can't thank you enough for writing this. You've given your teachers a lot to think about.

22

A VIRAL ARTICLE AND PARENTS WITH OPINIONS

It's later in the afternoon and I'm still super happy after my conversation with Mr. Brace. Even when Alexis, Carlay, and Vince started in with me by shouting a chorus of "Bucky Beaver" from the back of the bus, I couldn't have cared less.

"You must have had a good day," Mom had said when I got home. "What went on?"

But I didn't tell her about my article. Not yet. I wanted to enjoy the things that Mr. Brace had said and written before I told my parents about it. I'm not sure how they'll react to my having talked about resources. They might feel like it's too personal and that I'm airing the Family's Dirty Laundry, even though op-eds are literally *supposed* to be personal opinions.

"I think I know what I want to do for my journalism application, that's all." I smiled.

Even though everyone's home together for a change, it's quiet. Alexis went off to our bedroom to start her homework and Dad's on the couch watching TV before his shift. Mom's off from work today and preparing dinner and she said I could jump online to do some research for my Channel 5 application.

I'm wearing my jawbreaker and searching through Dean's blog to see if he says any more about bullying, but I can't find much. And the fact that he doesn't talk about it makes me feel like there is something really important for me to add to the story of kids who have to wear braces and jaw-breakers, and maybe get jaw surgery.

I click on a post called *post-surgery bliss*:

Hello, friends with facial anomalies! Just a quick note for anyone who's super scared about surgery:
I ate strawberry shortcake through a straw for dinner last night. Here's the thing: I'm seven weeks post-op, and my jaws are no longer clamped shut with these tight little wirelike rubber bands. While I can't eat every single thing I want yet, I can now eat a lot of things like pasta, mashed potatoes, fish, and finely chopped chicken. The doctor says that I don't have to eat anything through a straw anymore

(as long as I'm careful), and to be honest, that whole phase really flew by.

But last night, I chose to eat my cake through a straw. Why? Well. Throw some vanilla ice cream into a blender, add some milk and a hefty slice of strawberry shortcake, and tell me it's not the greatest thing that ever happened to you. I never would have discovered my favorite dessert if not for double jaw surgery!

Hey, I'm just trying to make you feel better about this whole thing.

Peace out.

Your friend,

Dean

I click on one of Dean's posts with pictures of his before-and-after jaws when Mom's cell phone rings.

"Hello? . . . This is she," I hear her say. "Uh-huh. Yes. *Really.*" She steps into the living room and looks at me, but I can't read her face. Dad's eyes dart back and forth between Mom and me, his face full of question marks. Alexis creeps into the living room, too, like her *Max is in trouble* gossip radar went off.

My mouth feels like sandpaper and my jaws start to throb. They pound like little heartbeats to the tune of *you're in trou-ble, you're in trou-ble.*

But then Mom's voice turns light and surprised. "Thank you, Dr. Dodge. We don't really use social media, but we'll check on it right now. I appreciate your call. Thank you! . . . Right. She's already started on her application, but we'll make sure she meets the deadline . . . Yes, you too. Thanks again!" Mom hangs up the phone.

"What was that about?" Dad yawns.

"Well," Mom says, sitting on the couch next to Dad. "A certain Max Plink wrote an op-ed that went viral today." She starts flipping through her phone. "That must be what these messages are about. I haven't had a chance to check them."

She smiles. "Shrynn's mom texted me saying that she read it and she thought it was great."

"I . . . she . . . what?" I choke.

"That was Dr. Dodge on the phone," Mom says, looking up. I don't remember the last time I've seen her so stinking happy looking. "He called to let us know that you wrote the most popular article of the year so far." She pronounces *popular* like *popul-ah*, and it makes me smile.

"Way to go, Jordan Slade," Dad says. He tugs on my ponytail. "Do we get to see this viral article?"

"Who's Jordan Slade?" Alexis grumbles.

"A famous journalist," Mom says.

"Boring," Alexis says. "What's for dinner?"

"I seem to remember that no one said your science project

was boring," Dad said. "And I seem to remember Max having nice things to say."

"No one *cares* what Max thinks," Alexis snaps.

"Obviously they *do*, if her articles are going viral," Dad says. It feels super nice to have him stick up for me.

"This is a big deal for Max," Mom chimes in. Her tone is sharp. "Would it hurt to be happy for her?"

"Whatever." Alexis doubles back into our bedroom and slams the door, but I don't even care. Nothing in the world can ruin the good mood I'm in.

"Let's see what Dr. Dodge is talking about," Mom says. I unplug the laptop and hand it to her. She logs into her social media account, which she hardly ever uses.

"Wow," she says. "They posted the article to the *Weiss Chronicle*'s social media page. It has over five thousand likes." She reads the title aloud.

"Sounds serious," Dad says, looking over Mom's shoulder. They read together in silence.

"This is really good, Max," Mom says after a few minutes. "Especially the part about how your teachers treat everyone as if they have the same exact access to the same resources. I can't believe some of them mark down if a student doesn't print their work." She looks at Dad. "And what about the kids who don't have internet access? We do, but by the skin of our teeth. It took this article forever to load." Mom hands the laptop back to me. "Not every kid has the things that schools think they should have. That's just reality."

"It's also reality that no one really cares what you have access to or not," Dad says. "If the car breaks down and I can't get to work on time, what do you think my boss would say? *Oh well, hey, you don't have access to a car, so take the day off?*" I mean, maybe he would, but then I don't get paid and we don't eat. Same for you, Jackie."

Mom's lips are in a thin line. "I think the point Max is making is that, for some people, it's easier to get ahead in life *because* they have easy access to important things that other people don't have. I mean," she says, pausing to light a cigarette, "we get by, but that's about it. *We get by.* What about the people who can't even get by because of things out of their control? Should schools just leave them behind? Should life just leave them behind? I don't think so. And that's what I think Max is getting at."

"You answered your own question." Dad rolls his eyes. "Life leaves people behind. Life doesn't care if you can afford the latest and greatest thing. If you can't, it's up to you to figure out how to get ahead. It's not the school's job to coddle these kids."

"These kids are *our* kids," Mom hisses.

"I stand by what I said," Dad says. "Life has always been easier for some people, and it's always been harder for others. Look at my entire family. My mother struggled until she died. Your family struggles. We struggle. Max is exactly right about that. But you don't see us asking for handouts."

Mom stands up and stubs out her cigarette in a nearby ashtray. "You have completely missed the point," she says. "Dinner will be in a half hour. Or maybe you should make your own, considering how you don't like handouts." With that, she disappears into the kitchen.

Dad bends over and kisses me on the cheek. "I'm proud of you, Maxi-Pie. You're doin' a lot more with your life than me and your mother ever did when we were your age." Even though he doesn't seem to agree with what I wrote, it feels good to know that Dad's proud of me. He calls out to Mom. "We might not have much, but we worked hard to get where we are. Shouldn't everyone else? Look at Max and Alexis. They work hard even *without* the kinds of things that other kids have."

"Thanks for making my point, Chris," she snaps from the kitchen. "Maybe they wouldn't have to work so damn hard if things were just a little easier. A little fairer."

"Well, life's not fair." Dad closes the door to the bedroom to get changed for work.

I don't know what to think. How can two parents work as hard as they do and still have a big fat red zero on the extras board, like that's the only thing we've actually earned? What would Dad say about that?

But I don't ask because all I can think about is: *Everyone's reading my article and I never want this feeling to go away.*

Mom calls out to me from the kitchen. "Max, please tell your sister that dinner will be ready soon."

"Can I check my phone?" I ask. I have the sneaking suspicion that I have a couple of text messages and I'm dying to check.

"Make it quick."

I grab my phone from the basket. Sure enough, there's a handful of messages. I click on the one from Shrynn first.

> Maxi! You're famous! If I print your article, can I have your autograph? Amy wants it, too ;)

I laugh as I move on to DeShaun's message.

> Plink-Meister! I never read the school paper because who cares, but I totes read your article. People are sharing it like cray!

My heart pounds as I see one from Keisha.

> Well done, Plink. Sorry again for the 'tude. I have a lot on my plate, including a Mom-shaped pain in my butt. But I totally knew you'd finally come up with something.
> Let me know if you wanna talk about the competition. Totally willing to share my brilliance. But you have just over four weeks, so you'll have to make it snappy.

I text her back.

Thanks, Keesh. Maybe we can work on
applications this weekend? At Shrynn's?

Let's plan. I can bring the equipment. Start
taking some b-roll.

Wutz b-roll?

Footage, Plink. B-roll is footage. It's a
5-minute essay, so you'll need a lot of it.

BTW—what's up with your mom?

I wait for what seems like a year and I'm about to put my

phone back in the basket when it dings.

Same old story. She just gets cranky and
takes it out on me. Not happy with me
unless I'm Little Miss Perfect. It's old.

You're lucky, Plink.

I put my phone in its basket because it's almost dinner-

time, and besides, I don't know what to say.

23

DR. WATSON JOINS TEAM MAX

It's been twenty-four hours since I found out that my article went viral, and I know by the way my jaw throbs that an appointment with Dr. Watson is around the corner. It's sort of like the way some people feel aches and pains when a storm is coming. The body just knows somehow.

So I wasn't surprised this morning when Mom reminded me that I had an appointment with Dr. Watson after school and that Alexis would be coming with us because Dad had to work overtime.

And she's not in the greatest mood because she and Dad got into another argument this morning about sharing the car.

"But something's gotta give, Jackie," he'd said to her. I hid in the bathroom, listening. "I can't be taking the train after working a fourteen-hour shift. I did an eighteen-hour shift last weekend. Would you want to be stuck without a car when you're done with the diner? I doubt it."

As I stood in the bathroom, crouched over the sink with the water running (so that they didn't think I was listening), I wondered how Dad felt about all his fairness talk now.

"Then buy me my own car," Mom had snapped. "Until then, your *family* needs to be able to get around when you're not home and taking car service everywhere we need to go is too expensive."

"Ever think of the bus?" Dad bit back. I heard the unmistakable sound of him putting on his heavy work boots and stomping toward the door.

"Oh, go to—" Mom's voice had been cut off by the sound of the door slamming against the frame so hard that I thought the roof might cave in.

I heard something fall in the hallway. When I opened the bathroom door, I saw the extras board lying facedown on the floor. I snatched it and hid it underneath the pile of newspapers that Dad shoves under the kitchen table when he's done with them.

So now Alexis is snarling in the back seat because she has to come with Mom and me to another orthodontist's appointment. I'm starting to notice that Alexis is even harder to deal with after Mom and Dad have it out.

I learned something about fight or flight in science class

the other week. When Mom and Dad fight, I hide in the bathroom because it's the only spot in the whole house where I can get privacy for a few minutes, but Alexis seems to get ready for the next world war—or at least for a fight with *me*. After Mrs. Neast's lesson, it all made sense. When things are rough at home, I want to flee, and Alexis wants to fight. Mrs. Neast said it had something to do with our lizard brains and the way we process fear.

"So you told me that you were going to do your project on braces, but you haven't said how you're going to go about it," Mom says. We're a couple of blocks away from Dr. Watson's office and I'm not sure, but I feel like I can detect a hint of pride in Mom's voice.

"I think I know what I want to do," I say. "Shrynn agreed to help because she wears braces and she knows what it's like." I'm careful not to mention the bullying part in front of Alexis.

"Yeah, like *you're* gonna be on the news," Alexis says. "And you should probably ask your newspaper teacher if *beavers* are even allowed to apply."

"Alexis, one more word and you'll lose your phone privileges for the rest of the week." Mom stops at a stoplight. "And you can forget about seeing your friends on Saturday. I've had enough of your mouth."

I hear a grumble that sounds like *whatever* as Alexis kicks the back of my seat, but this time, I'm not rattled. Mom's been sticking up for me more lately, and it feels super good.

"I have an idea for your application," Mom says.

My eyes grow wide. "What is it?"

"What if you asked Dr. Watson for her input? Maybe you can get footage of her working on your mouth and talking about why she wanted to be an orthodontist. We can tell her about the article you just wrote and how it went viral and stuff."

There's a burst of laughter from the back seat and I roll my eyes. "Why would anyone be interested in *that*?"

"Because a lot of kids *wear* braces," Mom says. "Adults, too. And don't think you're off the hook. You'll be in them in the next year or two, so you'll get to learn all about it whether you want to or not." She turns back to me. "You should ask Dr. Watson. See if she'd mind talking to you about it."

"But she always seems so busy," I say.

"She's an orthodontist, Max," Mom says. "You're not her only patient. Of course she's busy. But it can't hurt to ask."

"Can you ask her for me?" I say.

"Max Plink, you'll be thirteen years old soon. You can certainly ask your doctor for a conversation. I'll talk to her *with* you, but I'm not gonna ask her *for* you."

Mom parks the car and I'm kicking around her idea. It's not a bad one. I'm actually surprised at how good it is.

"How's it going, Max?" Dr. Watson breezes into the examination room and squeezes Mom's shoulder when we arrive. I'm sitting in the Chair of Doom, my jawbreaker resting in my lap.

"Hi, Dr. Watson," I say, feeling shy. Suddenly I'm not so sure about Mom's idea.

"How's the headgear working out for you?" she asks. She approaches me with a small mirror, which means it's time for the poking and prodding to start. I open my mouth. "Has Ms. Max been following the rules?" she asks Mom.

Mom smiles. "It seems that way. She wears it after school and to bed. I check on her after she falls asleep, and it's still right where it should be. She's doing good with it, in my opinion. She even has her own bottle of Tylenol. She takes it right after dinner if things are a little too sore."

I had no idea Mom checks on me in my sleep. And it's true, I only took the jawbreaker out of my mouth *once* in my sleep since the last time I saw Dr. Watson. Her idea about taking painkillers before bed seems to have worked.

"So, it's only been about a month since you began wearing the headgear," Dr. Watson says. "And it's way too soon to know if major progress is being made." She pauses as she pokes around my mouth. I can feel the mirror wedged between my back molars and my cheek. "Do me a favor, Max. Let's strap the headgear in." I do what the doctor says. "Now, how does it feel? Does it hurt? Do you feel pressure anywhere?"

"Actually, no," I say. "I mean, I can totally tell that it's there, but that's because it's protruding from my skull and kind of hard to ignore, you know?"

"Max, be serious." Mom's tone is a warning, but Dr. Watson smiles.

"That's good news. It means your mouth is getting used to it and we need to adjust the tension. So you'll be a little sore again, moving forward. And we'll probably have to do this with each visit, along with tightening your braces."

Oh, just awesome. I sigh. I hope Mom planned ravioli for dinner.

"Dr. Watson, we'd like to ask you something," Mom says, and my gut clenches.

"What's that?" Dr. Watson looks at me, smiling. I feel my face heat up. It's one thing to show up to a doctor's office so that they can do whatever they need to do, but it's another thing to, like, ask them to have a *conversation* with you.

"Max has a big project," Mom says. "It's an application to work with a famous journalist. Jordan Slade. Tell Dr. Watson about what we talked about, on the way over." The way Mom says *over* sounds like *ovuh*, and I never really think about it unless we're with people who speak all proper-like, like Dr. Watson.

I swallow. "I, I have to make a video essay." I pause. "And I have to pick a topic that'll be interesting to other people. And, the one I picked is, you know . . ." I swallow again.

"About braces?" Dr. Watson smiles. She reaches into her drawer and grabs a tool that looks like a mini wrench.

"Yeah," I say. "Because a lot of kids wear them and stuff. I was hoping I could, like, interview you. If it isn't too much trouble."

"I'd love to talk to you about orthodontia, Max. What would be interesting for you to know?" She pauses and lifts her protective eye gear up over her eyes and rests it on her head like a pair of glasses.

I hadn't really gotten that far. "Well, I . . . I don't really . . ."

But Mom rescues me. "Max may want to know more about why you decided to become an orthodontist, and how normal it is for kids to have braces, stuff like that. She was also hoping to get some footage of you working on her teeth during a regular appointment."

"Ah, yes." Dr. Watson is smiling really big now. "As far as normal, it seems that all the kids have braces these days. And more and more adults are getting them, too. Even some celebrities! There's a famous actress who just started treatment, too, but I can't remember her name for the life of me."

"So, like," I say. "Why did you want to become an orthodontist?"

"Good question." Mom smiles. At times like this, I forget

how rough our relationship can be. "By the way, Dr. Watson, Max wrote an article for her school's online newspaper that went viral. It's been posted all over social media. So she's really good at this stuff."

And now I want the chair to swallow me whole.

"*Really.*" Dr. Watson pats my hand. "I'll have to give it a look. It's always exciting to know what my patients are up to. As for your question, it's a very good one and easy for me to answer." Dr. Watson lowers her protective gear back over her eyes. "I promised myself that I'd never see another kid go through what I went through, growing up with severely misaligned teeth and jaws."

"What—what do you mean?" I ask.

"I hope it's not too personal," Mom says pointedly. "Max doesn't want to pry."

Dr. Watson waves a dismissive hand. "There should be no secrets when it comes to a doctor's motivations." She smiles again. "How about this. I'll work and talk at the same time. Can your mom take some footage?"

"Mom? Can you?" But her smartphone is already pointed at us.

"Rolling," Mom says with a smile. Dr. Watson positions her mini wrench in my mouth and begins to speak.

"There were six of us kids, and five of us needed braces. My parents couldn't afford that luxury. We couldn't afford much, to be honest. Not as many people worried about correcting their teeth back then, so my parents didn't think much of it."

It's weird, to get an insider view of your orthodontist's life. It's like, they're human with a childhood and stuff, but you don't really think of them that way when they're trying to move your teeth around.

"But the bullying was severe," she continues. "It started in elementary school and kept up straight through high school. So I put myself through college, but I also worked three jobs so that I could pay to get my teeth straightened. And along the way, I decided to become an orthodontist."

"Did something, like, specific happen that led to that decision?" I ask. I'm trying to channel my inner Keisha.

Dr. Watson lowers her eyes and bites her lip. "You're a journalist. I guess I should have seen that question coming, huh?" She smiles.

Mom jumps in. "Oh, don't worry if it's—"

"I had a friend in high school, Max," Dr. Watson continues, waving a hand to let Mom know that it's okay. "Anna and I had been best friends since middle school. Or at least I thought we were. But when she had her seventeenth birthday party, it seemed like she didn't want me in any of her pictures. It was a big party, you see. It was at her house, and there were lots of teenagers running around. Kids from school, and her family. And it seemed like she'd ask me to do something else whenever someone was trying to take group pictures. That's when people still brought their digital cameras to events, you know? So someone would point a camera in our direction, and she'd ask me to get something from another room, or to find a person she said she'd been looking for, stuff like that. And I was happy to help.

"I start to worry that I might not be in any of her pictures, and I figure Anna'd be upset about that. So I finally say, hey, let's take a picture together." Dr. Watson swings one arm off to the side, all animated-like. "And she flat out said *no*. Could you believe it?"

"Dr. Watson," Mom says. "I worry that we're taking too much of your time." I can't tell if Mom is legit concerned about the doctor's time, or if she's trying to get Dr. Watson to stop telling her story because it's sad and uncomfortable.

"No worries, Mrs. Plink. You're my last appointment. The one after you canceled, and it's a lot more fun talking with the both of you than filing paperwork." Dr. Watson smiles.

"So Anna basically said, *No, I don't want us in any pictures together*. And she said it's because they wouldn't be nice pictures, and she wanted only the best pictures for her last high school birthday before college. And I remember thinking, well, I'm dressed nicely. Even had a new pair of shoes. That day, my older sister did my hair for me and even gave me a manicure. And for a little while, I honestly didn't know what Anna meant. But then I found out later that she asked the others to make sure I wasn't in any pictures. Because she was embarrassed by my teeth. She had a perfect smile, you see. Never needed braces, what luck. And there was a boy in our class who wasn't very nice to me, but he and Anna were friends, and he made sure to tell me the truth about the whole thing the next time he saw me. Turns out Anna had a nickname for me." She pauses. "Jaws. My best friend called me Jaws behind my back."

"So what did you do?" I ask. I can't even imagine Shrynn turning on me like Anna turned on Dr. Watson.

"I became an orthodontist." She winks at me. "And I make sure that if a family decides against braces, it's not because they can't afford to have them, like my family. So a lot of families who think they can't afford treatment come to my office, and I see what I can do for them," Dr. Watson says. "If you'd like, we can set up an appointment so that we can talk more about it. Saturday afternoons work best, after the office is closed."

"Are you sure?" I say.

She smiles. "I wouldn't turn down Jordan Slade for an interview, so why should I turn *you* down? It's Team Max, all the way."

24

SHRYNN DOESN'T SEEM OKAY

It's the Saturday after my orthodontic appointment and five weeks until our competition applications are due. My interview with Dr. Watson is next Saturday and today I'm with Shrynn getting as much work done on it as I can.

"I've started collecting B-roll and data. I've also started writing the script," Shrynn says as she files her nails. She's sitting on the floor and leaning against her bed. "By the way, I finally chose a topic. I'm doing it on recycling." She looks up at me. "Did you know that schools are required by law to recycle, but they're really terrible at enforcing it? It's a huge problem, especially at Weiss. So I'm going undercover." She wriggles her eyebrows, and I laugh.

"And what about the divorce article?" I say softly. "For the paper?" I remember that Shrynn had mentioned wanting to write a feature on divorce, too. It's been at the back of my mind ever since she announced it.

She shrugs. "I just couldn't get into it," she says. "And it's not like I can just go up to other kids and say, 'Hey, are your parents divorced or divorcing? How do you feel about that?' It's just too personal and sad. So I'll write about recycling for the competition *and* the paper. I already told Dodge. We agreed that it seemed like a smart way to save time."

I still haven't told Shrynn about how my parents haven't been getting along.

She pops freshly made popcorn into her mouth. We're in her bedroom waiting for Keisha to arrive to give us pointers on our applications. "I already asked Mom's journalist friend, and she said that the recycling problem was a good idea. She even said she'd help me edit it!"

"I didn't know your mom had a journalist friend," I say carefully. My mouth begins to throb against my jawbreaker like it always does when I'm nervous. I don't want to sound like I'm jealous of the fact that Shrynn can get extra help with her project by an actual journalist, but I kind of am. And besides, this is exactly the kind of thing she would have told me about from the beginning.

"Oh, I just asked her a couple of questions when Mom was talking to her on the phone the other day." Shrynn shrugs. "It's not a big deal. I'm sure you can call her if you want to ask her something. What are you doing it on, anyway? I can't remember."

It's totally not like her to not include me on big things,

like asking for advice from a professional journalist. But it's like Shrynn's been in outer space lately.

Or like she doesn't care, right when I need her most.

I think it's time to tell Shrynn what's been going on at home.

"Shrynn, there are some things that—"

"HEY, MAX!" Amy bursts through Shrynn's door without knocking. She's wearing multicolored clips in her hair, black bangles around her wrists, and socks that match her clips.

"*A*-my," Shrynn says, swatting at her arm. "Not cool. You don't get to just charge in here like you own the place, okay? This is *my* room. Knock next time or I'm putting a lock on my door."

Amy throws Shrynn a cold stare. "It's not your house, Queen Shrynn, so I really don't—"

"MOM!!" Shrynn calls out at the top of her lungs. I feel the beginnings of a drool fest as my mouth hangs open. I've literally never seen Shrynn and Amy argue about anything.

"Okay, okay, *shush*," Amy says. "I just want to ask Max something, that's all."

"Promise me you'll knock from now on," Shrynn says with an edge.

"I *promise*, your highness." Amy bows and then turns to me. "Maxi, I need to ask you a question. You know I have to be in the science and technology showcase, right?

Because Neast the Beast and the rest of the science teachers are making all of the sixth graders do it."

"Amy, that's not nice," Shrynn says.

"Yup," I say. "So what's up?"

"Well . . ." Amy hesitates. "I kind of wanted to do a project on . . . my favorite planet. And I want to know if that would be okay with you."

My memory flashes back to when I showed the Li/Cheungs my jawbreaker for the first time. "You mean Saturn?" I ask.

"Yeah," she says.

"So why do you need my permission, Ame?" I ask. "You can do whatever you want!"

"I just . . . I wanted to make sure that you know that I'm not making fun of you. Because I think Saturn is totally cool, and I'm going to have to make a ring, and I'm going to be wearing it around my head and stuff. But you're the *inspiration* for it, because your headgear is so cool, and I want to call my project the Saturn Project. I'm gonna have a bunch of facts about Saturn printed on a T-shirt, and I'm also gonna make an interactive app that people can try out, to learn random facts about the solar system."

"Thanks, Amy," I say. "It's totally okay. I know you're not making fun of me."

"Okay, bye!" She spins on her heel and dashes out of Shrynn's bedroom. A second later, I hear Amy's bedroom door slam.

I'm really happy that Amy wanted to make sure that doing her project was okay with me. Not that she needs my permission, but she cared enough to make sure that I didn't take it personally.

My sister would never, not in a million years, go out of her way to protect my feelings. But honestly, I'm not sure I'd do the same for her. Not these days.

⸖ ☆ ⸜

"I studied the handbooks of middle schools across the city," Keisha's voice booms from her cell phone, all tinny-like. She arrived soon after the Amy invasion, and now the three of us are sitting on Shrynn's bed watching Keisha's winning Rising Star application video essay from last year. I've seen it a few times because Dr. Dodge threw a pizza party when Keisha won last year and played her video a bunch of times.

"In every instance, the dress code for female students was two to three to *four* times longer than the dress code for boys." Me and Shrynn watch as Keisha speaks into the camera. "I asked my principal for stats on disciplinary data based on dress code violations. He said they don't *disaggregate* that data, which I don't believe for a second. They keep stats on everything else, right? How do they not keep stats on why kids get called down to the office?" Keisha takes an authoritative step toward the camera and nods. "So I interviewed a bunch of people instead." A group of girls come out from behind Keisha and step in front of the camera. "These students were called down to the office for wearing the outfits they're wearing here." Some girls are wearing shorts that stop just above the knee while others wear ripped jeans and T-shirts. A couple of the other girls are wearing tank tops. Everyone looks like they're dressed for summer and it's hard to believe that it's even an issue.

"When the principal failed to comply, I took matters into my own hands," Keisha says as the lens zooms in on her face before cutting to footage of Weiss's hallways. I recognize the seventh-grade wing. The shot focuses on the boys and their outfits before cutting back to Keisha. She thrusts a microphone in front of one boy wearing plaid shorts that stop at the knee. She whips out a foldable ruler and holds it to his leg. "It looks like your shorts are in violation of the school policy. Jayce, were you called down to the principal for wearing this outfit?"

Keisha repeats that question with four other boys and the answer is *no* each time. "To be honest, this is a sting operation. For the cost of a pack of Twinkies, these students have agreed to wear clothes that are technically in violation of the school dress code, at least according to the rules for girls. And not to worry, I have signed releases from the parents of every kid featured in this video." Keisha pulls a stack of folded paper from her pants pocket and waves it at the camera. "The point is, it appears that there's a sexism problem at Weiss Junior High. And as a female student, I'm tired of being told that it's my job to keep boys comfortable. In fact, that's not my job. It's not any girl's job. But school dress codes seem to think it's our job." Keisha turns off her phone.

"I forgot how good your video is, Keish," Shrynn says. She rolls over and buries her head in her pillow. "Mine will never be as good as that!" She groans.

"Yeah, neither will mine," I say. I look at Keisha. "I've decided to do my project on bullying and braces."

"That's *fire*, Plink," she says. "I've *seen* what those kids do to you on the bus. Good topic."

"Yeah, but how would I do a sting operation about braces?"

"First of all, it doesn't have to be a sting operation," she says. Her teeth are pearly and straight and I feel a pang of jealousy. How did Keisha get to escape needing braces? It doesn't seem fair.

"My topic was good for that, but not all topics are. And you definitely don't need any special equipment. Just a phone with a good camera. Or a regular camera. Maybe a tripod. But that's it. And if you don't know how to edit your stuff, the programs are easy enough and you can use any computer to do it. The media lab has really easy software. The hardest part for me was bribing the boys to be in it." Keisha laughs.

"One of their moms *made* them do it because she liked my topic.

"The trick is to get numbers to back up your claims," Keisha continues, all teacher-like. She skips over to the white-board that hangs on the back of Shrynn's door and writes the word *numbers* in big red letters. "Numbers. Data. Facts. Plink, how many kids in the U.S. have braces?" she asks.

"I have no idea," I say. "Probably a lot."

"Well, look at us, for instance," Keisha says, gesturing to Shrynn. "Two thirds of us in this room have braces. The odds are, most kids wear them, right?"

"I guess," I say.

"Let's find out," Shrynn says, pulling out her phone. "How many kids in the U.S. wear braces," she mumbles as she types out the question. "Ah." She looks up. "Almost half. At least according to this one website."

"Okay," Keisha says. "We're getting somewhere. By the way, what kind of website is it?"

Shrynn studies her screen. "A doctor's office website."

Keisha frowns. "That's okay, but I'm sure there are better sources."

Shrynn scrolls through the results. "Here's one from the American Association of Orthodontics. More than four million Americans wear braces, and eighty percent of them are between six and eighteen years old."

"Great source," says Keisha. "As a rule of thumb, it's

always better to go with recognized experts when you need good data."

"But aren't doctors in doctors' offices experts?" I ask.

Keisha shrugs. "Sure," she says. "But literally anyone can have a website. The American Association of Orthodontics sounds more legit, like it or not. Now," she continues, "how many kids get bullied?"

"Yikes," I say. "How is it even possible to know that?"

"You start by looking it up." Keisha rolls her eyes.

"It says one out of every five," Shrynn says slowly, reading her phone. Keisha peers over her shoulder. I scoot behind Keisha and now we're all reading Shrynn's phone.

"Okay, so you might wanna poll kids at school, to keep it local. See how many of them get bullied, and—" Keisha's phone rings. She groans when she sees the screen. "It's my mom," she grumbles.

"Hello?" she answers. "Yeah, but—"

Keisha turns her back to us, but I can tell that she's upset, by the way her shoulders are hunched and her voice lowers to a loud whisper.

"But it's Saturday, Mom, and my homework's done and everything's done and Dad said I can. You weren't home when I left and I didn't know you needed my help. I'm helping my friends with their projects. It's for the—" Keisha pauses.

"Come on, Mom, really? Why can't you ask Ryan or Troy?" Even though her back is to us I know she starts to cry because I hear her sniffling. "Oh. I forgot when you asked me a week ago. I had a lot going on with school and the newspaper and— Yes. I know you work hard, too. I get it. I'll be home soon."

Keisha turns to us and wipes her eyes with the back of her hand. "I have to go," she says. "My mom needs me to do something. I should have known this would happen."

I nod.

"Sure, Keish," Shrynn says.

"She does this almost every time I go somewhere. Every time I try to see my friends, no matter what, she decides she needs something and that it's an emergency. That's why I ask my dad if I can go places, because my mom always says no."

"That's totally not cool," Shrynn says. "What does she need?"

Keisha rolls her eyes. "What does it matter? She always needs something, and she always needs *me* to do it, even though my brothers and dad and younger sister are home to help her. She just doesn't think I'm good enough, you know?" She snatches her book bag off the carpet and angrily hoists it onto her back. "No matter what I do, what kind of grades I get, how much I do at home, no matter how much I try to prove myself, it's never good enough."

"What do you mean?" I ask softly.

"The boys in my family are treated like gold," she growls. "I see it with my brothers and cousins. They're basically allowed to do whatever they want, and they don't get nearly as many chores as I do, and even after I do everything she asks, I have to fight to see my friends for a couple of hours. I mean, it's not like she yelled at me or anything, but I forgot to do something that she asked me to do last weekend, and she sounded so disappointed. I don't *always* forget things, just when there's a lot going on at school. But then she turns it into a thing about trust, which it's *so* not, and—" Keisha sighs. "She's just impossible sometimes, you know?"

Shrynn and I glance at each other. I don't know what to say, and I can tell Shrynn feels the same.

"Just text me if you have any questions about the project. If I don't answer, it means Mom's holding my phone hostage." Keisha laughs, but it's a hopeless laugh.

"See ya," she says as she walks out of Shrynn's room, her shoulders hunched and her head down.

"So bizarre," Shrynn whispers. "Keisha always seems so cool. Perfect, even. She walks into every room like she owns the place and Dodge treats her like she's queen of the universe."

"I thought so, too," I say, and then I realize that's exactly what I think of Shrynn. My Perfect Friend With the Perfect Life. Except, I'm starting to wonder if I'm wrong.

25

SISTERS AT WAR

"I think the best way to get people to participate in a poll is to make one online," Mr. Brace says. It's the Monday after Shrynn and I worked on our applications and he's sitting at his desk eating lunch. His feet are propped up on his desk and his plaid shirt, red beard, and tall frame make him look like a lumberjack.

"Here, take a look." He tilts his computer monitor toward me. "This is the website I use for the polls I ask you guys to take in class. You just enter your questions here, and when you're finished it gives you a link. If you send me the link, I'll ask the homeroom teachers to administer it to their students."

He turns to me. "You'll be anonymous, but I'll have to tell the teachers that one of my English students is working on an important project for the newspaper and that they have my full support as their sponsor. Kids seem to take it more seriously that way."

I shrug. "That sounds fine. I guess . . ."

"What's on your mind?" Mr. Brace asks. "Are you worried it sounds too complicated?"

"No, that's not it," I whisper. "I mean, do you think people will take the poll? Like, what if no one responds?"

"If no one responds, we can figure out a way to incentivize it."

"But how would I do that?" I ask.

"Let's worry about that later," he says. "In my experience, people like to take polls, especially when they know that their favorite teacher is asking them to do it, and especially when they know that they're allowed to take out their cell phones during class."

"Can I make it now? From here?" I gesture to the class computer that sits in the corner of the room.

"If you can do it in fifteen minutes before your next class, I don't see why not. Just show me when you're finished and I'll look it over."

I head over to the class computer. I find the website and navigate the super easy instructions. I try to channel my inner Keisha to come up with the best possible words:

Do you wear braces, or will you wear them in
    the future?
Have you experienced bullying at Weiss
    Junior High in the last week?

> Have you experienced bullying at Weiss
>   Junior High in the last month?
> Have you experienced bullying at Weiss
>   Junior High in the last year?
> Have you ever been bullied because something
>   about you is different? Please explain.

I finish the questions and show them to Mr. Brace. When he gives me a thumbs-up I finally feel like I'm about to make real headway on my project.

⋛ ☆ ⋚

"You think you're such a hotshot."

We got home from school an hour ago and I was doing homework on my bunk when Alexis hopped down from hers to go work on her science fair project. The art portion—her painting—was just about finished, two weeks ahead of schedule. She added color and descriptions to the different brain parts, and I heard her telling Mom she's now making the 3D version on a computer at her friend Kristy's house.

"What are you talking about?" I ask.

"With your stupid article going viral, and now with that dumb poll you asked the whole school to take. Who do you think you are, train-wreck face?"

"Whatever," I say. Mr. Brace sent out the poll to the homeroom teachers right after I sent it to him. He told me to give it a few days to see how many responses I'd get. I thought I wouldn't get *any*, but by the time I got home from school today almost one hundred students had responded to it. "How'd you know it was me, anyway?"

"Because who else would ask those stupid questions."

"Whatever," I say again. I reach into my backpack and as I pull out another book the picture of Shrynn, me, and Amy falls out and flutters to the floor next to my bed.

Alexis's face twists into something ugly, like she wants to laugh and growl at the same time.

"Why do you have a picture of *them*?" she snarls.

"Because Shrynn's my best *friend*," I bite back.

"You could have at least taken off your train-wreck-face costume." She's laughing now, like a fricking hyena. "I can't even believe they wanted to be in a picture with you looking like that. Look at your teeth! Look at your face! You're surrounded by metal!"

I think back to what Dr. Watson told me. *So Anna basically said, No, I don't want us in any pictures together.* Except this isn't a friend. This is my sister.

The TV news story on bullying, the episode from last year, flashes across my memory. *Yes, your child can become bully proof. They should respond and behave in a way that signals to the bullies that their attempts at abusive behavior have been unsuccessful.* Right. That's all. Easy-peasy.

It didn't work the last time I tried. But I give it another shot.

I get up from my bed. My fists are clenched as I make my way over to Alexis. "I'm sorry you don't like my face," I say hotly. My voice trembles. "But Shrynn and Amy don't mind it. In fact, Amy *asked* me to put on my jawbreaker, and she's doing a whole *science* project about it, so you can take that and shove it."

"If they think you're so awesome, then maybe you should go live with *them*," Alexis cackles. "It's not like anyone wants you around *here*. Or anywhere else."

"Maybe I *will*." Once again, my attempt at bully proofing myself is a total failure. "Because Shrynn and Amy are more like sisters to me than you'll *ever* be. Because they're nice *people*, ever think of that? They're actually good, decent people. And Shrynn can't even believe that you act the way you do. She sees it in the cafeteria, she sees it in the halls, and I tell her what you do on the bus. But the joke's on you because everyone knows that Vince and Carlay aren't your friends. Not really. And you look like a total joke hanging out with them. And everyone sees how pathetic you are, thinking that you're Miss Popularity."

Dad's at work and I hear Mom puttering around in the

kitchen, which is only literally about twelve or fifteen feet from my bedroom.

I feel like I should lower my voice but I'm on a roll.

"You're a sixth-grade-loser-jerk-bully who can't even come up with an idea for your own science project. Maybe you should ask Amy for advice on how to think for yourself. And while you're at it, maybe you should ask Amy and Shrynn about how to be a good sister, a good *person*, because you know what, Alexis?" My saliva is flying and I see some of it land on her shirt, but she doesn't seem to notice. "You suck. You suck as a sister and you suck at life because only people who *suck* act like you do. And you can say whatever you want about me, but everyone knows what a pathetic excuse of a sister you are."

I went too far. I know I went too far.

Alexis grabs the picture of Shrynn, Amy, and me off the floor.

"Hey!" I yelp, but it's too late. She rips it directly in half, right down the middle, and rips it in half again. Then she takes the side that has Amy on it and rips it to total shreds. She throws the pieces at my feet before stomping out of the bedroom. I hear Mom call to her to help in the kitchen. Part of me worries that she'll tell Mom about our fight, but then I remember that if we're caught fighting, Alexis will just get in trouble, too.

We both know better than to tell our parents if something bad is happening.

I drop to my knees and sift through the pieces of torn and crumpled photo. The only piece that's still intact is my face, surrounded by a metal orb, my teeth and braces and jawbreaker on full display, my lower lip slick with drool. I chuck the pieces into the little pink garbage pail that sits underneath Alexis's easel.

How can something as normal as braces change everything?

And then I notice that Alexis's jars of paint are open, stinking up the room.

The black jar is the biggest, and there's a thick, brand-new paintbrush sitting next to it. I know I shouldn't do it. But that doesn't matter to me right now. I hear Mom and Alexis clinking around out in the kitchen. *Stop slamming things*, I hear Mom say. It's less than a week since my last visit with Dr. Watson so my teeth and jaws are still sore, which means more pasta for dinner. My bedroom smells like a mix of macaroni and cheese and cigarettes and paint. Whenever Mom cooks, the whole apartment knows it. Same for when she smokes.

I grab the paintbrush and dip it into the black paint, getting it all nice and gooey. Alexis's project looks about finished. She signed her initials at the bottom right corner, like she always does when she's about done with her Masterpieces.

I run my finger over the brain. It looks like the kind of picture you'd see in a magazine, or on a website. It's really, really good. Probably the coolest thing she's ever created. There's no doubt in my mind that she'll win a prize, especially if her interactive 3D brain is just as good.

I take the paintbrush and draw a thick black X over the project, corner to corner. And then I draw another. And then another. And I don't stop until Mom calls to me, to say that dinner's ready.

26
GROUNDED FOR LIFE

The words Mom spat at us after the Battle Royale last night bounce around my brain.

No friends, so don't even think about it. No phone, except for emergencies. You will leave the house for school and doctors' appointments. Nothing else. I don't have time for this bull and you'll earn back your privileges when the two of you figure out how to get along.

We are *so* grounded, me and Alexis. I knew it would happen.

First, there was a shriek after Alexis stormed off to our bedroom after dinner. And then a wail. Mom's glass of water crashed to the floor next to the couch.

"Alexis!" Mom had yelped. I heard her race toward the bedroom. "Are you hurt?"

I kept washing the dishes (it was my turn). I had ten

seconds before Mom stormed into the kitchen, her eyes blazing.

I washed a fork and then a cup. I counted down. Ten . . . nine . . . eight . . . The portrait of younger me, the one Alexis sketched a few years ago, mocked me from its spot on the wall, as if to say, *Remember when we used to get along? Now we don't, and it's all your fault.*

Mom's voice had cut through the apartment. *Max, get your butt out here, NOW.* I turned off the water. I dried my hands. I took my time.

Mom doesn't care who started it. She never cares who started it.

After she ordered us to go to bed *or else* (at 7:30 P.M.), I heard Mom call Dad. *You better leave work and come deal with your daughters*, she'd hissed. She must not have liked his answer, because she hung up on him. The apartment reeked of cigarette smoke. It was gross, like an ashtray. I hid my head under the covers so that I wouldn't have to smell it. The comforter put pressure on my jawbreaker. It hurt. I still smelled the smoke. I can't stand the smell of cigarette smoke. Cigarettes should be outlawed.

Sisters should be outlawed.

I tossed and turned and I couldn't fall asleep because I heard Alexis crying in the bunk above mine. But I didn't cry. I was too tired to cry, too worn out.

In my family, someone's always fighting with someone else. Someone's always storming off and disappearing for years. Like Mom's sisters we haven't seen since Alexis and I were in, like, first and second grades. Like Dad's brothers who never call. Someone's always saying something they shouldn't say or doing something they shouldn't do. And there's always So. Much. Noise. Too many bad feelings. It doesn't feel like there's a lot of love in my family. Hardly any at all. Just yelling.

I want one day without noise.

≳ ☆ ≲

"So when do you think you'll be able to come over again?" Shrynn asks.

"I have no idea," I say. "I guess when Mom decides that she's not mad anymore?"

It's the next day and Shrynn and I are at lunch, at our usual table in the cafeteria. The one closest to the main exit. Shrynn's eating a cheese sandwich. Mom made me a turkey sandwich, but I'm not really hungry. She didn't say anything to us before school, except to remind us that we're grounded and to not even think about making plans with our friends this week or next.

The walk to the bus stop was quiet (Alexis walked ten

steps in front of me) but the bus ride was not. I sat in the first seat behind the bus driver, and Alexis, Vince, and Carlay went straight to the back.

"Well, hello there, Bucky Beaver," Vince had said when he walked past me. "Your teeth are extra big today. Run out of wood?"

"Hi, Horseface from Bucky Beaver town." Carlay smirked.

Clever, I thought to myself.

"Loser," Alexis grumbled.

I ignored them.

I crouched in the seat and stared out the window and thought about my face. I keep waiting to look like a different person, like someone who doesn't need surgery to literally have her face rearranged.

"But you won't tell me *why* your mom's mad at you," Shrynn says from across the lunch table. "It's totally not like you to not share all the gory details with me."

"It's not important. Same old, same old, you know?" To be honest, I'm too ashamed to tell Shrynn about what I did to Alexis's project. In Shrynn's world, older sisters don't destroy their younger sisters' science projects. And younger sisters don't rip up pictures of their older sisters. And moms don't get in their kids' faces without talking things out and dads don't say that they're too busy for their families because the Bills Won't Pay Themselves. This time, it just seems like things are a little too crazy to share, a little too far out there, even for my best friend.

"Hey, by the way." I'm dying to change the subject. "How's your video essay going? Have you worked on it anymore since we came over?"

I've made some headway with mine, but not much. The idea of the deadline being just a few weeks away makes me super nervous.

"I actually—" she begins, but we're interrupted by a boy, a super tall sixth grader with fiery red hair and braces who comes up to our table. He's holding a plastic bag out to me.

"This is for you," he says.

"For me?" I ask. "What is it?"

He shrugs. "I dunno. Someone said you needed pencils really bad. So a bunch of us donated pencils. Do you need them or not?"

"I'll take them," Shrynn says, jumping to her feet, her eyes like thunderclouds. She snatches the bag from the boy, and he shrugs again and walks back to his table on the other side of the cafeteria.

"Shrynn, what—" I begin, but she interrupts me. "I'll be right back." She zips over to the nearest garbage can and chucks the bag of pencils in there.

"What the heck was that about?" I ask, but then, all at once, I know exactly what it's about. I hear Vince's voice and Carlay's cackle from a few tables away, and I remember Vince's words from the bus.

Your teeth are extra big today. Run out of wood?

They couldn't collect trees, so they collected pencils. A real good joke. A laugh a minute. Totally clever.

I look at Shrynn. Her eyebrows are narrowed in a V and her cheeks are red and she's as angry as if it had happened to her.

That's the thing about best friends.

"I think we should eat in the media lab from now on," Shrynn says. "Or the library. Or Mr. Brace's classroom. You know he lets kids eat lunch there if they have work to catch up on. We don't have to come here. Not ever again."

I appreciate what Shrynn is trying to do. I really do. She's trying to protect me, exactly like a sister would. Exactly like a sister *should*.

⟩ ☆ ⟨

It's later in the day—just a few hours after I received the pencil "donation"—and Dad's awake when we get home from school.

"The way you girls are with each other is no good, do you understand me?" he growls. "*No good.* Put your stuff down and follow me."

"But I have a lot of homework," Alexis whines. She shoots me eye daggers. We're both in for it.

"We're going for a ride." His tone is no-nonsense and tough. He's wearing a cutoff T-shirt and baggy work pants and big, heavy protective boots. His shoulder and arm muscles are bulging.

Dad takes us to the pizzeria even though it's not Friday night. We drive over in silence.

We place our pizza order and find a bench outside, next to the chain-link fence. "What were you thinking, Max? What the *hell* were you thinking when you destroyed her project?" Dad taps his head above his ear, as if to ask, *Where is your brain?*

"If I went to Mom, instead of handling it myself, nothing would have happened except some, *Alexis, don't touch your sister's things. The two of you better knock it off.*" I mimic Mom's tone and the way her lips purse when she's scolding us.

"Well, you'll never be able to ruin my projects again because I'm doing all of them at school now," Alexis says from the end of the table. She's leaning right up against the fence, like it's the only thing keeping her from escaping. "I told my art teacher what you did and she's letting me take class time to do it over." Alexis folds her arms in front of her chest.

"Oh yeah?" I say. "Did you tell her you deserved it? Did you tell her you're a pathetic excuse for a sister and that you *deserved* it?" Any remorse I'd felt over destroying Alexis's project is gone.

"Max, I want you to apologize to your sister." Dad takes a bite of pizza. "And Alexis, I want you to apologize for ruining Max's picture. And then you'll shake on it, and we can eat and go home and put this whole thing behind us."

"*What?*" I say. "I'm not apologizing to her. She started it."

"And I'm *not* shaking her hand," Alexis snarls. "I'm not touching her, so you can forget it."

"Well, I don't want you to touch me," I hiss, "because I'm not sorry and I hope you fail the project."

"Girls—" Dad begins.

"Wipe the drool off your face, Bucky Beaver. And by the way, we'll see who's pathetic."

"*Girls*—" Dad says again.

"And what's that supposed to mean?" I'm not really a violent person but a part of me wants to reach across the table and claw Alexis's face off.

"It means that you'll—"

"ENOUGH!" Dad pounds his fists on the table. "THAT'S *ENOUGH*. Do you two think I have time for this?" Dad takes an angry bite of his pizza. "Do you really think me and your mother got nothing better to do than to constantly play referee with you girls?"

The outdoor eating area is suddenly silent, exactly like you see in the movies when someone drops a tray of dishes.

I don't have to look around to know that people are staring at us.

"The two of you need to keep your hands off each other's things," he continues, quieter now.

My pizza's sitting in front of me. Two slices of plain. But I can't touch it. My mouth still hurts from my last visit with Dr. Watson, which Dad would know if he bothered to ask. Plus, I'm tired of pizza. We have it every single week and I'm tired of it.

I'm tired of *everything*. But not too tired to tell Dad what I'm really thinking.

"*She* shouldn't have touched my stuff," I growl. "*She* started it. And if she touches my stuff again, I'll find something else to destroy."

"I'm telling *Mom* you said that," Alexis spits back. I ignore her.

"You're being a little dramatic, Max," Dad says, devouring his last bite. "No, she shouldn't have touched your picture," he says, glancing at Alexis. "But you destroyed her project. Her *school* project. That's important. What were you *thinking*?"

"Well, the picture was important to *me*, Dad! It was a gift from my best friend!" I still haven't touched my pizza.

"Drama queen," I hear Alexis mutter through a mouthful of food.

"Finish your food and let's go," Dad says. "I've had enough of the both of you."

I scoot toward the end of the picnic table. Dad pulls out his phone and scrolls as he eats. Alexis flips me the middle finger from an angle where she knows Dad won't see her.

I ignore the both of them and stare at my pizza while they finish eating in silence.

I know Dad probably thinks he solved the problem because he yelled at us, but I have the feeling that it's not over yet.

⤜ ☆ ⤛

As soon as we get home Dad gathers his things for work.

"*Your* turn," he tells Mom.

Mom shoots me a look and then Alexis. "What do you *mean*, my turn?"

"If these two wanna be at each other's throats, you can deal with it now. I have other things to do."

"Oh, you mean you had to be a parent for a few minutes?" Mom says, dripping with fake sweetness. "You had to get off the couch and actually *deal* with something? Golly gosh, Chris, are you sure you don't need a vacation?"

Dad grabs his keys.

"You don't have work for another hour," Mom says. "Where—"

But Dad slams the door behind him. Mom shakes her head and plops into a chair at the kitchen table, where a

bunch of papers are spread out and her phone is set to cal-
culator mode. A cigarette burns next to her, tilted in the
black-stained ashtray, and it makes me nauseous.

I wonder where my dad went. I have my suspicions, but
if I think about them hard enough my heart hurts. If Dad's
not home he's at work, and if he's not home or at work, he's
out drinking. I'd heard Mom tell him the other night that
if he came home smelling like that again she'd get a second
job if it meant she could throw him out.

And now I'm wondering if fights like what happened over
dinner make Dad want to drink, and that maybe he wouldn't
have left early if me and Alexis would Just. Stop. Fighting.

"Can I use my phone for a few minutes?" Alexis asks Mom.

"No." Mom exhales and a cloud of smoke covers her
face. "You know better than to ask."

"Oh please, but it's for school," Alexis begs. I'm about to
close the door to our bedroom when I hear her say, "I have
to call Carlay. It's about joining the AV club."

It's one thing for Alexis to sit with Carlay on the bus or in
the cafeteria, but it's another to, like, call her on the actual
fricking phone.

"I don't know who this Carlay girl is, but make it fast,"
Mom sighs as she caves. "Use the house phone, though."
Alexis smirks at me before she locks herself in the bathroom
with the phone.

I think about telling Mom who This Carlay Girl is, but

I'm too tired to have a conversation about it. Instead, I ask Mom if I can jump online to read more of Dean's blog for my Channel 5 application.

"You have twenty minutes," she says.

I pull up his site and go straight to his contact page, where his email address is posted. *This is what real journalists do*, I remind myself. I open a blank email.

Dear Dean,

    My name is Max. I have braces and headgear. I know your blog is mostly about surgery, so I hope you don't mind my questions that are about other things.

    I'm doing a school project on braces, and I saw your post on bullying and was hoping you wouldn't mind telling me more about what you went through. What were the kids like? What were the things they said to you? How did you deal with it?

Thanks for everything,

Max

I close the laptop lid and retreat into my bedroom for a few more minutes of privacy. If Mom and Dad won't help with the whole Alexis thing, then maybe someone else will, even though he's a total stranger.

My jaws and teeth throb as I slip into bed. When Alexis barges in a few minutes later, I pretend to be asleep.

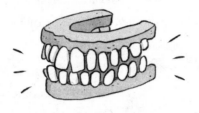

27

DR. WATSON GETS IT

It's the day of my interview with Dr. Watson and four weeks until my Channel 5 application is due. I've been writing the script for my video and trying to collect a bunch of data that I might use for the project and visiting the media lab during lunch to try and pull some of it together.

"It's really good to see you again, Max." Me, Mom, and Alexis are in the waiting room when Dr. Watson comes out to greet us. "And great to see you, Mrs. Plink. And Alexis! It's been a while."

"Thank you for taking the time," Mom says, but Alexis doesn't respond. She just glares at *me* while Dr. Watson smiles at her.

So rude.

Dr. Watson walks me to her office. She offers me a bottle of water and a chair across from her desk. I take off my coat, swig some water, and position a notepad and pen on my knees.

She takes off her white doctor's coat. She's wearing a heavy-looking red turtleneck, even though it's springlike outside. When we arrived, the waiting room was completely silent. Even Lucy, the lady who works the front desk, was gone. I've never heard it so quiet here. And it's totally weird to be in Dr. Watson's office and not in the exam room.

It's small, and slightly messy with papers and pamphlets strewn across her desk. There are a couple of plants near the windows and some paintings hanging up on the walls. The paintings are colorful and abstract, and I feel like Alexis would love them. There are also a couple of pictures on her desk and shelves.

"So tell me about the *Weiss Chronicle Online*," Dr. Watson says. "I perused the website earlier this morning. That's an impressive publication you have there! And I love your recent op-ed. Brava!" She claps her hands. "More students should speak out on important things like equal access to school opportunities."

"Thanks," I say. "The paper wins awards and stuff, and we have a really good staff. But this story"—I hold up my notepad—"isn't for the paper, exactly. It's for Channel 5's Rising Star journalist competition."

"Wow," Dr. Watson says. "That sounds quite serious." I nod. "Well, let's try to get you a winning application."

"Can—can I film us?" I say. I take a deep breath. "More footage, to add to what we did during my last visit. Because it should look like a real news story. Like what you see on TV. I mean, after I edit it." Mom let me use her phone for the filming part, and I even have a tiny tripod so I don't have to hold it the entire time.

Dr. Watson says yes, then helps me find the perfect spot for my phone. Once I start recording, I begin to ask her my questions, stuff like how many kids actually wear braces, and what's the worst case she's ever seen. Keisha helped me come up with a few questions during newspaper club the other day, and even Mom and Dad helped think about what I wanted to ask, from the parents' point of view. They seem to get along better when they're helping us with homework and school projects.

Dr. Watson said that if I wanted to sound really scientific, I'd use the word *malocclusion* to describe why a whole lot of kids—and even some adults—come to her in the first place. *Malocclusion* basically just means that you have crooked teeth or a poor bite. She said that almost no one is born with a perfect bite, and something like 90 percent of kids have a malocclusion.

"Some cases are more complicated than others," Dr. Watson says. "But there's no such thing as having the worst case." She forms air quotations around the word *worst*. "There are severe cases, and not-so-severe cases, and longer cases versus shorter cases, but it's my job to figure out all kinds of cases, a bit like a jigsaw puzzle. And it's very gratifying for me to help both children and adults with complicated bone structures. Sometimes I'll even consult with another doctor for a second opinion, just to have another brain on the case."

"Is my case really severe?" I ask. "I mean, it feels like the worst case ever, because I don't know anyone else who has to wear a jawbreaker or who might need surgery and"—a tear slips down my right cheek.

They don't tell you how hard it is, when you get braces. No one ever said, *Okay, Max, you might be severely bullied and sometimes you're going to feel really different and even ugly, but it's not true, no matter what the other kids say.*

Dr. Watson smiles the warmest smile I think I've ever seen.

"I'm going to be honest with you, Max, because I think that's why you're here, okay?" She hands me a tissue, then folds her hands on the desk in front of her. "You have a complicated case. There's no sense in not being real about that. You have an unusual bite, a bit of a tongue thrust, and you might need surgery and possibly even speech therapy down the line. Or you might not. When we begin a case, we can guess where we will end up, but we never quite know for sure. That's just how it works, in the wondrous world of orthodontia." She throws her hands above her head and flicks her wrist, as though orthodontics truly is some magical realm.

I wouldn't go that far.

"Let me show you something." She stands up from her desk and pulls a plastic, see-through box down from her highest shelf. There's a mold of someone's teeth inside it. It looks like it's made of cement, and the front and side teeth are shooting out all over the place, and they jut out way over the bottom teeth, which are all crowded and set way back. "This was my very first mold, from right before I got braces all those years ago. I was nineteen, I think. I asked my orthodontist if I could keep it, and he let me. He would have just thrown it out anyway, when he was finished with it."

I gasp. "Those are *your* teeth?"

She smiles broadly. "Yup! Can't you tell?" She positions the cement teeth next to her face.

I study the mold. "Wow," I whisper. I remember having to get my own mold done. Dr. Watson's assistant put all of this pink gooey stuff on a tray and then she shoved it in my mouth and basically told me to sit there until it dried. The goo doesn't taste like anything and basically looks like something you put over holes in the wall.

"That overjet is really something, isn't it?" Dr. Watson says. "I pull this out of my bag of tricks when I know I have a patient who's having a hard time. It's my prized possession."

Her eyes turn serious. "I'm afraid I haven't taken enough time to educate you about what your experience might be, and I'm sorry for that. You came to me at a busy time. I've been doing a lot of community work. My services are less expensive than the average office, for reasons I think I told you about before." She smiles. "That means I have to take on more clients, and I'm pretty much a one-man band, with the exception of a couple of assistants. And business has really picked up over the last year."

She puts the mold back on the highest shelf. "But I've been there, Max. Where you are now. And your case will depend completely on how your teeth and jaws respond to intervention. But in a couple of years," she continues, "no matter what has to happen, it'll look like nothing ever happened in the first place. And that's my goal. To correct your bite and get you comfortable in your own skin and feeling like it's all behind you, as quickly as possible."

I scratch notes down on my pad as fast as I can because Keisha taught me to not rely on just using video, in case something happens to the digital file and I lose everything.

"But I have the feeling you have other things on your mind, too," she says softly. I swallow. "This whole thing has been giving you a really hard time, hasn't it?"

I nod.

"The kids at school?" she asks.

"A few of 'em," I whisper.

"And your sister," she says, but not like a question. She must have seen Alexis glaring at me out in the lobby.

"How did you know?" I squeak.

Dr. Watson smiles. "I've seen it time and time again," she says. "It's one of the sadder things I've seen, honestly. When siblings fall out. It can get nasty."

I nod.

"When a child starts treatment, it's like their entire world changes. They have to be more careful than they've ever been, they can't play certain sports without worrying, they can't play certain instruments as easily, they can't eat a lot of their favorite foods and snacks until it's all over and they have my permission. And if there are siblings with only one child in treatment, suddenly all of the attention turns to that child. It could start to feel really unequal at home, you see. Especially if the child runs into some trouble at school with bullies, or if money gets tighter. Sometimes it's as simple as the younger children not wanting to go to the appointments only to wait around out there until everything is over." She gestures to the waiting room that's at the other end of the hall. "These appointments can be really long. I'm sure it's not fun to sit in the waiting room for two hours and I understand their frustration. But that's no excuse to behave badly. We all have to do things we don't want to do sometimes."

My pen actually drops to the floor as I listen to Dr. Watson. It's like she's describing my life and *sticking up for me*. But I never thought of how I might be getting more of Mom's and Dad's attention now, especially because of the jawbreaker and the whole question about surgery. And after I get my braces tightened, we have pasta and other soft foods for four or five days straight. All of us do, because Mom says she's not a restaurant and everyone is gonna eat the same thing or not at all. But I never really thought of how it actually *feels*, to have to do a bunch of things differently just because of one person.

Just because of me.

Dr. Watson clears her throat. "Does any of that sound familiar?"

"Yeah," I whisper. I pick up my pen from beside my feet.

"It's a very big deal to begin treatment," Dr. Watson says. "It's a big, complicated, expensive deal. And in some homes, things really can change. But each family finds their own way through." I'm scribbling, and she pauses. "Have I given you good stuff so far, for your application?"

"Yes!" I say, a little too loudly. "Yeah," I say, softer. "This is really good. Can I ask you one more question?"

"Of course."

"You talked about this friend you used to have . . ."

"Anna," she says with a smile.

I nod.

"We eventually went off to different colleges, did different things, you know. The way people do. But after that high school party, she and I didn't talk much. I was pretty heart-broken about the whole thing. Betrayed might be a better word. Self-conscious is another. It's not okay for people to attack you just because of how you look. I was really disap-pointed in her. I cried for a long time."

I scratch on my notepad, and Dr. Watson pauses. "But there's a twist," she says. I look up.

"I found out later that her dad lost his job and had a lot of trouble finding another one. So a whole lot of things had changed for Anna overnight. The family could no lon-ger afford to send her to the college of her choice. They also had to move from their home into a place they could more easily afford." Dr. Watson slaps her hands against her desk. "And that's when I finally understood that Anna's behavior wasn't entirely about me. She was going through a lot. I was her best friend, but I didn't know any of it."

"How did you not know?" I can't imagine Shrynn going through all this stuff without my knowing.

"I'm not sure," she says, and looks sad now. "I was prob-ably too far inside my own head to pay much attention to anyone else. I had really low self-esteem, and I spent a lot of time feeling sorry for myself. When I thought about it hard enough, I decided many years later that I owed Anna an apology."

"She's the one who says that you're not good enough to be in her pictures, but *you* owe *her* an apology?"

Dr. Watson shrugs. "Maybe I didn't owe Anna anything. But I owed it to myself to go back to her and apologize. Because it helped me reclaim my power, and it allowed me to be the person I want to be in the world. Someone who can recognize the role she played, and someone who doesn't have to be right about everything."

Could something be going on in Carlay's and Vince's lives that makes them act like complete jerks? Something I'll never know about?

I glance at the clock that hangs on the wall behind the doctor's desk. We've been talking for almost an hour. I think about Mom and Alexis sitting in the waiting room. They've been sitting out in the waiting room this whole time, waiting on me.

Waiting on *me*, because of *my* braces and *my* project. On an early spring Saturday, when Alexis probably wants to be at her friend Kristy's house because she lives right around the corner and Alexis goes there almost every week, exactly like I used to with Shrynn. And Mom probably wants to be doing chores or even something for herself, which she almost never gets to do.

"So, did you ever actually apologize to Anna?"

"We apologized to each other. Profusely, I might add."

"When did that happen?"

"About ten years later," Dr. Watson says. "After she married my sister."

"Wow!" I gasp. "So, you're friends again?"

"Better than that." Dr. Watson winks at me. "We're family. Oh, and Max?"

I look up at her after I reach over to turn off the camera.

"Let's keep the Anna stuff off the record. Privacy and all that."

"You got it, Dr. Watson."

She walks me back out into the waiting room. Alexis is slouched in a chair and playing with Mom's cell phone while Mom reads a magazine. They both look bored. I notice Mom check her watch before she sees us coming.

"I think we're all finished," Dr. Watson calls cheerfully.

"Thank God," Alexis grumbles.

We say goodbye and head to the car. After talking with Dr. Watson, there's something I feel I need to do. That I owe it to Alexis to do. No, that I owe it to *myself* to do for Alexis. Because that's the kind of person I want to be.

"Mom," I say. "Can we go to the art supply store?"

"Yes!" Alexis cries. "Please! And then can I go to Kristy's?" Alexis brings her hands together like she's praying. "We're not grounded anymore, right?"

Mom looks surprised. "I don't see why not, if it's okay with Kristy's mom. Max, do you have a project coming up?"

"No . . ." I don't know how to say it. "I wanted to replace some of Alexis's paint. After what happened. I mean, after what I did. I'll use my birthday money. If you cover me, I'll pay you back when we get home."

"It can be expensive," Mom says. I can see her shielding a smile.

"That's okay."

"What do you say, Alexis?" Mom says as she starts the car. I see something in my sister's face. It looks likes surprise, but also guilt.

"Thanks," she grumbles. And she doesn't look at me for the entire car ride. She doesn't act grateful, but that's okay. I don't need her to. I feel good about doing the right thing.

"What colors do you think you'll get at the art supply store?" Mom asks Alexis.

"Well, I'm kind of low on black paint," Alexis says. She makes a face at me in the sideview mirror, but it's not a nasty one. It's a playful one.

Maybe, just maybe, things will be better from this point forward.

28

SHRYNN'S SECRET

When we get home after my appointment, Dad's no longer on the couch where he was when we left.

"Where'd Dad go?" I ask Mom. "It's, like, three hours before he has to leave."

"He's doing overtime," Mom says softly. She doesn't look at me.

When Alexis takes off to go to her friend's house, I jump on the computer to work on the results of my survey. The internet connection is moving even slower than usual, so this may take a while.

I see that a few more students took the survey for a total of 250, which is way more than I expected. I start making little charts that I'm going to include in my application. It turns out that a lot of kids at Weiss say they get bullied on a pretty regular basis.

I review the written answers, even though there aren't

many of them—just a couple of sentences here and there about kids who say they're being bullied at the bus stop, on the bus, or in the cafeteria. The places where teachers or other adults don't always see things.

I check my email to see if Dean wrote back. He hasn't, but I have a message from Amy with a subject line that makes my breath catch in my throat.

Maxi, we need to talk, the line reads. And then:

Hi Max,

   This is kind of hard to talk about so bear with me, ok? Lately, your sister's been really mean to me. Like, a total jerk. She's been calling me names and stuff, and tripping me if I walk by her, so I'm trying really hard to stay away from her and I also asked the teacher if I could change my seat. I asked her to put me closer to the board so that I could see it better (which is a total lie, I have the eyesight of an eagle, and I know this because Neast-the-Beast is super into eagles. Did you know that an eagle's eyes are the same size as human eyes? So cool!).

   Anywayz, I just thought you should know about this and I didn't really know how else to tell u. I haven't told Shrynn about Alexis because with everything going on lately I know she'd get super-upset and confront u about it. Ever since our parents told us they were getting a divorce, Shrynn's been a totally different person. I think we both have. But I'm really worried about her.

Anywayz, cud you plz tell Alexis to stop being such a whippersnapper? (That word is in a book I'm reading for English and I think it's so funny!) Wish me luck on my Saturn-is-the-best-planet-ever project! I can't believe it's just under a week away!

Love,

Amy, the Way Cooler Cheung Sister

PS-I snuck through Shrynn's account to find your email address, so don't tell her about this email, ok? But it's totally ok if you tell her that I told you about the divorce because I'm sick of being secretive about it and you were gonna find out anyway. Just tell her that I told you at school. Besides, she's always mad at me these days so what's one more thing?

Shrynn's mom and dad are getting a *divorce*? And Shrynn never told me? And Alexis has been bullying Amy?

Everything is starting to make sense. The way Shrynn's been zoning out in class and that time she was absent for almost a whole week. And when she snapped at Amy for barging into her bedroom, even though Amy's barged in a million times before. And also the way she hasn't been as quick lately to respond to my texts.

My best friend is going through something huge, and I knew nothing about it. Some friend I am.

I shut down the laptop and find Mom in the kitchen. "Can I go to Shrynn's?" I ask. It was such a good day at Dr. Watson's and then at the art store, and with Alexis at Kristy's, I feel like I can ask.

"Take your phone, but also see if she'll meet you halfway," Mom says. I notice how easygoing Mom can be sometimes, and I think of Keisha and how her mom is so strict with her. I guess in some ways I really am lucky.

I text Shrynn.

> Wanna hang out for a bit?

Shrynn writes back.

> Sure. Amy is really on my nerves. Let's go to the park. Maybe a handball court is open.

I ask Shrynn to meet me up the street. I have no idea what I'm going to say when I see her. I'm hoping I'll figure it out on the way.

⋛ ☆ ⋚

"So what's going on?" I say carefully. "Why is Amy on your nerves?"

"She's just been so annoying lately. She won't leave me alone. I have to lock my door because she won't stop bugging me. She wanted to come with us to the park and I said *forget* it. She has *no* boundaries. She's been my shadow and I just don't want to talk all the time, you know?"

Shrynn bounces the blue handball on our way to the park.

"Not even to me?" I ask.

"Well, that's different. Of course I want to talk to you, *always*." She smiles. "You're my best friend."

I stop walking.

"What's the matter?" she asks.

"If I'm your best friend, how come you didn't tell me about your parents?"

My heart feels like it's going to pound out of body and leap straight into the gutter.

"And how did you know about this?"

I know I have to be honest. "Amy told me."

Shrynn's lips form a straight line. "*When*."

I know for Amy's sake that I can't tell Shrynn about the email. "At school. I ran into her, and we talked for a few minutes. She mentioned it then."

Shrynn throws her hands in the air. "You two are unbelievable!" she shouts.

"*We're* unbelievable?" I sputter. "You don't tell me, your best friend, about this hugely important thing going on in your life, but *we're* unbelievable?"

"Maybe if you weren't so wrapped up in *yourself*, I would have told you *weeks* ago. Maybe I need help sometimes, too. But no, everything is about *your* jawbreaker, *your* sister, *your* life. Our entire friendship has been about *you* lately, and you have no room in your head for other people's problems. That's obvious. But Amy had *no right* to tell you before I did."

"Shrynn, first of all—"

"Just forget it, Max," she snaps. "I don't feel like going to the park anymore. I mean, think about it. You have your problems, but *your* parents are still together. My dad moved out *weeks* ago." Her eyes spill over. "You have no idea how lucky you are!"

Her dad moved out already? "Hey, I didn't—" I reach for her arm, but she shakes it away.

"Good luck with the journalism competition."

"Shrynn," I say, "wait, don't—"

"The deadline is almost here, so we don't have to work on it together at this point. Just leave me alone, okay?" Shrynn chucks her ball into the sewer, turns on her heel, and storms off in the direction of her house, leaving me behind.

29
MAX'S WORST NIGHTMARE

I take my time walking home. If I get back too early, Mom will ask why and I'm too embarrassed to tell her. This is the first big fight I'd ever gotten into with Shrynn, and I can't help but feel like she may be right about a couple of things. I guess everything really *has* been about me lately, to the point where Shrynn felt like she couldn't tell me her problems. And I have no idea how to fix this.

But I do know how to fix the situation with Alexis bullying Amy. At least, I think I do.

I get home an hour after Shrynn stalked off.

"You could've stayed longer." Mom looks up at me from her chair at the kitchen table. A cigarette burns, stinking up the air.

"Oh, Shrynn needed to do some things for her mom," I lie. "And I have homework." I head to my bedroom before Mom can reply.

I sit on my bunk, waiting for Alexis to get home, and I pull out my phone. Shrynn might not be in the mood to hear from me yet, but I'm reminded of Dr. Watson's story about Anna. I want to apologize because that's the person I want to be. I send Shrynn a text.

> I'm sorry I've been too into myself to see what's going on with you. I promise to work on that. I hope you can forgive me.

I hear Alexis come home before I can think too much about whether Shrynn will respond. And when she enters our bedroom, I position myself inches from her.

"Amy told me what you've been doing."

"What are you *talking* about?" Alexis flings her sweatshirt onto her bed.

"I know you've been bullying her."

Alexis eyes me up and down. "And what do *you* care?"

I take a deep and shaky breath. "If you can't be nice, stay away from her. And if you don't stay away from her, I'm telling Mom and Dad and I'm going to show them the email Amy wrote to me. And trust me, you don't want them to know about the things she said."

Alexis pauses. "Fine," she finally grumbles. "Just drop it, okay? You don't have to tell Mom. I'll stop." The way Alexis backs down so quickly makes me wonder whether Amy told me all that there was to tell about Alexis's behavior.

"And I want you to apologize to her," I say. "The first chance you get."

She rolls her eyes. "I will on Monday, if it matters that much to you."

"It does."

"I'll take care of it Monday," she says again, before walking out of the room. And I let out a breath I didn't know I'd been holding.

≳ ☆ ≲

"Do you really think my project is good enough to win?" Alexis asks softly. We just got to the bus stop. It's been two weeks since our talk about Amy, which means it's also been that long since my fight with Shrynn.

Things are better between Alexis and me, but things never felt worse with my best friend. She says hello and smiles in class but never responded to my apology text.

Maybe she needs time. Or maybe I lost my best friend.

"I don't see why not," I say. "Especially because you tied art to its scientific benefits for the brain."

It's Friday, the day of the sixth-grade science and technology fair. Mom and Dad are going to be there for it. The fair starts right after lunch, and my math teacher is taking us, which makes me happy, because anything to get out of math.

I see Carlay and Vince on the corner laughing about something. Alexis, instead of running over to them, ducks into the deli. She's been keeping to herself these past couple of weeks, except for a few weird phone calls she made.

Maybe she's just nervous about the science fair. Or maybe this is as good as things are ever going to be with my sister.

I climb into the bus in front of Alexis. Today, she sits one row behind me.

"Hey, Horseface," Carlay calls. I hear her voice from where she's sitting all the way in the back with Vince.

"I think you mean dog face," he responds.

"The face of a dog, the teeth of a horse?" Carlay cackles.

"Maybe, but I think snaggletooth might be more accurate," Vince says. "Alexis has literal fangs."

Alexis? Unbelievable. They're not talking about me. They're targeting my sister.

I look over at her. She's wedged against the window with her hood pulled over her head.

⤜ ☆ ⤛

My math teacher brings us down to the gym where the fair is being held, and by the time we get there it's loud and swarming with students and parents. It seems like a million projects are set up on rows of tables covered in white cloth and blue trim, our school colors. A lot of the projects are super fancy and hooked up to speakers and laptops. One student even has five iPads set up so that people can try out her new app, and I understand why Alexis was so nervous about having to compete with kids who have the resources for these things.

Four large flat-screen TVs hang up high in each corner of the gym, and I see Alexis standing underneath one of them, next to her project. Her 3D brain is pulled up on a clunky AV club laptop and her new painting—the one she made after I ruined the first one—sits displayed behind the computer, bright and textured and impressive. It's the only piece of actual art at the entire fair.

I start to make my way over to her when I notice Mom and Dad enter the gym through the double doors at the back. They weave through the crowd to find Alexis, and I wave at them just as the lights dim.

"Good afternoon, all!" Mrs. Neast is standing on a makeshift stage with a microphone and a large projection screen suspended behind her. "If I can just have your attention for a minute or two. Thank you, friends and families, for coming to Weiss Junior High's inaugural Science and Technology Showcase!"

A few people clap and an excited buzz travels through the room.

"Before I set you loose to learn about what our future

scientists, inventors, and thinkers have been up to, I wanted to remind everyone that each science teacher picks three winners from their classrooms for first, second, and third place. Prizes include gift certificates to the local bookstore and an afternoon at the local science museum!"

There's more clapping and a whoop-whoop.

"Also, I would like to take this opportunity to thank the AV club and the *Weiss Chronicle Online* for their help with the video montage, which will display on the overhead projector here, and the TVs, which we purchased and installed specifically for this event!" With one arm she makes a sweeping gesture around the gym. "The montage is a compilation of pictures of science in action at Weiss Junior, so please enjoy! And a heartfelt thank-you to Dr. Gregory Dodge, adviser of the *Chronicle Online*, and Ms. Denise Lipkin, adviser to the AV club, and their dedicated students for collecting the perfect images. The montage will run on a loop across the hour, so if you have to step out, don't worry about missing anything."

The lights are turned back on. Mrs. Neast walks over to a laptop and the noise in the gym picks up as people start to mingle among the projects. The montage begins its slow loop of images, kicking off with the small garden that the sixth graders planted just outside the school. This picture of a super small plot of soil (it is the city, after all) with sunflowers reaching to the sky is followed, after about five seconds, by a bunch of eighth graders wearing goggles and filling beakers with a cloudy liquid.

I'm halfway to Mom and Dad when I see Shrynn a few feet away. "Hey," I say, gently tugging on her sleeve.

"Oh, hey," she says, but she quickly looks away. "My parents are here to see Amy and I want to catch up with them. See ya later." She pushes through the crowd toward her mom.

I finally make it to Alexis's table, and Dad's hugging her. "I'm so proud of you, Bug. Good job with this. Isn't this a good job, Max?"

"Yeah," I say. "You can see the painting from across the room!"

"Really?" Alexis asks.

"Really," I say. "It totally stands out."

"Why don't you tell us about it," Mom says.

"But I did already, at home," Alexis says, playing with her fingers. She won't look at us.

"That's not the same." Mom smiles. "Talk to us like we're seeing your project for the first—Max, what's the matter?"

My attention is drawn to the montage as it shifts from a picture of kids filling recycling bins to an image of a beaver, and then another, and then a picture of a group of beavers building a dam and then one of a beaver sharpening its teeth on a tree stump.

Each screen projects a picture of beavers for what seems like hours. I stand frozen as the montage next displays a picture of a couple of beavers mating. Then there's a gasp and then a shriek and the noise in the gym dies down all at once. And that's when I see it, that's when *everyone* sees it, and there's no stopping it.

"What on earth—" I hear Mom say.

My face and jawbreaker take up the entire screen. I recognize the image immediately. It's from the photo of me, Shrynn, and Amy, from the day that Amy asked me to wear my jawbreaker. But I can also see that this is a picture *of* a part of a picture, and that the edges are all ripped and torn and the picture itself is rumpled from that day, that terrible, no-good day. The day that I ruined Alexis's project in retaliation for her destroying this photo.

The words THE SCIENCE OF BEEVERS sit below my face in big black letters. The seconds tick away as the montage refuses to shift to the next picture. I can't blink. I can't move. I feel myself drool but I forget that I'm supposed to mop it up before anyone can see it. I can barely breathe, and my eyes are blurry with tears.

The montage finally turns over, back to the beginning with the picture of the school gardens.

"I'm sorry, folks," Mrs. Neast says. "There appears to be a problem with the display. I'm going to shut it down for now, so please do—do, um, do enjoy the remainder of the showcase." She clicks a button on the laptop and slams it shut before exiting the makeshift stage. She pushes her way through the crowd toward Dr. Dodge, who's standing on the other side of the gym with Keisha. Keisha's throwing her hands up in the air and I can't hear what they're saying but it looks like an urgent conversation. Keisha helped gather pictures for the montage, but she wasn't in charge of putting the final file together. That was the AV club's job.

"Who did this, Max?" Dad's voice is a growl.

"Alexis, do you know anything about this?" Mom snaps.

"I, I . . ." Alexis's voice trembles. I don't stick around to hear what she has to say. There's now a whisper traveling across the gym and the only thing I want to do is leave. Run. Hide. I turn on my heel. Mom reaches for my arm, but I wriggle away from her and half sprint, half push my way to the exit. The gym opens out into a wide hallway, and the hall empties out into a maze of classrooms, offices, and lockers. I'm sure I can find somewhere to hide.

There has to be somewhere to hide.

"Did you *see* that?" I hear a boy chuckle, like the only thing he's missing is popcorn.

"I'd never come back to school if that happened to me," a girl I recognize from the eighth grade responds.

"So embarrassing," another girl says.

"I can't believe the things that kids do to each other," an adult voice says, probably someone's mom.

"Max! Max, come back!" That voice belongs to Shrynn, but I don't care.

I taste bile as I charge through the doors. There's a restroom right there—the same one where I first introduced Shrynn to my jawbreaker. I slam my way into the nearest stall and throw up.

30

HUMAN SHIELDS

"Maxi, let me in." Shrynn's banging on the bathroom stall.

"*Why*," I gulp. "Just go away. It doesn't matter, okay? Besides"—I can't help but take a shot at her—"it's all about *me* again, right?"

"Max." Shrynn's voice is small and teary sounding. "I knew it was bad, but I really had no idea . . ."

I open the stall's door just as a girl pushes her way into the restroom, sees us, and then exits just as quickly.

"Why didn't you tell me things were that bad? I mean, I knew they bugged you in class, but . . ."

"What else was I supposed to say?" I snap. "You saw it with your own eyes and you *still* didn't think it was that bad?"

She looks away from me. "I guess I didn't want to believe it," she says. "I'm so sorry."

I don't say anything.

"Do you think Alexis had anything to do with it?" Shrynn asks carefully. She bites on her thumbnail.

"I know she did," I say. "Don't you recognize the picture?"

"I do," she says. "That's why I asked. She must have gotten her hands on it."

I lean on the edge of the sink. "She got her hands on it weeks ago." I spill my guts about everything that's happened between Alexis and me, even the super embarrassing stuff, like how I destroyed her project.

"Ugh, Max." Shrynn puts her hand to her mouth. "I wish you would have told me sooner."

"Do you really?" I say. After what Shrynn said two weeks ago, I find it hard to believe.

"*Yes*," she says. "I was mad before, okay? Really mad. Mostly at Amy for telling you about Mom and Dad. I wanted to be able to tell you myself, when I was ready." She looks away from me. "I'm sorry."

"I'm sorry, too," I whisper. "I wish I would have known about your parents. What happened with them? They always seemed so happy."

Shrynn stares at her feet. "I honestly don't know. One day, a couple of months ago, they sat us down and said they were breaking up. That sometimes this happens with marriages and it's perfectly normal. But it doesn't feel normal." I can tell she's holding back tears. "It hasn't felt normal since that day."

"I'm sorry I didn't know about this, Shrynny," I say. "I'm really, really sorry."

She shrugs and smiles, her cheeks wet with tears. "I'm sorry I blamed you for not knowing. I actually wasn't ready to talk about it. And I regret that now, because I know things were kind of weird for both of us at home. I should have told you."

There's a pause. In a school bathroom, it's almost like you can *hear* the silence.

"But how are you doing?" I finally ask.

Shrynn shrugs. "As well as I can be, I guess. This is the first time I'm really talking about it with anyone. I don't talk to Amy about it. She was super upset, and it just makes me even more upset to see her like that." She leans against a sink. "I'm really angry at my parents, you know? Things seemed completely normal, and then they just dropped it on us. There was never any fighting and almost no arguing. It's like they just want to make this huge change, and they don't even care about how it affects us." Fresh tears slide down her cheeks. "They think that living apart would be better for the family. Like, are you kidding me?"

"I'm sorry," I whisper again. "But I get it."

"You do?"

"I really do." I pause, not sure of whether to tell Shrynn more about what's been going on at home. I don't want to turn the conversation back to me and what I've been through with my parents, but this feels like the right moment to share.

"Mine haven't been getting along at all." My voice is getting choky. "Dad's been on the couch, and they've been fighting constantly. And . . ."

"And?" she says softly.

"They fight a lot about my dad drinking. And sometimes I think I can smell it on him. But they haven't talked about it with us."

"Yikes," Shrynn says. "Are you sure?"

"I've heard my mom yell at him about it, so I'm pretty sure. And he hasn't been home much. Mom said he's working a lot, but I don't believe her."

I jump at the sound of the restroom door slamming open. Keisha comes charging in.

"Plink," she says. Her tone is gentle, like she wants to wrap me in a hug.

"Keish." I shrug and wipe my eyes.

"I feel like it's my fault," Keisha says.

"*How?*"

"Yeah," Shrynn says. "We know you had nothing to do with that."

"I should have asked to see it first, before it went live. I double-check everything. But I figured, this was such an easy project, and I saw an earlier version—before they added all that awful stuff." Keisha looks really sad. "Not very becoming of an editor in chief."

"It's *not* your fault," I say.

"The kids who did this give a whole new meaning to the word *troglodyte*," she says.

"What's *that* mean?" Shrynn asks.

Keisha whips out her phone and punches in the spelling. She holds it up for us to see. "Prehistoric cave dweller," Shrynn reads slowly. She looks at me. I look at Keisha. And the three of us smile.

"Your parents are looking for you," Keisha says quietly.

"Where are they?" I ask.

"They're still in the gym. I saw your sister with them, and your mom's talking to the principal. I overheard Mr. Green say that they need to find you and have a conversation." She extends her hand out to me while Shrynn takes the other. My human shields lead me out of the bathroom, down the hall, and back to the science fair.

☆

Mr. Green, the school principal, invited my family back to his office for privacy.

"So you weren't the only one in on this?" He leans way over his desk and peers at Alexis. His eyebrows are black and furry and narrowed into a V shape with a bushy black beard to match. His starched white shirt glows against his brown skin and it's buttoned tight around his neck underneath a scratchy-looking red vest. And of course I notice that his teeth are perfectly straight.

I'd never been inside the principal's office before. The carpet is a dark blue, and there are floor-to-ceiling shelves littered with books and stacks of paper. A bobblehead doll of a famous baseball player sits on his desk, swaying gently next to a glass paperweight and a cup of pens. A laptop sits closed, off to the side.

Mom and Dad have always said that if the school principal has no idea who we are, that's a good thing. We've never been in trouble at school, and even though I didn't do anything, that's never mattered to my parents before. When Alexis gets in trouble, I always do, too.

But there's no way they can hold me responsible for Alexis's behavior. Not this time.

"It—it wasn't my idea," Alexis finally says. Her face is red and splotchy. Mr. Green had to pull two more chairs out of the kitchen next to his office so that we could all sit. Mom and Dad are wedged between Alexis and me, their faces grim and angry looking.

He looks at my parents. "I take misconduct very seriously," he says. "And while a lot of this sounds like a family issue that I'd prefer to leave to you to sort out, Alexis has clearly broken a school rule. We make it abundantly clear in the handbook that there are consequences for any Weiss student who uses technology to bully other students, on or off campus. I must say that I've never come across an issue involving siblings, though. Not on this scale."

Dad leans forward. "What happens now?" he asks. "Obviously we'll be having discussions at home, but what happens on your end?"

"There's normally a three-day suspension involved in this sort of thing," Mr. Green says.

Dad looks shocked, but Mom says, "That sounds reasonable."

Is Alexis about to receive a consequence for the first time *ever*? And I'm not about to go down *with* her?

"*Reasonable?*" Dad says.

Mr. Green's clock ticks from where it hangs on the wall next to the window. Mom massages her temples while Alexis stares at the floor, and I see a muscle in Dad's cheek twitch.

"In a way," Mr. Green says, "Alexis is lucky that her victim is related to her. Had this been someone else, the family easily could have taken this further—and they would have received my full support. The next step would be the superintendent's office, and thanks to laws about school bullying, the step after that consists of legal channels. It all depends on the history of abuse, of course. But I prefer to work toward solutions directly with families, if possible." He pauses. "I spoke briefly with Dr. Dodge and one of the newspaper club members just after this happened. The fact that Alexis doesn't seem to be the only one involved complicates the path forward a little, but I'm confident that we'll get to the bottom of that, too."

"Mr. Green," I begin. "I think I know who else is involved. Carlay Prince and Vince Mazza."

He turns to Alexis. "Is that true?"

She stares at the floor and nods.

"Then that makes my job easier." He pulls a pen from his drawer and writes their names down on a piece of paper.

I could hug Mr. Green. I've never heard anyone refer to bullying as abuse or bullied kids as victims, and this is the first time in a long time that I feel supported by an adult whose literal job it is to protect kids.

"I'm sorry, Max," Dad says. "I guess maybe I don't know what to do. I never had help with this sort of thing, and now I don't know how to help my own kid."

For what seems like a century, no one says anything.

"Chris, Alexis used this picture to bully Max," Mom finally says. "We always said that the things our own brothers and sisters did to us growing up, and the way it was for us with the bullying and taunting and the violence would never happen in our house, and now it's happening. I know you think that what you went through with your brothers was worse—"

"Of *course* it was worse, Jackie," Dad interrupts. "We

got into knife fights with each other. My mother was addicted to pills, and I never knew my father. How is that not worse?"

"You *got into knife fights*?" Alexis says. It's the first thing she's said since denying that the montage was her idea.

"If I may, Mr. and Mrs. Plink," Mr. Green says carefully. "We know much more about bullying now than we did years ago. And part of why I take this so seriously—apart from the senseless, abject cruelty of it all—is because of what we know of the impact of bullying on children's mental health. The implications for depression, anxiety, and low self-esteem are clear. It's a serious issue warranting serious consequences."

There's a long pause before Mom turns to Dad. "It's not a competition over who had it worse," she says, even putting her hand on his leg, and for a quick second I feel something tender pass between them. "At the end of the day, we want the girls to respect each other. To *love* each other."

Everything's starting to make sense. My parents don't know how to deal with these things because they never learned. They never had good examples with their own parents. So it's like these really tough relationships just sort of get passed down and around families, like an heirloom that no one wants.

"In truth," Mr. Green says, then clears his throat. "Three

days is not a hard and fast rule. I need to know more about Alexis's involvement." He turns toward my sister and says in a softer tone, "Why don't you tell us how this came to be?"

Alexis doesn't say anything, like she's afraid.

"Unless of course you want to make things difficult." He taps his fingers on the desk. "Here's the thing, Alexis. Your participation may warrant a three-day suspension. I haven't decided yet. But if you don't tell me what you know about how this situation came to be, we'll just keep to the standard policy and call it a day. Either way, I will find out the rest of the story."

"Alexis," Mom hisses, "out with it. Or a three-day suspension is *nothing* compared to what you'll get at home."

"Nothing at all," Dad chimes in.

"It was Carlay and Vince who started it, okay?" Alexis snaps. "They've been bugging me for a picture of Max and her headgear for weeks."

"And what was your role, specifically?" Mr. Green asks.

"They just said to get them the picture and they'd do the rest." Alexis's eyes spill over and she's a sniffling mess.

"So they created the montage?" Mr. Green says. "You didn't help?"

"I—they—" Alexis hiccups.

"*Now*," Dad barks.

"They found all the beaver pictures and added those to the end of the real montage. After the school science pictures.

And when the AV club adviser asked to see it, they showed her the file of the real montage, without the beavers. But they uploaded the beaver file to the laptop that Mrs. Neast used. Plus the picture of Max."

"Is that it?" Mom seethes. "Is that *all* of it?"

"This is your last opportunity for complete honesty," Mr. Green says.

"They showed me the final version, on the bus," Alexis whispers. "I knew it was gonna happen."

Mr. Green puts his pen down. "So, Alexis played a key role in this, but it sounds like the two other students are the masterminds. Beginning Monday, this will be a two-day suspension. One for providing the picture, and one for endorsing the final product. I'll also talk with her science teacher about disqualifying Alexis from award consideration."

"Wait, what?" Alexis squeaks. "But I worked—"

Mr. Green holds up his hand and Alexis shuts her trap. He turns to my parents. "Offering Alexis one of the showcase awards would be akin to rewarding misconduct. It's up to her science teacher what grade she'll get on her project, and I have nothing to do with that. Alexis should pass science if her grades warrant it. But an award, in my opinion, would be inappropriate under the circumstances."

Mom nods. Dad throws his head back and looks up at the ceiling.

"Wait, I didn't *endorse* the final product," Alexis growls.

"But you knew about it and you did nothing to stop it, correct?" Mr. Green says matter-of-factly. "Did you tell a teacher? Did you tell your parents? Did you tell anyone in a position to intervene?"

"No." Alexis's voice is a whisper.

"Which is exactly why you're in this situation," Mom snaps.

"And what about her academic record?" Dad asks.

"If she stays out of trouble, the violation won't follow her to high school," Mr. Green says. "But that's up to Alexis, of course.

"Mr. and Mrs. Plink," he continues. "Respectfully, I think the rest is a family issue. We can spend all day talking about *why* this happened, but I don't think that's my place. I hope it gets resolved soon, though. Do please let me know if you'd like to see the resources on bullying that inform our school district's policies. In the meantime, I'll be dealing with the others and their parents as soon as possible."

"And *we'll* be dealing with this at home," Dad says.

As we leave the office, Mr. Green's voice booms over the intercom like thunder. "Vince Mazza and Carlay Prince, report to my office immediately."

31

DAD FINALLY GETS IT

"WHAT HAS GOTTEN INTO YOU TWO?" Dad explodes as soon as we're home. "You two do nothing but fight. Every week there's a new issue. And now me and your mother are being called into the principal's office. WHY?"

"Family meeting," Mom barks. "On the couch. Now."

"Dad, I'm not . . ." I plop myself down on the couch and stop talking because I don't even know what I want to say. Of course Dad would try to blame us *both* for something that the *both* of us aren't guilty of doing. And when did I stop being Max, and when did Alexis stop being Alexis? When did we just become *you two*?

"Chris," Mom says, "this is *not* Max's fault." She turns to me. "We really had no idea."

I take a shaky breath. "Maybe you would have if you just paid attention to the things I've been trying to tell you?"

Dad takes a deep breath. "I know it's not your fault, Max. I'm sorry. And you're right, maybe I don't understand." He turns to Mom. "I'm at a loss, Jackie. I'm at a complete loss. The two of you seemed to be getting better. What happened?"

It did seem like things had gotten better, especially this past week. But my parents still need to know the truth.

"It's not just the picture," I say. "It's pretty much been going on all year. Alexis, Vince, and Carlay start in with me on the bus, and then Vince and Carlay keep it up in class. And when I come home, I get it even more from Alexis. She acts just like them." Alexis doesn't say anything. She sits on the floor with tears streaming down her face.

"But why, Jack?" Dad rubs his temples. "These ain't our girls. Our girls don't hang out with bullies and ruin each other's schoolwork and go after each other like wild animals and embarrass each other in front of hundreds of kids."

"This isn't an *each other* thing, Dad," I bark. "Not this time. It's her teaming up with other people to do this to me."

"I tried to stop them," Alexis whispers. We turn to her.

"Yeah, I gave them the picture after Max destroyed my project. They said I could sit with them at lunch and on the bus and stuff if I helped them. And I wanted to get back at Max for what she did. But after she bought me new paint and I finished my project, I didn't want to get back at her anymore. I just wanted to forget everything. But it was too late. I tried to get the picture back." She looks at me. "I promise, I tried. But they wouldn't give it to me. And when I asked them to not run the montage with your picture or the beavers, they laughed in my face."

Alexis takes a shaky breath. "I thought they were my friends. But after I gave them what they wanted, they completely turned on me. Now I can't even walk by without them doing or saying something really mean." She stares at her fingers as her voice breaks and tears drip off her nose and down to her pants. "You hear them on the bus." She's talking to me now. "They totally turned on me."

"Is that true, Alexis?" Dad says. "Why are you tryna be friends with kids like this? What's gotten into you?"

Alexis shrugs. "I dunno," she sniffles. "Vince can be funny sometimes. Carlay isn't always a total jerk. And she likes art, same as me. Besides, they're popular."

"With who?" Dad says. "The police department?"

I catch Mom hide a smile. When Dad gets it, he really gets it.

"So what did this teach you?" he continues. His tone is somehow sharp and gentle at the same time. "If you wanna be friends with a bunch of wise guys they'll turn on you eventually, right? It's like my mother used to say. *You play with poop, you smell like poop.* No two ways about it. And I especially don't want you tryna get in good with people who are mean to your sister." Dad turns to me. "That goes for you, too. If they can't be good to the *both* of you, they're not welcome around here, you got that?"

Alexis and I glance at each other. "Yes," we say.

There's a long pause. The only sound in the room is Alexis, sniffling.

"Let me make myself clear," Mom says to her. "You are to stay away from Carlay and Vince. I don't want you sitting with them on the bus, at lunch, or so much as looking at them in the hallways. They don't exist, do you understand me?"

Alexis nods.

"And after this science fair business you lost your phone privileges for a month," Mom adds.

"But—" Alexis gasps.

"You won't be seeing any friends outside of school, either," Dad interrupts. "It'll give you plenty of time to think about what happened and how to do better."

I want to cheer but I don't dare say a word. For the first time ever, my parents aren't punishing the both of us for something only one of us has done.

32

EVEN MORE CHANGES

Keisha points her cell phone at me. "So, a tripod's great, but holding the camera by hand also brings a realness to the video. Sort of like reality TV."

It's Monday afternoon, and more than a week since the science fair. The application for the journalism competition is due one week from today, and Dodge allowed Keisha and Shrynn to take newspaper club time to help me film some final footage for my Rising Star application. I'm going to put the last bits together this weekend and submit it. Shrynn's letting me use her laptop because our house computer has been crashing literally every five minutes, and she's even going to help me edit it. Mom and Dad are also letting me spend the night at Shrynn's house this Friday so that we can get a ton of work done. It's my first sleepover ever.

"By the way, Plink, did you hear about what happened to Carlay and Vince?" Keisha asks.

"No," I say softly as I fiddle with the camera. I haven't seen them at all since the science fair and I've been trying not to think about them. Dad told me not to let them live in my head rent-free, and I've been trying really hard to follow that advice.

"Well, for tampering with school equipment and using technology to bully you, they got suspended for three days. Everyone's talking about it. Someone heard Carlay's mom scream at the principal last week, something about what they did not being a big enough deal for kids to be suspended. According to my sources, Carlay was *mortified*. And I heard Vince's parents are super mad at the principal, too, and might put Vince in another school. They did their time last week but, to my knowledge, they haven't been back." That's Keisha for you. Forever in reporter mode.

"I'd heard about that," Shrynn whispers to me. "But I didn't bring it up because I figured you wouldn't want to talk about it. I couldn't imagine getting suspended from school and everyone talking about it. So embarrassing. Oops, sorry, Max."

I'd told Shrynn about Alexis's punishment, but I guess she'd forgotten that she'd also been suspended. Alexis had spent the entire two days in our bedroom, reading, doing homework, and sulking. It was weird, knowing that she was home not because she was sick, but because she'd gotten into trouble at school. For something she did to me.

"It's fine," I say.

I guess it explains why I haven't seen them on the bus or in class.

"You know what I think," Keisha says. "If you really want Jordan Slade to remember you, you'll wear your headgear in the video."

"Wait, what?" I say.

Shrynn gasps. "That's such a good idea, Keish!"

"Think about it," Keisha says. "You were so afraid of people seeing you in that thing, and now *everyone's* seen you in it. I think you need to own it."

Shrynn tugs on my sleeve and nods. "You so should. And by the way . . ."

"Yeah?" I say.

"I'll help you film it."

"That would be awesome," I say.

Shrynn smiles.

"Do you want to come over this Friday, Keish?" she asks. "Max is sleeping over."

Keisha pauses for a long minute. "I won't be able to stay over," she says. "But maybe I can come over for a little while. I'll ask my dad. He usually says yes. At least, he says yes a lot more than my mom does."

"It would be great if you could come," I say. "It would be so much fun!"

"We'll see," Keisha says. "The good thing, I guess, is that my parents got into a huge fight over me recently."

"That's a *good* thing?" I ask.

"This time it was. My dad told my mom to stop treating me like an inmate. That I work just as hard as she did when she was my age, and that I've earned a little freedom. He also said something about her rebelling against her parents because they had her on lockdown all the time, and that I'm not nearly as rebellious as I could be."

"Wow," I say. "It's great that your dad stuck up for you."

"Yeah," she says. "We need more men joining the fight for women's rights, you know?"

We laugh.

"We're having pasta and ice cream on Friday," Shrynn says. "I really hope you can come."

"Me too," Keisha says.

⧽ ☆ ⧼

When I get home from school, Mom and Dad are sitting on the couch. As in, next to each other. But the TV's not on and Mom looks like she's been crying.

"Why don't you put your stuff down and sit with us for a minute," Dad says. His voice is hoarse. "And get your sister, too."

I take off my windbreaker and fling that with my back-pack onto my bed. I'm wearing a T-shirt that says *Was that really necessary?* and Alexis is on her bed reading a book in her pajamas.

"Mom and Dad want us in the living room," I say.

"What *now?*" she grumbles.

"I have no idea," I say, except that maybe I do. Is it finally going to happen? Are Mom and Dad about to drop the Divorce Bomb?

Alexis and I make our way into the living room. I sit on the couch and Alexis sits on the floor and leans against our bedroom door.

Mom and Dad look at each other. Dad nods slightly. Mom speaks first. "We want to talk about some changes that are happening."

Dad looks at us. "This . . . this is really hard for me to say, but I want to say first that I love you girls. And I want you to know that."

I watch Dad as his head gets sweaty and he taps his foot rapidly. I've never seen him so nervous.

"What's wrong?" Alexis's voice is small.

"I have a—I've been getting help for my drinking problem." He spits out the words like they tasted sour and rotten. "This is why you haven't seen me around as much."

"What do you mean, your *drinking* problem?" Alexis asks.

"I have an addiction." Dad's voice is low. "And we—your mom and me—we recently decided that I needed to get help." He pauses. "I've been going to support meetings.

It's called Alcoholics Anonymous. They're meetings for people who struggle with abusing alcohol. I started about six weeks ago. And those meetings are why I haven't been home as much lately."

"So what does this mean?" Alexis asks. "You go to meetings and then you don't have a problem anymore?"

Dad smiles weakly. "I'm afraid it's not that easy, Bug," he says. "But the AA meetings are supposed to help me work through my addiction. My dependency on alcohol. I come from a long line of substance abusers, so there may be a genetic component. Which is why I'm getting help. I owe it to my family to get better, and to do what I can to protect you girls." Dad clears his throat.

"I stopped drinking and I don't intend to start again. I'm taking it day by day. The meetings give me tools to cope with stress and other issues," he continues. "To be honest, I should have started going a long time ago."

"And your dad will be attending more meetings soon, each week, and sometimes on Friday afternoons, so things are going to change a little bit, from week to week," Mom says, "and we wanted you to know so that you wouldn't wonder where he was."

"But I was *already* wondering where he was," I blurt. "Why didn't you tell us sooner?"

"Yeah," Alexis chimes in. "You always say he's working overtime. Is that not true?"

Mom looks away from us. "Sometimes it was true, but sometimes it wasn't."

"We wanted to protect you girls," Dad says again.

"We didn't intend to upset you," Mom says. "We did what we thought was right."

"What you thought was *right*?" I bark. "What if one of us lied about something hugely important?"

"*Yeah*," Alexis says.

"Well, we hope you won't do that," Dad says. He rubs his temples. "Besides, this is a little different."

My eyes are blurry with tears. "But we knew, Dad. We *knew* something wasn't right. We *heard* you both fighting in the middle of the night. We *heard* the things Mom said to you about your drinking."

"Max, try to see things from our perspective." Mom's tone has hints of frustration, the way it always does when I challenge her. "We don't believe in coming to children with adult issues, at least not without there being a really good reason. But with Dad being gone more, we figured it was time."

"*Your* perspective?" I say. "Well, here's *my* perspective. You never told us the whole story about what was going on, and for months Alexis has blamed me for the way you act toward each other." I glance at Alexis. She's staring at a spot on the floor. "She thinks you and Dad hate each other because of *me*."

"There's no way you can believe that. Either of you. Are you serious?" Dad says.

"That is absolutely not true," Mom says sharply. "How could you think such a thing?"

"Well, you never told us why Dad's on the couch," Alexis says. "Everything is about, *We're making changes around here*"—she uses air quotations and mimics Mom's voice—"but you literally never tell us why. And every time you and Dad fight it's about money, and Max's braces cost a lot of money and it's all you ever seem to talk about, so . . ."

"And I've heard you yell at Dad over smelling like a six-pack or a bar when he comes home from work," I say. "And Dad, I *know* I've smelled it on you, too. And I've also wondered if you drink because of us."

Mom glances at Dad before getting up from her spot on the couch. She sits on the floor between Alexis and me. "You girls come up with some ridiculous stuff sometimes, but this really takes the cake."

"What do you mean?" Alexis sniffles.

"I think you needed someone to blame for what's been going on, so you chose Max," Mom says to Alexis. And then she looks at me. "And you blamed yourself."

There's a long silence before Dad says, "Jacks, I think we messed up here. Big-time." Even though this is a hard conversation, probably the worst conversation ever, the way he calls her Jacks, like he used to, makes me feel hopeful. "We didn't do this the right way."

Dad turns to us. "Girls, me and your mom are working

on some problems we've been having. And to be honest, getting home really late at night and sleeping on the couch is easier because then I don't wake up your mom too early before her shift. And yes, we argue, a little too much sometimes, but it has nothing to do with you. And I don't ever want to hear that you're blaming each other for my drinking or our fighting or this family's money problems ever again." He looks at Alexis. "None of this is Max's fault, just like none of it's your fault. Do you understand?"

"Yes," she mumbles.

"We want to move forward as best we can," Dad says. "Can you girls help with that?"

Alexis speaks first. "Yes," she says.

"Yes," I say. "But while we're talking about changes, I want to make some, too."

"What sorts of changes?" Mom asks.

"Take Shrynn's house, for instance," I say. "I used to go almost every Friday, and then suddenly I wasn't allowed because you and Dad had a fight."

"We were just trying to find more ways for me to spend time with you girls, Max," Dad says.

"Well, I like going to Shrynn's, and it was our thing for years. And you just took it away."

"We can rethink that," Mom says. "Especially when your dad has meetings on Fridays."

"We just want you both to be honest and fair," I say softly.

"Pinkie swear," Dad says. "And let's not forget it works both ways. We want honesty from you both, and fairness with each other."

"Speaking of honesty," Mom says. "Would anyone like to tell me where the extras board might be hiding?"

"That was me," I say softly. "It's under the old newspapers. I put it there when it fell off the wall."

"But *why?*" she says, surprised.

"I think I know," Dad says. "Jacks, we all know money has been tight. The constant reminder wasn't necessary."

"And it was *embarrassing*," Alexis says. I nod, noticing how nice it is when she and I agree.

Mom sighs. "I thought it was a good way to teach you girls some financial responsibility. But maybe it wasn't a good idea after all."

"Girls, I have to start getting ready for work," Dad says. "Before I leave, I want to know that you understand that none of this is your fault. I'll work on recovery, and your Mom and I have also talked about starting family therapy. There's nothing set in stone, but you'll be the first to know as soon as we know more."

Alexis and I glance at each other and nod. "We understand," I say. I'm sad for Dad, but hopeful for my family.

"And I'll send the extras board out with tonight's trash," Mom says.

33
NO MORE SECRETS

"My parents finally told us about Dad's drinking problem," I say to Shrynn. It's Friday and I've been looking forward to my sleepover at Shrynn's all week. We're sitting on her bed and going through my script before we pull the last bits of my application together for Monday's submission.

"That's really hard, Max," she says softly. "I'm sorry."

Mom's at work and Dad dropped me off with my overnight bag on his way to an AA meeting. Alexis is at home by herself. Dad convinced Mom to let Alexis stay home because he'd only be gone for a couple of hours. They agreed to it without fighting.

To be honest, it's a relief to know the truth about Dad. I wonder about the kids at school, and whether any of them have a mom or dad who struggles with drinking too much or using drugs. But I've never heard anyone talking about these things, which makes me think there's a lot of shame about it.

"But at least we know the truth now, you know?" I say. "The reasons for why everything seemed to change over the last year or so."

"I don't really know much about substance abuse," says Shrynn. "I mean, like, I know what it *is*, but I don't know how it feels to watch someone going through it."

"And I know more than I wish I did." I offer a sad smile. I feel like I already know what it means to have an addiction, because we learned in health class this year about how addiction is a disease. And how some diseases can't be cured, but they can be managed.

But the health teacher didn't teach us about the other stuff—the important stuff. The way that some kids might feel like their parent's addiction is their fault, or the way that some families break up over it or how the words *rehab* and *recovery* and *family therapy* are brand-new topics of conversation.

"When my dad left, all I could think about was how lucky you are. That even though things were weird, at least everyone was still under the same roof."

"Yeah," I say. "I used to think you were the luckiest person in the world, too."

"I guess we were both wrong," Shrynn says. "Is there anything I can do?"

"Just keep being you, I guess," I say, pausing. "Actually, there *is* something else you can do. You haven't told me much about *your* mom and dad lately." I want to do better about making sure Shrynn knows I care as much about her life as she does about mine.

Shrynn looks away from me, but I see her eyes fill with tears.

"Want to tell me more about what's been going on?" I whisper. She pauses for a long minute.

"We found out that Dad was leaving right around the time that Dodge announced the Jordan Slade competition. Dad got an apartment on the other side of the city. Amy and I started spending some weekends there. I hate it. He tries to act like things are totally normal, but it's, like, nothing's the way it was before.

"Mom and Dad want me to go see someone. A doctor or counselor or something. To talk about my feelings, I guess. I have my first appointment next week. Amy, too. They think it'll help with . . . things. Especially my relationship with Amy. We've been fighting *so much* lately." She lets out a pained laugh. "My parents are worried, but it's just stupid stuff. I mean, Amy needs to figure out how to stop barging into my room. I didn't think we needed to call the National Guard about it."

"I hope you're not mad at Amy anymore for telling me," I say carefully. "She was just trying to help."

"Oh, I'm not," she says. "She apologized after I got home that day." I know she's talking about the day of our Battle Royale. "She trusted you the way I should have all along."

Shrynn pauses. "Don't tell anyone about this, okay? I really don't want anyone else to know yet."

"Of course," I say slowly. "You know I'd never say a word. I hope you go to therapy, though." Just last night I overheard Mom and Dad hold a whispered conversation about calling a family therapist, and how expensive it might be without having good insurance (whatever that means). "I think we're going to therapy, too, from what my parents have said. I mean, most people say that therapy is supposed to be super helpful, right?"

Shrynn nods. "I guess so."

It's funny, how there are all different kinds of doctors for all different kinds of problems. I see an orthodontist for my Complicated Teeth and Shrynn's going to see a therapist for her Complicated Feelings.

"I was so upset with my parents, you know? They weren't fighting hardcore or anything. I didn't have a *clue*. It came out of nowhere and it seemed really unfair."

It's so weird, how we're going through the same thing in a completely different way.

"I still can't talk about my parents without crying." Her tears spill over and she grabs a tissue from her nightstand. "You're the only person I feel comfortable talking to about this. I can't believe I didn't know until recently that you were going through something hard, too."

Me neither, I think. Me and Shrynn could have leaned on each other this entire time if one of us had the guts to say something.

She takes a deep breath. "No more secrets, okay?"

"No more secrets," I whisper.

Shrynn's phone buzzes. "It's Keisha," she says, reading her screen. "Her dad gave her permission to come over but her mom got home just as Keish was leaving and said she was only allowed to stay for forty-five minutes." Shrynn looks at me. "Wow. Her mom sure doesn't let her get out much."

I'm sad for Keisha. Having hard parents is, well . . . hard.

"She'll be here in about twenty minutes," Shrynn says. "So let's get to work. Do you have your jawbreaker?"

I pull my metal orb out of my overnight bag. "Right here," I say.

Shrynn's staring at me. "What?" I ask.

"I'd be lying if I said I didn't want to win this thing," she says slowly. "Like, I'd love to work with Jordan Slade."

"I know," I say softly. "Me too. I hate competing, especially with you. It's kind of awkward, right?"

"It is." She shrugs. "But if you win, I'll be super happy for you!" She throws a pillow at my arm. "Put that thing on. It's time to introduce Jordan Slade to Max Plink in all her glory!"

34

MAX'S GOOD NEWS

"When do you think we'll find out about the competition, Keish?" I say. We're in newspaper club working on stories for this week and I'm sitting at my usual table with Shrynn and Keisha. I'm wearing a T-shirt that says *Is it over yet?* And drafting an op-ed on cyberbullying for our next issue, and then I'll be conducting a separate interview with Mr. Green about his experiences with students who use technology to bully other kids. It's been two full weeks since I submitted my video essay to Channel 5.

As soon as I was finished with my project, I emailed Dodge with my ideas for the next pieces I wanted to write.

I'm sorry you've had to deal with this yourself, he'd replied. *And by the way, welcome back to work.*

But even with newspaper deadlines to distract me, I can't help but obsess over the competition results.

Like . . . *what if I win?*

"From what I remember, it took them around two or three weeks to announce the finalists?" Keisha says, peering at her computer screen. "Once the deadline passes, they're super fast. First, they called my parents to tell me I was one of four finalists. They told us when the winner would be announced on the air so that we could watch. And then about a week later, they played clips of the finalists' video essays on the morning news and Jordan announced the winner afterward. You remember that part, right? We all watched it in here."

"Wow," I say softly. "Yeah, I remember that. It felt like the room exploded when Jordan said your name on the air."

"So exciting!" Shrynn squeals.

"But is it even possible for me to win?" I say to Keisha. "I mean, after you won last year? Would they choose another person from the same school?"

Keisha shrugs. "I have no idea. I don't see why that should matter. A good story is a good story."

"No matter what happens," Shrynn says, "I think we need to have a party at my house. With the newspaper club. I'll ask my mom tonight. And with Amy winning third place at the science showcase, I bet Mom'll let us!"

"She won? Cool!" I say.

"Yeah, she's really proud."

"Well, a party is a super great idea," I say.

"I'm thinking something fancy," Shrynn says. "Maybe there'll even be a dress code!"

"What kind of dress code?" I ask.

She shrugs. "You'll have to wear something other than a T-shirt that says *Don't* or *Bye* or *Get out of my face* or *Good grammar saves lives* or something. That's all."

What? I always thought she liked my collection. But when she smirks at me, I realize she's kidding.

"Don't be jealous of my T-shirt collection," I finally say.

Shrynn laughs and we start party planning when I notice Keisha staring out the window.

"What's wrong?" I ask.

"I just hope I can come," she mumbles.

"But you have to come," Shrynn says. "It's almost the end of the year. The best time to celebrate."

Keisha's expression is sad. "Tell that to my mom."

⋛ ☆ ⋚

After school, Alexis and I walk home from the bus stop together. It's one more small thing that's changed since the science showcase, and it feels nice.

"I was thinking of starting another painting," she says softly. "I wanna know what you think."

"What of?" I ask.

"I'm not sure," she says. "But I'm thinking something abstract. Something that represents substance abuse, you know? Addiction. My teacher announced some kind of art fair. It's for junior high school students. High school, too, but that's a different category. The community college is holding it, and I think I want to submit."

"Wow," I say. "What do you think that might look like?"

She sighs. "I have no idea. But there'll probably be lots of black and gray." She looks at me with a playful smirk. "And I should have enough black, unless you have other ideas."

"I won't touch it," I say. "I promise."

"I know," she says. "I was kidding."

When we turn the corner we see Mom standing outside our apartment building in her diner uniform. She's waving her cell phone at us, all frantic-like.

"Guess what?!" Mom shrieks. She throws her apron to the ground and takes giant steps toward us.

Alexis looks at me. "Do you think we're in trouble?" she asks. "I know I haven't done anything. And besides, I only have another week to go before I'm not grounded anymore and I'm not trying to mess that up."

"I don't think I've done anything," I say.

We quicken our pace.

"What's wrong?" I ask Mom.

"*Well*," she says, breathless and smiling. "Producers with

Channel 5 just called. You're a finalist for the Rising Star competition."

"*Really?*" I squeal.

"That's cool," Alexis mumbles. It's still awkward between us, but we're trying. We're definitely trying.

"They'll be showing your video on Friday's morning news, along with the other finalists," Mom says. "And the winner will get a personal phone call from Jordan Slade within two weeks after she announces the winner."

"Can I use my phone?" I'm practically shouting. "I have to send some texts. And then can I get on email for a second? I need to tell Dr. Dodge."

"Yes and yes, as long as you text your dad first. He's at an AA meeting, but he'll see it as soon as he gets out." Mom smiles. She turns to Alexis, who's staring at her feet. "This is very exciting for Max," she says. "For *all* of us. So what's the matter?"

"Well, I'm a week away from not being grounded any-more . . . ," she says. "So can I use my phone, too?"

"Yes," Mom says, hiding a smile. "I think I can manage that."

"And then can I go to Kristy's?"

"Don't push your luck." Mom turns to me. "Your dad's going to work directly from his meeting tonight, but I thought we could have a nice dinner, the three of us. Should I order a pizza?"

"No!" Alexis and I shout at the same time. We look at each other and smile.

"How about ravioli?" Mom says.

"No!" Alexis and I shout again. I see Dr. Watson in two weeks and don't want to eat any more pasta unless my teeth and jaws are on fire.

"Um . . . grilled cheese?" Mom asks.

I think about that. "Maybe?" I say.

"Well, I'm out of ideas," she says. "What do you feel like having?"

"I don't know." I shrug. To be honest, I don't really care what we have for dinner, as long as it's not pizza or ravioli.

"We have pizza and ravioli all the time," Alexis says. And now I know the exact right thing to do.

"What if Alexis gets to pick?" I say.

Alexis and Mom head into our apartment in front of me, Alexis rattling off all of the gourmet meals she wouldn't mind having for dinner tonight.

35

EVERYTHING IS PERFECT

It's Friday, the morning of Jordan Slade's decision. All
the reporters were given permission by their teachers to
spend first and second periods at a special meeting with
the *Weiss Chronicle*.

Me and Shrynn stop by Mr. Brace's class to say hello
and get the homework. "I am so, so excited for you,"
Shrynn whispers as we step into the room. According to
Dr. Dodge, I'm the only finalist from Weiss. And Shrynn
told the truth when she said she'd be happy for me no
matter what happened.

"Thanks," I say. "But I wish we could both be finalists."

"It's okay," she says. "I'll try again next year. And
maybe we'll be able to celebrate your win at my party
next Saturday." Earlier in the week Shrynn's mom had
given her and Amy permission to have friends over next

weekend. *It's a formal affair*, Shrynn had said, mimicking a British accent. *So wear your best T-shirt.*

"Good luck today, Plink-Meister!" DeShaun calls out. "Woot-woot!"

I laugh with the others as Mr. Brace hands us some worksheets.

"This is what we're doing today," he says. "Try to turn it in Monday, if you're not too busy celebrating this weekend." He smiles at me as Shrynn grabs my sleeve and lets out a soft squeal.

There is literally nothing more exciting than getting out of class to find out whether you've won a city-wide contest.

"Oh, and Max?" Mr. Brace says as we turn to leave.

I turn around. "Yeah?"

"We're all rooting for you, right, guys?" And the whole class stands up and applauds and I take an exaggerated bow.

Today just feels so huge. Today *is* huge. Mom even let me take my cell phone to school so that I can text her with the news either way, if I don't hear from her first.

Shrynn and I race across the school to Dr. Dodge's room.

We're almost there when we pass by the glass art showcase that sits outside the main office. Alexis's brain painting—the art portion of her science project—is smack in the center, the best one in the whole display.

"Hey, one sec," I say to Shrynn. "Let me take a picture of this and send it to my mom."

A few seconds later we're racing down the hall again. As we get close, I hear what sounds like laughter and a blaring TV. I also smell sugar.

When we arrive, Dr. Dodge is there with Keisha and the rest of the club. There are rows of doughnuts and bottles of juice spread out on a far table by the windows. The TV that hangs from the ceiling in the corner of the room is set to Channel 5 and blasting with morning news. Even Mr. Green is here.

"When we have staff members who throw their hat into this competition, it's cause for celebration, no matter what happens," Dr. Dodge is saying to Mr. Green.

"Yes, very impressive, very impressive," Mr. Green says. He's smiling and balancing a plate with two jelly dough-nuts and a cup of orange juice on a clipboard.

"All right, everyone." Dr. Dodge claps his hands. "It's about to start! Channel 5 received four applications from Weiss Junior, and only two were from members of the newspaper club. No matter what happens with the results, let's give it up for finalist Max Plink!"

The class erupts in applause and all my organs are doing cartwheels.

"Yes, very impressive indeed," Mr. Green mumbles through a mouth full of doughnut.

"Shh, shh, everyone." Dr. Dodge turns up the TV. "Here's Jordan Slade."

Jordan Slade appears on the screen in a beige suit. Her curly hair is soft and springy looking and taking up a large part of the screen. When she smiles at the camera, I notice that her teeth are straight and pretty.

"And now we turn to Channel 5's Rising Star journalist competition, a program I began five years ago to support junior high school students from Brooklyn, New York, who think they might want to pursue careers in news media." She's smiling at the camera and sitting on a fluffy pink chair with a large window behind her. There's a shot of the Brooklyn Bridge off in the distance, backed up with rush hour traffic. "I truly love this program," Jordan says. "It's our opportunity to honor our talented young journalists.

"Every year we receive dozens of applications from across the city, and it gets tougher and tougher to choose our next group of Rising Star finalists," Jordan continues. "But without further ado, here are our four finalists." My skin prickles with excitement as Shrynn squeezes my wrist.

Jordan introduces a clip from an application about climate change and how it's affected the city. The finalist had a really great video. Professional looking and smart, like the kind of story you'd see on actual news.

"That was a good one, but yours is better, Plink," Keisha says.

"Yeah," Shrynn whispers. "We all know about climate change. It really didn't add anything to the conversation."

I can totally count on my friends.

Jordan announces two more finalists from two other schools and by the time she gets to mine I can barely breathe.

"Our last finalist submitted a video essay that hit close to home for me." Jordan's dark eyes pierce the camera. "It's a fine example of investigative journalism, and I know exactly what this applicant is going through. You see, I wore braces as a child, and then again as a young adult." I had no idea that some people wear braces more than once in a lifetime. That sounds like the literal worst. "The experience was interesting, to say the least." And then I see my face, my jawbreaker, fill up the screen.

Shrynn squeals and wraps her arms around me and Keisha claps and Dr. Dodge pounds his fist in the air and the staff members cheer around me and Mr. Green says *very impressive, indeed.*

"Yeah, Plink!" Dodge calls out, holding his cell phone high in the air to take a picture of us as we cheer. "Okay, hold on, everyone. Let's listen."

In the video, I'm reading off stats from the survey that Mr. Brace helped me with. *Two thirds of the kids at Weiss Junior High School wear braces*, I say into the camera. I'm trying not to think of how all of New York is now watching me wear my jawbreaker.

I have what's called a Class II malocclusion, which basically just means that my jaws don't fit together correctly. And when kids started bullying me about my braces, I decided to try to find out how many other kids get bullied at school, too. It seems that Weiss Junior High School has a bullying problem, and I'm here to break down the numbers for you.

About seventy-five percent of the students who responded to my survey said they've experienced bullying at least once since they started Weiss Junior. Approximately fifty percent say they experience bullying occasionally, and around thirty percent have told me that they experience bullying chronically. My video cuts away to a colorful bar graph. *For the record, I define* chronically *as at least once a week. And that's the category that I fit into.*

But I'm not ashamed to talk about this anymore. Because according to my orthodontist, complicated teeth are normal. My video cuts away to a slice of my interview with Dr. Watson before returning to me.

I'll just say that the fact that I have to wear this jaw-breaker thing is totally out of my control, but it's gotten me a whole lot of attention that I never even asked for. But like my friend Keisha says—and I know she's right because she's right about everything—I need to use my mouth to take my power back.

So, my name is Max Plink, and yeah, I have this stupid skeletal deformity or whatever but that's beside the point because there's a bullying problem at Weiss Junior. A huge bullying problem, and it's time for something to be done about it. Because no kid is safe from bullying unless all kids are safe, and we deserve a safe school. I, um, hope you like the sound of that because I, along with my friends Keisha and Shrynn, came up with it ourselves. And no one should have to look perfect just to be treated well.

I finish my story with some more clips of Dr. Watson and a bunch of details about how bullying affects mental health and self-esteem and even brain function, and then the show cuts back to Jordan. I might just be imagining it, but did Jordan play my video for just a couple of seconds longer than the others?

"And with that, I think it's the perfect time to announce that Max Plink is the winner of this year's Rising Star journalist competition. This is also the first time in Channel 5 history that the same school is represented two years in a row. Well done, Max. We'll see you soon." She smiles and nods at the camera before the screen cuts away to a commercial.

There's a brief silence before the club bursts into applause and Shrynn and Keisha ambush me in a bear hug and Dr. Dodge's smile is huge and I hear my phone chiming in the pocket of my book bag and, and . . .

Mr. Green approaches me. "You've been through a lot this year, Max," he says. "More than I think I realized." *It's never a good thing when the principal knows your name,* Dad has always said.

"Th-thanks, Mr. Green," I say.

"And you're a true inspiration. I'm going to review our school's bullying policies, to see whether we need to be clearer about the policies here at Weiss. Maybe I'll even send a note home to families, clarifying our position. Great job, and congratulations again." He grabs another dough-nut before leaving the room. "Time for me to get back to the business of principal-ing."

I turn to find Shrynn and Keisha right behind me. Shrynn hands me my phone.

"I hope it's okay that I went into your bag to get it," she says. "It's been blowing up."

I have five missed calls from Mom and one text from Dad. Before I can check Dad's text, another one comes through. It's from Mom.

> Dad will pick up U and Alexis from school. We'll have early lunch at diner. I'll make sure they get UR favorite burger and milkshake going. Tell Alexis that grilled chz is waiting for her. My manager turned all the TVs to the news this morning and everyone clapped when she said that U were my daughter. We're so proud of U, Bean. C U soon. Xo Mom

"Everything okay?" Shrynn says softly.

"Perfect," I whisper. "Everything's perfect."

36

DESHAUN IS KING OF THE BACKYARD

It's Saturday, just over a week after I won the competition, and it's the afternoon of Shrynn's party. I'm standing on her front stoop in a brand-new T-shirt, a blue one with white letters that says, *Ready To Boogie*.

When Shrynn and Amy answer the door, Shrynn looks so pretty in a new blue-and-yellow-striped dress and Amy has sparkles on her face.

"I need to talk to her first." Amy pulls me by the arm into their hallway. Shrynn rolls her eyes but smiles.

"I should've said something sooner, but thanks for talking to Alexis about everything," Amy says. "She hasn't bugged me since. She's even been nice to me, and we sit together in class sometimes. So thanks. I thought about inviting her to the party, but I'm not sure we're there yet."

"*Yet.*" I smile.

Amy shrugs. "You never know, right?"

"Well, I'm glad it's over and done with," I say. I never asked Alexis about Amy since that day. I trusted that she'd leave her alone.

"Aaand, now it's my turn." Shrynn comes up from behind and pulls on my other arm.

"Thanks again, Maxi," Amy whispers before heading through the kitchen and into the backyard.

☆

Shrynn's backyard is about the size of a shoebox, but that's Brooklyn for you. It's big enough to fit a picnic table and a couple of plants and a grill. And just past the yard there's a train that runs underground every ten minutes.

"Amy claimed the backyard for her friends, but we can go out there, too," Shrynn says. "There are some snacks in the kitchen so let's stop there first."

She grabs my hand as we make our way toward the kitchen. Her dad is at the sink filling a vase with flowers. When he sees me, he smiles and says hello before disappearing into the living room to make a phone call.

"Your dad's here?" I whisper.

Shrynn shrugs. "It's not like they don't get along. And Mom needed help setting up, so she asked him."

I don't know what to say. I guess there are some things

about Shrynn's family that will always seem perfect, at least to me.

Some friends from newspaper club had already arrived, including Keisha. She's wearing a long black gown with white flip-flops and her hair is all in tiny braids pinned up in a twist and she is fancier than I've ever seen her.

But I'm most surprised to see DeShaun standing near the refrigerator scarfing down gummy bears. He's not in the newspaper club and I actually didn't know that he and Shrynn were *hang out at each other's house* kind of close. I look at Shrynn. Her cheeks are glowing a light pink.

DeShaun's wearing suit pants, a T-shirt with a cartoon character on it, and a striped bow tie. Only DeShaun can make an outfit like that look cool.

"Plink-Meister!" He lifts his hand for a high five.

"Everyone, let's head outside for some snacks," Shrynn's mom says. "It's a tight fit, but we'll make it work. And pizza will be here within the hour."

When we get to the backyard, Amy is laughing hard at something another sixth grader said. I take a seat at the opposite end of the picnic table, in between Keisha and DeShaun and across from Shrynn. The table is loaded with bowls of chips and candy, and also a bowl of oranges.

"It looks like everyone's here," Andra says. She's passing out paper cups full of sparkling cider. "And I just wanted to congratulate all of you on such a successful year so far. There's been so much good news, about the *Weiss Chronicle*, the science fair, the journalism competition. It seemed like the perfect time for a little get-together."

"Thanks, Mom," Shrynn says.

"Yeah, thanks, Mom!" Amy says.

"Thank you, Andra," everyone says in unison, and we all laugh as we sip from our cups.

"Hear ye, hear ye," DeShaun stands up. "Mrs. Li, with your permission, I'd like to teach a vocabulary lesson," DeShaun says. Andra smiles. "Listen up, sixth graders!" he says. "As your Weiss Junior High student body president, I have something to say."

Keisha narrows her eyebrows. "We don't have a student body president."

"We do for today, cuz," he says.

I almost spit out my soda. "You guys are *cousins*?!" I shriek.

"Don't tell anyone," Keisha says, hiding a smile. "I have a reputation to maintain."

I turn to Shrynn. "Did you know they were cousins?"

"Doesn't everyone?" She shrugs.

"All right, sixth graders," DeShaun continues, "you may not have heard of this requirement, but there's one thing you need to do to officially graduate to the seventh grade.

It's a top-secret rule published in the DeShaun Manual for Peak Coolness."

"Oh, for the love of—" Keisha interrupts.

"Shh, shh." DeShaun snaps his fingers in Keisha's face. "Quiet, commoner! I'm king of the backyard for the next ten minutes."

"I'll be counting," Keisha says.

"Are you sure, Mrs. Li?" DeShaun asks.

Andra winks at him. "I am if you are." She removes everything from the table except the bowl of oranges.

"Oh, I'm sure. With Mrs. Li's help and that of your new eighth-grade comrades, I'm going to teach you soon-to-be seventh graders the greatest word on the planet. Everyone, take an orange and start peeling as fast as you can." Andra passes around the bowl of oranges. Shrynn grabs one the size of a baseball and looks at me and smiles. I think we both know exactly what DeShaun is up to.

"As soon as you're finished peeling, take your orange and hold it in the air." DeShaun holds his peeled orange high above his head. "Now, repeat after me. Orb-isc-u-late." He says the word slowly, syllable by syllable.

"Huh?" Amy says. "I've never heard that before."

"If you're smart, you'll repeat after me," DeShaun says. "Orbisculate. Say it three times. Orbisculate, orbisculate, orbisculate."

The sixth graders look curiously at one another but they do as he says. *Orbisculate, orbisculate, orbisculate,* they chant, their oranges above their heads. Amy is especially serious and determined, never one to miss out on a lesson in cool.

"And now . . . ," DeShaun whispers. All the sixth graders' eyes are on him, and I hear a train approaching in the distance, which is kind of the perfect soundtrack for what I know is about to happen.

"SQUEEZE! YOU'VE BEEN ORBISCULATED!" DeShaun squeezes his orange and sticky liquid and fruit fibers shoot across the table and then everyone's squeezing their oranges at each other and before we know it we're all covered in juice and it's messy but it's also amazing.

"That's the coolest word ever!" Amy says. "I'm gonna use it as much as I can."

"*Great,*" says Shrynn, rolling her eyes but smiling, too.

"I brought extra hand sanitizer for exactly this occasion!" Andra says, passing around wipes, paper towels, and a bottle of floral-smelling liquid.

"Did you know he was gonna do this?" I whisper to Shrynn.

"He asked for our help," she says. "He's so hung up on this word for some reason. But that's DeShaun."

"My cousin is a fool," Keisha says, wiping orange juice from her arm, but she's smiling. Her phone chimes with a text. Me and Shrynn look at each other. I remember what happened the last time Keisha's phone went off when she was here.

"My mom wants to know if we're having fun." Keisha looks at DeShaun.

"I told you she'd let you go if she knew I was coming," DeShaun says. "Maybe she's starting to chill out."

"Maybe." Keisha smiles. "I hope so. She was really impressed with the latest edition of the paper. She even told me she was proud of me."

"Of course she is." DeShaun shrugs. "Aunt Kathy might be strict, but she's always been super proud of you. That's obvious to anyone."

"Let's get this table cleaned up before the pizza arrives," Andra says, passing out more wipes. I look at the ground around my feet to make sure I picked up all my orange peels, and that's when I notice Shrynn and DeShaun holding hands under the table.

37
LETTING GO

It's Saturday, one week after Shrynn's party, and Mom and I and are leaving for Dr. Watson's soon. I overheard Dad say that he'd take me but he'd have to miss an AA meeting, so he offered to take me next time. Mom was okay with it. Dad says he hasn't had a drink in over a month and things are different at home. Lighter. My parents haven't been arguing as much and Mom seems happier, too.

To be honest, I can't wait to see Dr. Watson. The day I won the competition, her office manager, Lucy, called Mom's phone and left a message about how everyone in the waiting room clapped when Dr. Watson's face popped up on the TV. And Lucy congratulated us on behalf of Dr. Watson and the office and said they really looked forward to seeing us soon because it's like I'm a famous celebrity or something.

Alexis is in our bedroom listening to music and texting her friends. Mom's been letting her stay home by herself a bit more, especially if she or Dad are only going to be gone for a short time.

Before we leave, I hop on the computer. I want to watch the video of Jordan Slade again, the one where she announces my win. I've probably watched it twenty times. And as long as I only have one window open, it won't crash on me (hopefully). The computer started behaving a bit better once Dad ran a couple of updates.

But I check my email first. Mr. Green sent a bulletin to the whole school about bullying and I want to read it again. He'd talked about how he's had to reckon with the fact that bullying was a huge problem at Weiss and that all students who participate in acts of bullying against other students will be referred to his office, and that he's drafting a new policy that all students and their guardians will have to sign off on so that there are no misunderstandings. Every kid at school is going to be sent home with a copy of it.

But before I click on Mr. Green's email, I notice an unopened one with the name Dean.

I hold my breath and click on his name.

Hi Max! Sorry it's taken me so long to get back to you. I really don't check my blog that much anymore. It's amazing how quickly life moves on after surgery. And I still can't believe that people actually read my story!

Thanks for sending your questions. I'm super sorry that you've had to deal with bullying. To be honest, kids can be really cruel (not to tell you something you already know). I didn't really write much about it for the blog because I never wanted to give them the satisfaction, you know? And besides, I just really wanted to focus on the surgery and recovery aspect.

Here's the deal: Yes, kids can be terrible, but you can't let it define you, you know? You can be the most perfect-looking person in the world (not something I have *any* experience with!), and other kids will still find a way to bring you down. My mom taught me to feel sorry for that type of person. It can't be easy to wake up and be at war with all the world.

I dealt with a lot of this sort of thing, too. The only thing I can say is that it passes. I just try to remember that sometimes people are who they are for reasons that have nothing to do with us. So really try to lean on your friends and family and just keep being a good person. That's all that matters. And if it's really, super-duper bad, you should tell your parents or a teacher who you totally trust and ask them for help. You shouldn't have to deal with it alone.

By the way, I posted your question to my blog. You should check it out. Thanks for the inspiration,

and thanks for writing, Max! You seem like a good
person. Don't let anyone drag you down, okay
kiddo?
Peace,
Dean

"Max, are you ready to go?" Mom calls from the kitchen.
I close the laptop and dash into my bedroom to get my jawbreaker. It's as much a part of my appointments as my teeth
and jaws, and that probably won't change for a long time.

But it's all good, because I actually feel like I'm floating.
Like I can fly.

⋛ ☆ ⋚

Both Dr. Watson and Lucy start off our appointment with
a huge bear hug, which is kind of awkward because we've
never hugged like that, but it's also kind of nice.

"You did a brave thing, Max," Dr. Watson says. "I mean,
I knew you were going to do a story on this, but I had no
idea you'd be wearing your headgear! So brave. I'm proud
of you!"

"Thanks," I say. "I never thought it would happen. Not in
a million years." But I'm not actually sure that I believe my
own words. Maybe I *did* think it would happen, if I tried
hard enough, and dreamed big enough.

"We can't thank you enough for all of your help," Mom says.

"The pleasure is mine," Dr. Watson says. "And by the way, my phone's been ringing off the hook! I might have to tell people that I'm full soon!" She gestures to the examining chair. "Now, let's get down to business."

"Max," she says after a few minutes of poking around, "if I didn't know any better, I'd think you were wearing your headgear twenty-four hours a day."

I smile, even though there are mirrors shoved up against my back molars.

"She's been wearing her headgear between twelve and fourteen hours a day," Mom says proudly. "And we haven't had to remind her in *weeks*."

"Her commitment shows," Dr. Watson says. "This progress is looking really good. So, we'll tighten today and take some X-rays next time. I'll also adjust the headgear a tiny bit, so make sure to have your Tylenol handy if you need it." She asks me to close my mouth and then open it again. "I'd say it'll be another four to six months before we're able to really know what we're dealing with as far as surgery, and I can't promise that we're out of the woods. But for now, just keep doing what you're doing, kiddo. Your maxilla is responding."

I remember that maxilla means Upper Jaw. *Max's maxilla*

is responding, thanks to that stinkin' jawbreaker. I look over at Mom. She smiles and nods, as if to say, *good job*.

"I think it's time to give Dr. Watson her gift." Mom smiles as she pulls a box from her purse and hands it to me.

Dr. Watson gasps. "This was so very unnecessary! Thank you both!"

She examines the box. It's wrapped in silver paper with a pink ribbon. Mom's really good at wrapping gifts. "Can I open it now? I'm like a child when it comes to presents."

I laugh and nod as Dr. Watson rips into the box and pulls out the mug that Mom, Alexis, and I designed for her. It's made of black porcelain and has the word *jawbreaker* in large hot-pink letters scrawled all the way around it. Thanks to Alexis, there's also the outline of a smiling cat face wearing braces and a bow tie. And on the bottom part, a message:

For Dr. Watson, Coolest ortho ever. From, Max Plink.

The mug is practically the size of a bowl, too, so she can even use it for soup or cereal or whatever she wants.

"Max, this is my favorite gift ever. Thank you so much. And thank *you*, Mrs. Plink."

"You've been such a help," Mom says. "We wanted to show our appreciation."

"Nonsense." Dr. Watson waves her hand. "I appreciate that, but Max did the hard stuff. I just told her a couple of wild little stories. Besides, it was good for me to think back to those days, and how hard they were sometimes. I think it helps me to be a better doctor for my patients who are going through the same thing. A lot of kids are in headgear these days and facing the possibility of surgery. Max, you did a great thing by destigmatizing such a common issue. I hear it's around fifteen percent now. That's a lot of kids getting surgery!"

I make a mental note to look up the word *destigmatize* when I get home.

"For now, though, you're doing great. Like I said, we're not out of the woods, but if you keep wearing your headgear exactly as you need to, we can see where you are in a few months. Hopefully we'll know more about whether you'll need surgery by the fall, okay?"

I swallow hard. "Okay," I say. It's tough to imagine going through the summer and not knowing exactly what's going to happen. But that's the way these things are, I guess. And I'll always have my friends and my family to help me with the difficult stuff.

"So let's tighten up these wires and get you out of here, kiddo," Dr. Watson says. Ten minutes later Mom and I are walking back to the car.

"You seem quiet," Mom says. "You okay?"

"I guess," I sigh. "I mean, I'm used to the jawbreaker and

everything, but I just want it to be over. I want to know what's gonna happen."

"I know, Max," Mom says. "But life doesn't always work that way. We all have to be okay with uncertainty. Me, your dad, Alexis, everyone. And it's hard, but you have to let go of some of that control, you know?"

I look at Mom. I can tell by her face that she's had to take her own advice, and now I *know* I can be okay not knowing what the future holds. If Mom can do it, I can do it, too.

"Yeah," I say. "I'll try."

"Let's head home," she says. "You have the whole summer ahead of you, and you'll get through this. Besides"— she taps my knee—"there's nothing a big plate of ravioli can't cure."

We drive home with the windows down, and the warm spring air reminds me that everything's going to be okay.

Acknowledgments

I am overflowing with gratitude for my editor, Joy Peskin. You appeared in my world out of thin air at exactly the right time and I am still pinching myself. To my mind, we clicked from that first phone call (I was so excited to meet you that I did not sleep the entire weekend before our chat). Thank you for helping me find the courage to be vulnerable in my storytelling, and for believing in Max. In so many ways, I consider it Our Story. I hope very much that *Jawbreaker* is the beginning of a long literary journey together.

I have immense gratitude for my agent, Erin Murphy. You have worked magic in my world, and your candor, support, and kindness have sustained me. Thank you for giving me the courage to stop seeking out Rules and Parameters That Don't Exist (I meant it when I said I was holding on to that email forever). I am a braver and smarter writer because of you.

To the team at Farrar, Straus, & Giroux Books for Young Readers: Hannah Miller, Linda Minton, Ilana Worrell, Veronica Mang, and Celeste Cass. With your talent and dedication, you brought this story to life. It really does take a village. I am indebted.

Grace Li, Elizabeth Lee, and Alexus Blanding, your feedback helped me immeasurably. I am so grateful to you all.

James Lancett and Meg Sayre: Your vision brought me to tears. Thank you for your stunning artwork and design.

I have a group of friends, old and new, who have been with me every step of the way. You know who you are. Thank you for your love and support. I love you.

To my family, from Michigan to New Jersey to Maryland to Washington to Canada. You, too, have been there every step of the way. Thank you. I love you.